Assassin's Heart

Isabella Norse

RedHeadedViking Publications

RedHeadedViking Publications
202 North Davis Drive #249
Warner Robins GA 31093

Publisher's Note: This is a work of fiction. Names, characters, places, and incidents are a product of the author's imagination. Any resemblance to actual people, living or dead, or to businesses, companies, events, institutions, or locales is completely coincidental.

Book Layout ©2013 BookDesignTemplates.com

Cover designed by Melody Simmons, ebookindiecovers.com

Assassin's Heart/ Isabella Norse. -- 1st ed.
ISBN 978-0-9912371-1-1

*This book is dedicated to my husband,
the man who teaches me what love is every day.*

ACKNOWLEDGMENTS

Many thanks to:

The readers and reviewers on Fanfiction.net. Your positive feedback gave me the courage to begin writing original stories.

Chris Baty and the staff of The Office of Letters and Light. National Novel Writing Month turned my "someday I'm going to write a novel" into Actually. Writing. A. Novel!

Melody Simmons, cover designer extraordinaire. Your pre-made cover is so perfect, I can't wait to see what your custom covers are like!

Terri Valentine, writing instructor and copy editor. You have a remarkable ability to teach, correct and encourage.

1

My breath caught in my throat as I fled down the servant's staircase, pursued by bloody corpses. Well, not *actual* bloody corpses, but the memories of them. I would have almost preferred the real thing – I couldn't outrun memories.

My bare feet slapped against the cold stone of the stairs and I careened off of the walls in my haste, bruising my arms. I was numb, as if the nightmare had drained all vestiges of warmth from my body.

The massive kitchens were lit only by the glowing embers of the fires that had been banked for the night. Their flickering light drew me closer with promises of warmth and safety. I stood on the hearth, as close to the coals as I dared, letting their heat soak into my body.

I rested my head against the mantel and closed my eyes. A big mistake – Lord Landry's blood-soaked form once again appeared. I jerked my eyes open, bile rising in my throat. Even after all these years, the memory of the feel - and sound - as I slipped my dagger into his body made me ill. To make it even worse, I had to stab him three times before inflicting a fatal wound. Oh, I knew the mechanics well enough - I was thoroughly trained in human anatomy and well versed in the use of a blade. However, when the time came to use my years of training to actually take a life, my hand shook so badly that it impaired my aim.

I was an assassin. For years, I had specialized in the murder of pedophiles. At eighteen, I could no longer pass myself off as a child as easily as I once could. Vido, my guild master, felt that the time had come for me to prove myself with my first non-pedophile hit, which was how I now found myself serving as a maid at the royal palace, waiting to kill the heir to the throne.

In truth, I felt no remorse for the deaths of Lord Landry and his ilk; they were monsters in human form and deserved far worse for the crimes that they had committed. The only regrets that I felt were for me and the life that I was forced to live – a life not of my choosing. Although I had killed many times, it never got easier - each death took a piece of my soul. I was afraid that this death - the death of an innocent man -

would destroy me completely, turning me into the soulless killer that Vido wanted me to become.

"You look like you could use a drink. Would you like some tea?" an unfamiliar voice asked close to my ear.

Startled, I whirled to face the speaker and looked into the bluest eyes that I had ever seen. Time stopped, my breathing stopped, and even my heart skipped a beat. Once I could tear my gaze away from those captivating eyes, I examined the rest of his face - fair skin, black hair pulled back in a queue, a roguish grin and, heaven help me, *dimples*. He was dressed in the drab grey garments that identified him as a servant, like me.

Time and somewhat ragged breathing resumed. I hoped that he had not noticed the lengthy pause as I studied him.

"You scared me!" I finally managed to say. "I didn't realize that anyone else was here." My hand flew to my chest as if to keep my heart from pounding its way out.

His eyes widened at my reaction. Placing his hands on my shoulders, he guided me to a nearby bench. Once I was seated, he pressed a cup of tea into my hand then rushed to the pantry. The muffled clinking sounds emanating from behind the door indicated that he was searching the shelves. Moments later he emerged with a triumphant grin on his face and a bottle in his hand. He uncorked the bottle with strong, even, white teeth and poured a healthy splash of something into my cup. Before I could ask what it was, I was overcome by fumes strong enough to make my eyes water – Southron whiskey.

"Are you crazy? Cook will have your hide if she finds out that you have raided her stores."

"Not a chance. I have Cook wrapped around my finger." He extended his pinky in demonstration as he slid onto the bench next to me. "Now, drink up. You need some color in those cheeks." He reached out as if to press the cup to my lips.

He was right. I did need the drink. Yet, I balked at being told what to do by someone not much older than me. I tended to be somewhat contrary by nature. Apparently he saw the dangerous glint in my eyes and raised his hands in surrender.

"Sorry! I'm just trying to help. You got so pale I was afraid that you were going to faint." He stared at me curiously. "Lillie, isn't it? I've seen you around."

I flashed him an apologetic look, took a big swallow of my tea, and choked as the harsh whiskey hit my throat. I waved away his attempts to assist me. I finally managed to croak "Yes, I'm Lillie." As I wiped away the tears streaming down my cheeks, I cocked my head and surveyed him openly. "You've seen me? I'm afraid that I don't recall seeing you."

He grinned widely, dimples deepening. "You don't? I'm crushed." He bowed with a flourish, no mean feat considering that he was seated. "My name is Nef. I'm a stable hand - I've seen you when you come to visit the animals."

Now it was my turn to grin. "How did you know my name? The animals didn't tell you, I'm sure."

He shrugged. "Simple. I asked. I am intrigued by the striking young woman who spends so much of her time with the strays."

Intrigued? By me? "I'm pleased to meet you, Nef." I extended my hand. Instead of shaking it as I expected, he grasped it firmly and raised it to his lips, pressing a warm kiss onto its back. The heat from his lips seemed to radiate throughout my entire body. Or, maybe it was just the whiskey.

Blushing, I struggled for something to say as I attempted to extricate my hand from his. "Um, what brings you to the kitchens at this hour?" My traitorous voice quavered wildly, revealing the impact that his touch had on me.

His eyes twinkled as he released my hand, then he yawned and stretched, the fabric of his shirt pulling taut and treating me to a tantalizing glimpse of the muscles lurking beneath its surface. "One of the horses wasn't feeling well, and I have been taking care of her."

I jumped to my feet. "Which one? What's wrong? Can I see her?"

"Easy there." He motioned for me to calm down. "It was Elah. She's better now - which is the only reason that I was willing to leave her for a few minutes. What about you?" He pulled me into the dim light from the embers and stared far too intimately at the area of my groin. "Are you all right? Did you get burned?"

Only then did I realize that my sudden movement had caused the last of my tea to slosh into my lap. I shook my head and grabbed at his hand, urging him to his feet. "No, I'm fine. Please, let's go to the stables."

He sighed, gulped down the last of his tea and led me through the darkened room and into the courtyard.

Although the harsh Ramaldan winter was slowly loosening its grasp on the country, the nights were still cold and our breath made puffs of fog. The palace was silent, the only sounds the whistling of the guard as he made his rounds and the clinking of a chain as the watch dog scratched at an errant flea. A full moon peeked around a solitary cloud to light our path, causing the frost on the stones of the yard to glitter like gemstones.

I had thrown on my robe when I bolted from my room, but had failed to grab my slippers. The warmth from my feet melted the frost, leaving a trail of footprints behind me. We were about halfway to the stables when I stubbed my toe on a loose stone. Stubbing a toe at any time hurt - the fact that my foot was cold made it even worse. I swore in pain.

"What's wrong?" Nef looked at me in consternation; glancing down, he noticed my bare feet for the first time. "Are you nuts? You're going to catch your death of cold walking around out here with no shoes on!" Before I realized what he intended, he swept me off of my feet and into his arms, giving a startled *whuff* as my weight settled against him.

I felt it too. Heat bloomed from my shoulders to my thighs where they pressed against Nef's broad chest. I glanced down, half expecting to see a glow like the one from the fires that we had left behind. Nope, no sparks – well, no visible ones, at least. And now I knew for sure. It definitely wasn't the whiskey.

Nef grunted, shifting me slightly.

"Surely I'm not that heavy!" I grumbled.

"You, heavy?" He laughed, his teeth flashing white in the moonlight. "Not at all." He dropped his head briefly to look at me, his expression hidden in shadow. "You are, however, very... unexpected."

I fell quiet as I pondered that statement.

When we entered the stables, he sat me on the nearest flat surface, grabbed a rag from the stack reserved for cleaning tack and began chafing my feet to warm them up. Some people find having their feet rubbed soothing; being unbearably ticklish, I found it to be just shy of torture. Finally satisfied that I had suffered nothing worse than a bruise, he led me to the stall of the ailing horse.

Elah, an aging grey mare – and one of my special favorites - stood in the stall, her head hanging in exhaustion, sweat shining on her flanks.

"Poor baby! Are you feeling better now?"

At the sound of my voice, she looked up, stepped to the stall door and lowered her head for me to pet her.

Nef entered her stall and began to wipe her down. "The worst is past." He patted her affectionately on the rear. "Just a touch of indigestion. Someone left the feed bucket in her stall after filling her trough and she decided to help herself."

"You silly girl! Haven't I warned you about that appetite of yours?"

She rested her head against mine as I rubbed her muzzle and spoke soothingly to her. The last dregs of tension flowed out of her and she sighed, her breath warm in my ear.

Nef lay back on the pile of clean hay in the corner of the stall and watched with a smile as we girls visited. The next time I glanced over at him, he was asleep.

So handsome. Why had I never noticed him? I gave myself a mental shake. I couldn't allow myself to become complacent.

I stayed with Elah until she too began to nod off. Now that I knew she was truly all right, I entered the stall quietly, covered Nef with the blanket that was lying on the hay near him, picked up the lantern and made my way back to the main building. In spite of his concerns and my lack of shoes, I was fine – I wasn't nearly as delicate as my looks would have people believe. Although, I must admit it was nice to have someone seemingly so concerned about my well-being.

The least I could do in return was clean up the signs of our middle-of-the-night visit to the kitchens – just in case Nef wasn't in as good with Cook as he thought.

My efforts weren't completely altruistic however; I was also postponing my return to my bed and the ghosts that awaited me there.

2

The chamber pot shattered, splattering its contents all over the floor, bedspread, and me. Wonderful. Now, chamber pots were not known for their ability to spontaneously explode, nor was this one the first of its kind to do so. This detonation was aided by the foot of one Lord Narvel, a minor noble with a major ego.

"As you clean, perhaps you can ponder the consequences of rising above your station," he snarled, or more accurately, squeaked. His pig-like eyes glared at me out of his round, pock-marked face. "I expect no signs of this to remain when I return." With that, he raised his snout, or rather *nose*, in the air, took his wife's arm and waddled from the room.

My head was bowed as was proper for a servant being addressed by one of their "betters," but I raised my eyes in time to see the apologetic look that Lady Adele threw my way as she went by. As they proceeded down the hall, I stepped to the door and watched them walk away.

My day just wasn't getting any better. First, no sleep; now this.

"What a pathetic, sniveling, excuse for humanity he is," I mumbled to myself. My posture had changed; I was no longer the good little servant. My head was now up, green eyes blazing, and my hands were clenched into fists at my side. It was too bad that I was unwilling to take the life of an innocent man – surely the world would be a better place without Lord Narvel.

A low chuckle sounded behind me. "You know, he would have you beaten if he saw you looking at him with such effrontery. He would also volunteer to do the beating himself - as long as you were naked and tied to the bed frame."

Nef.

I dropped my posture back into appropriate servant mode. He laughed.

When I turned to look at him, his eyes shone with good humor. He leaned against the stone wall, his arms crossed casually over his chest and one foot propped on the wall behind him.

"Don't give me that. It's too late now - I've seen the real you. You did everything except stomp your foot. It suits you."

As he pushed himself upright, his gaze traveled slowly down my body; his scrutiny was almost palpable. When he raised his eyes back to mine, a subtle challenge lurked in their azure depths.

I returned his stare evenly and gave him an almost imperceptible nod. *Challenge accepted.*

"Are you lost?"

"Being a stable boy means being among the lowest of the low - and doing pretty much whatever anyone else tells you to do. I get around." He stepped closer and wiped splattered filth from my cheek, his fingertips leaving a trail of fire in their wake.

"However, I'm here because I wanted to see you. Thank you for tucking me in last night."

"You're welcome. You looked quite sweet sleeping in the hay." *Where did* that *come from?* "Um, thank you for taking me to see Elah."

He struggled manfully not to grin at my gaffe and nodded at the mess left behind by my least favorite lordling instead. "So, what did you do to incur the wrath of His Narvelness?"

"He came into the room and caught me speaking with Lady Adele. She is frequently here when I come to clean - she seems lonely and likes to talk to me. Today, she was asking my opinion on which jewels she should wear - this did not go over well with Lord Narvel. He is a proponent of the school of 'servants should be neither seen nor heard' - and they should *definitely* never be spoken to." I glanced down the hall again. "I feel sorry for Lady Adele, being married to such a...troll."

He shrugged. "Such is the life of a woman born to nobility - especially lesser nobility. Their families consider them nothing more than chattel - brood mares to be bought and sold to strengthen bloodlines and move them closer to the higher ranks." He met my eyes directly. "Even the younger male nobles are frequently used in similar fashion. Being a servant is a definite plus in my book." Gesturing toward the mess, which was beginning to develop a distinct odor, he added, "Let me help you with this."

I placed my hands on my hips and surveyed the damage. "I know I'm supposed to say 'Thank you, but I can manage it myself' - but to be honest, I would appreciate the help." I gave him a grin. "I'm not exactly the largest person in the castle."

He laughed and stepped closer - the top of my head barely reached his shoulder. "Yeah - I noticed." He motioned toward the room with his head. "Let's get started."

First, we gathered the pieces of broken pottery and placed them on the apron that I had removed. Then Nef lifted furniture so that I could roll up the rush mat covering the floor – most of the nastiness had soaked into it. We talked as we worked, getting to know one another better.

"How long have you been at the castle?" The muscles in his arms bunched as he lifted the corner of the bed; a scattering of dark hair dusted them.

I watched him through my lashes, wondering what that hair would feel like, as I tugged out the mat. "About six months. I was fortunate enough to get a job assisting the cook – but it was quickly discovered that I have no skills in that area. It was decided that I would be moved to another area before I accidentally poisoned someone or set the kitchen on fire."

Nef chuckled.

"Conveniently enough - for me, not for her - it was discovered that one of the upstairs maids was with child. She was hurried of to an unknown destination and I moved into her position." I scowled. "I hope she is all right. I feel sure that the child was a result of a liaison with one of the nobles."

He snorted as he continued to move furnishings. "Some of the nobles are actually decent men. Others are not. As you saw displayed earlier."

Now it was my turn to snort. "Narvel. Who would name their child 'Narvel'? Growing up with a name like that has got to leave some sort of scars on the psyche."

The mat was finally rolled up and ready to be moved. I looked at the debris covering the floor and couldn't help but laugh.

Nef was surprised. "What on earth can you find humorous about all of this?"

I pointed. "Look. See the colors?" The sunlight coming through the beveled glass in the window was casting rainbows of color throughout the room. "There is beauty where you least expect it - you just have to look for it."

He looked around. "You're right. I hadn't even noticed - I'll keep that in mind. I think I like your attitude, Lillie." He gave me a smile. "Now, what should I do with this thing?"

"It needs to go to the laundress - she will have to determine if it can be cleaned or if it will have to be burned. I personally vote for burning. I'll walk with you." I indicated the apron full of pottery shards. "I've got to discard the remains of the chamber pot and get a new one."

We made our way down the servant's staircase to the laundry room.

"I really appreciate your help - you saved me a lot of time." I suddenly felt inexplicably shy and ducked my head. "And I'm sorry that I didn't notice you before."

"All is forgiven." He dumped the mat in the laundry room before giving me a wink. "Watch out for exploding chamber pots." With that, he turned and walked away, his easy stride marking him as someone who was comfortable in his own skin.

As I watched him, I wished that I felt that same sense of confidence in myself. Recently, I had begun to feel as if I no longer knew *who* I was.

"Girl, I've got more than enough work to do! What else are you bringing me?" The laundress scowled at me somewhat belligerently.

"There was an accident with Lord Narvel's chamber pot." I shrugged as I indicated the ruined mat and broken pot. There really wasn't anything else to say.

"Lord Narvel, is it?" She snorted in disdain. "If anyone deserves a roomful of shit, it's that one. However, we need to make things nice for Lady Adele. That woman is one of the sweetest people in the kingdom." She placed thin arms roped with muscle on her hips and looked at the mess. "Leave those things with me and go finish cleaning. I'll have some of the men bring up a new mat later." She shooed me away. "Go on, girl. You've got things to do. And thanks to you, I've got even more." She glared at me.

I wasn't worried – I knew she was all bluster.

I returned to Lord Narvel's quarters and wiped up the rest of the nastiness then swept the room. Once the floor was free of debris, I brought in the sweet sand and scrubbed the remaining stain to remove the lingering odor.

Don't let anyone kid you - being a maid was back-breaking work. I was glad that it wasn't my regular job. However, I would miss this place when it was time to move on. I had made friends here - a rare thing in my life.

I let the laundress know when I was finished so that the mat could be replaced.

"Child, you stink!" She wrinkled her nose as she pressed a clean uniform into my hands. "Go change. But bring those soiled garments back as quickly as possible," she admonished with an accompanying wag of her finger. "The quicker I can wash them, the greater the chance that I can salvage them."

After a quick stop by the kitchen for warm water, I made my way to the servant's quarters and the small room that I shared with Maerie - a fellow maid. The room was empty, much to my relief. I quickly stripped, tossing my stained, smelly garments into a pile on the floor. The lack of clothing revealed a secret - the dagger that I carried strapped to my outer thigh. The location allowed easy access through the pocket slit in my skirt and the corresponding slit in my shift. No one knew that I carried a knife and I wanted to keep it that way - if Maerie were to see it, everyone in the castle would know within minutes. I completed my ablutions quickly, dressed in the clean clothes, and returned the dirty ones to the laundress as promised.

"You look exhausted." She gave me gentle push toward the door. "Go on - get something to eat before the men come in and take all the good stuff."

As I turned to walk away, she stopped me.

"Don't you worry none about Lord Narvel; this isn't the first time something like this has happened." She sniffed. "His high and mightiness hasn't realized that we keep him in the rooms with the rush mats instead of the nicer woven rugs for a reason."

I gave her a smile of thanks and went to the kitchen. Once there, I waved at Cook and loaded up my clean apron with food. I picked up the moldy cheese and bread and the pieces of bruised and battered fruit that Cook set aside for me, then added a few good pieces of the same. I bore my gleanings across the yard and into the stables, to share with my fur-covered friends.

I loved everything about the stables - the warmth, the smell of the hay, even the smell of the animals. Several of the horses nickered at me as I entered. I walked by their stalls, stroking their warm muzzles.

"Hi, everyone!" I greeted them quietly. "I'm glad to see you; it's been a rough day."

The horses nosed my hand and rolled their eyes at my apron.

I laughed. "You know the rules - I eat first, then you."

I walked to the end of the aisle and the large pile of clean hay stored there. I climbed midway up the stack, laid back, closed my eyes and inhaled the smell of sunshine and warm fields that rose around me. Soon, a quiet rustling began nearby. I opened one eye and cocked my head in time to see Tiny, one of the barn cats, slowly creeping toward me. Once she was close enough, I reached out a finger and gently scratched her head; she closed her eyes in bliss. It had taken a while to earn Tiny's trust; even though she still darted away if I made any sudden moves, she would now let me pet her.

I opened my apron and began munching on bread, cheese, and apples, washing everything down with swigs of cider from the leather pouch that I had grabbed at the last moment. I ate slowly, enjoying the peace and quiet. Gradually, more of the barn cats came and joined me, watching my movements and waiting their turn.

Once I finished my meal, I tore the moldy cheese into small pieces and scattered it on the ground around me. The cats moved in for their treats. Most of them were quite comfortable with me and rubbed up against me in thanks - and for attention. I petted them all, calling them by the names that I had given them, hoping that I had brought some brief pleasure into their lives. At least for a short time, they could enjoy not having to fight and scrounge for food and be loved simply because they existed. We should all be so lucky.

Once I finished with the cats, I moved on to the horses – starting with Elah.

"How's my pretty girl?" The old mare tossed her head and whickered, pulling her lips back in anticipation of a treat. "Feeling better, are you?" I pulled out my knife and made quick work of slicing an apple which I fed to her slowly. "Now, no more over-eating," I admonished. "You gave me a scare last night." I stroked her muzzle in farewell before working my way through the remaining stalls, doling out fruit and affection.

Lastly, I crumbled the dry moldy bread and scattered it on the ground in the stable yard as a treat for the wild birds that nested in the nooks and crannies of the stable roof.

The door to the kitchens had been thrown open, casting a warm, inviting light into the darkening night. I let it draw me closer, but I paused in the growing shadows, listening to the conversation that flowed out with the light. Loud and soft, high and low, the voices blended together in a song that spoke of home and hearth and love. The speakers may have been servants, invisible to those they served, but they were also a family – a family that had welcomed me and accepted me as one of their own. When they learned the truth about me, they would be shocked and outraged. I did not like deceiving them; this place was the closest thing to a true home that I had ever known and leaving it would be the hardest thing that I had ever had to do. The memories of my time there were precious to me - I stored them away as an animal stockpiled food for the winter.

I stepped through the doorway.

"Lillie!" Maerie rushed up and grabbed my arm. "Where have you been?" Her freckled nose wrinkled. "Never mind. I can tell that you've been with the horses again. Wait until you hear about my day." She led me to our room, talking incessantly.

Maerie was full of dreams. She was convinced that some handsome young noble would fall in love with her, take her away to his manor and make her his lady - completely overlooking her commoner birth. I hoped she was right. I would hate to see the light in her eyes die if she were to give herself to some lordling only to learn that he wanted her body, but not her soul.

As we prepared for bed, Maerie finally took a deep breath and insisted that I tell her about my day. I did, making sure to include as many details as possible - she lived for the details.

She gasped in horror as I described the shattering chamber pot and sighed when I described Nef.

Her blonde brows furrowed. "I don't recall seeing him around the castle."

"You wouldn't," I teased. "You only have eyes for the lordlings, not a mere stable boy."

She swung her pillow at me. "Maybe so, but I am always willing to look at a handsome face, no matter what its rank."

I removed my uniform and hung it carefully on the hook on the wall at the end of my bed before pulling my nightgown over my head; I used its soft folds to hide my dagger as I wriggled out of my shift.

Maerie rolled her eyes. She was convinced that I suffered from extreme modesty; nothing could have been further from the truth.

As I pulled back the covers and moved to get into bed, Maerie cleared her throat. I ignored her.

"Ahem!" she repeated, louder.

"What?" I sighed, turning to face my roommate. I knew what was coming.

"You know the rules." Maerie gestured pointedly toward the end of the room.

We slept with the high window in our room slightly ajar to let in fresh air. I moved my clothes to hang in front of it.

"I'll never understand you," I grumbled as I returned to my bed. "Horses and hay smell wonderful."

Maerie simply snorted before blowing out the candle and plunging us into darkness.

3

The clattering of hooves on cobblestones jarred me from a much needed, dreamless, sleep – there was a definite downside to sleeping with the window open. I lost precious time as I struggled out of the bedclothes that had a stranglehold on my legs and staggered across the room, yawning. I had to stand on my tiptoes in order to see over the windowsill – a dangerous stunt when still half-asleep. However, my efforts were in vain – no horse or rider was visible. Light from the open kitchen doorway flowed into the courtyard; I suspected that the mysterious caller had been invited within. The horse would have been taken to the stables; if its arrival was any indication, it had been ridden hard and would be in need of attention. A faint lightening in the eastern sky indicated that dawn was approaching; attempting to return to my slumber would be futile.

The kitchen staff was already up and busily prepping the mountain of foodstuffs required to feed the occupants of the palace on a daily basis. The peeling and chopping of vegetables may have kept the hands busy, but the mouths associated with the hands were free to gossip. I was sure that I would be able to find someone who would be eager to tell me about our early morning visitor. I took an extremely quick, extremely cold sponge bath and dressed before venturing downstairs. I had no sooner entered the room before Cook, looking exceptionally harried for so early in the day, pressed a heavily laden tray into my hands.

"Thank the Makers! I asked for an extra set of hands and here you are!"

I was pretty sure that it was the first time that I had been the answer to a prayer.

She shoved me none too gently toward the table nearest the fire and its lone occupant. "See to it that his needs are met until I can find the mistress."

"His 'needs'?" My footsteps faltered.

Cook rolled her eyes in exasperation. "Nothing like that, child! Food, tea, whiskey – any needs that can be met from our larders." Without further ado, she scuttled out of the room as quickly as her ample frame would allow.

Reassured, I greeted our rather disheveled, extremely dusty visitor. "Good morning, sir. Cook has prepared a selection of edibles for you. Can I get you something to drink?"

"Coffee? In the name of all that is holy, please tell me that you have coffee!" He rubbed a strong brown hand across the stubble on his cheeks before peering at me blearily through bloodshot eyes. "The stronger, the better."

A quick glance at the hearth showed the battered kettle hanging in its usual location over the flames. It was the work of only a couple of moments to pour a cup of the steaming black brew for our guest. I was glad he liked it strong; Cook made it no other way.

After locating the sweetener, I gave the beverage to the stranger. He shoveled several heaping spoons of sugar into the cup and gave it a quick stir before tossing back a healthy swallow. I cringed, certain that he had scalded his throat.

"Thank you, lass." He sighed and swiped his arm across his mouth. "That's the best thing I've had since the whore in..." A grin split his face, revealing teeth in need of a good brushing and a genial disposition. "Hells, I've been on the road so long all of the towns are running together. Well, wherever she was, she was the best piece of ass I've had in quite a while." He raised his cup in salute. When he put it down, he simultaneously pulled me onto the bench beside him and pushed the tray toward me. "Here - I hate to eat alone."

I glanced over my shoulder.

"Don't worry. I'll tell 'em that I twisted your arm." He reached out and gently twisted my wrist in demonstration just as my stomach growled loudly in response to the aromas drifting off of the platter. He laughed as he grabbed a pastry and offered it to me.

I accepted it gratefully and smiled back as I bit into it. I liked this man – whoever he was. I excused myself long enough to make myself a cup of tea. When I returned, I learned why he hated to eat alone – it meant that he would have no one to talk to. I didn't know if he was always talkative or if his current need was fueled by his forced solitude as he traveled. He carried the conversation, never staying on one topic for long. I simply listened as I ate, occasionally interjecting a noncommittal grunt. He continued to talk long after my hunger was sated, pausing only intermittently to eat or drink. I was beginning to wonder how I was going to extricate myself from his attentions so that I could begin my daily chores when a shadow fell across the table.

"Jehrold. As verbose as always, I see."

Neither of us had heard Mistress Lalane enter the room. "Mama L," as she was lovingly called by those in her employ, was the head of household, responsible for the entire palace staff. She was more than fair and treated her staff like family; however, those who shirked their duties did not last long in her service. While she cared for all of her staff, she took a special interest in her youngest charges. She truly wanted them to do well and succeed. She was currently focusing most of her attention on Maerie. I think she was concerned by Maerie's fantasies of being swept away by a lordling lover; she knew such fancies had the potential to end badly. Mama L was the one person in the palace that made me nervous; her gaze always held a certain coldness when it fell on me. I was convinced that she was suspicious of me and was simply biding her time before exposing me.

Jehrold leaped to his feet and bowed, surreptitiously wiping his mouth as he did so. "Mistress LaLane - just the person that I was looking for!" As he pressed his lips to her hand, he eyed her appreciatively.

It was understandable. Mama L was a striking woman, no stranger to the admiring looks of men. Tall and slender, yet not without feminine curves, she wore her white hair pulled into a loose bun. Her violet eyes were calm and steady at all times. The white hair was deceiving; most people assumed that she was older than she really was. Mama L was no more than forty – if that. However, something about her seemed older than her years. Some would say that she had an old soul. Even now, she was perfectly composed, no hint of the early hour reflected in her face.

To say that I was surprised at the flush of color that flooded her cheeks at the touch of Jehrold's lips would be an understatement. My eyebrows attempted to work their way into my hairline as I witnessed their exchange.

She laughed indulgently at his mannerisms and squeezed his fingers gently before releasing his hand. "To what do I owe the pleasure of your visit?"

"Marcus wished me to tell you that he will be returning to the palace as soon as the snow melts in the high mountain passes. Based on what I experienced in my travels, you have approximately six weeks, if no additional snow falls."

My ears perked up. Marcus was the king's most trusted advisor and the man charged with selecting a suitable heir. He and a contingent of the royal guard had left the palace several months ago to begin the process. Several families of noble blood had sons of an acceptable age. Each of the families would be interviewed to determine which would be given the "honor" of providing the heir to the throne. It was my understanding that the selected to heir would be taken from his family even if it was against their will. Not exactly the best way to win the approval and acceptance of the one who would have nothing to lose by killing the king and taking his throne for their own. But that was just my opinion.

"Six weeks?" One slim hand floated gracefully to her chest. "He does like to keep life exciting, doesn't he? Ah well, we will be busy, but it will be time enough. Please, finish your meal." She gestured for him to return to the table and his food. "I do hope that you will stay long enough to rest and let us replenish your supplies."

"I'll do better than that." He actually had the audacity to wink at her. "I am under orders to stay and assist with preparations in any way that I can." He pointed to his pack. "You know Marcus – he sent several lists of details that I am to ensure are taken care of." He shrugged. "As if it you would plan anything that would be less than perfect."

"It will be a pleasure to have you at the palace again – it has been far too long. I'll have a room prepared for you."

"Don't go to any trouble on my account, sweetling. I would be more than happy to share your bed."

Mama L responded with a girlish laugh.

I gasped and choked on a crumb. Jehrold pounded me heartily on the back until I was able to draw in a gasping breath. Tears streamed down my face as I struggled to regain my composure.

"Lillie, since you have already eaten, I would like for you to ready a room for our guest." Amusement tinged Mama L's voice.

I had to take several swallows of my now cold tea before I was able to croak a response. "Yes, ma'am."

I raced up the stairs and burst into my shared room, the door slamming against the wall.

"What? Who..." Maerie sat bolt upright, her sleeping cap hanging jauntily from one ear. "Lillie! What's going on? Is there a fire?"

"No — nothing like that! I'm pretty sure that Mama L has a lover — and he is in the kitchen right now! I'm supposed to ready a room for him."

"A lover? Are you sure?" She was already out of bed and dragging on her clothes.

"Pretty sure. The clues were subtle, but they were there."

Maerie ran from the room, only to reappear, grab her cap and apron and leave again.

One task down, one to go. Since Mama L did not specify which room I was to prepare, I put Jehrold in the vacant room closest to her own.

Word of Jehrold's news spread quickly — the excitement among the servants was almost palpable. While it seemed that almost everyone was eager to gossip and speculate about the heir, I simply wanted to be alone to consider what the implications of the news were for me. Fortunately, my duties as a maid were somewhat solitary and gave me the excuse that I needed to avoid the whispered conversations taking place around almost every corner. Routine tasks such as sweeping allowed me plenty of time to think as I worked.

I had settled into my life, and my role, in the castle easily enough. My training allowed me to be equally comfortable in the part of a noblewoman or a servant, and anything in between. It was easier than most would think. If I dressed myself in the drab garb of a servant and took on the mannerisms expected of one - eyes down, spoke only when spoken to - everyone assumed that I was a servant. However, if I were to strip off the servant's clothing and slip into a lady's gown with jewels at my throat and in my hair and greet those that I met with confidence - and possibly a slight air of disdain - they would assume that I was a noblewoman. In truth I was both and neither. I was who I chose to be.

Unfortunately, I was struggling to find out who that was.

Manah's throne was handed down through the male bloodline. The reigning king had no male heirs, although it wasn't for lack of trying. He had several daughters, each by a different mother. It was dangerous to be a female that caught the eye of His Majesty - there was a very real chance that to do so was a death sentence. Each wife that had produced a daughter had been put to death, as had each wife that failed to bear a child. His Majesty had a cruel streak and delighted in finding new and creative - also known as cruel - ways to kill each wife. Somehow, he failed to see that *he* was the common denominator in each of these "failures."

The nobles had grown restless at His Majesty's inability to produce an heir and were threatening to replace him with someone with the proven capability of doing so. Therefore, he had decided to adopt an heir. The nobles, a touchy bunch at the best of times, turned on each other without hesitation – many families willingly offered their sons as sacrifices on the altar of politics. The power that would be theirs if the successor were selected from their lineage far outweighed anything as trivial as familial loyalty or love.

This was where the Va'Shile – the assassin's guild – and I came in. The Va'Shile cared not who was in power. They cared only for the coin received for their assistance in facilitating change when needed. Vido had secured my position as cook's assistant; the rest was up to me. Once the heir had been chosen and publicly acknowledged, it was my job to kill him.

The sound of arguing broke into my reverie. Stepping into the hall, I found a small group of maids in heated discussion. Hair-pulling and face-slapping seemed only moments away.

"What in the name of the Makers is going on?"

The tallest of the group pointed at one of the others, a rather round girl with freckles and a saucy grin. "*She* thinks that the throne should be allowed to go to a female. Whoever heard of such a thing? A female on the throne. Ridiculous!"

"If you are going to risk your job by arguing where you might be seen by one of the lords, the least you can do is argue over something important!" I turned my gaze on the saucy one. "The law says that the throne can only be held by a male."

An I-told-you-so look began to spread across the face of Tall Girl, until I turned to her.

"But, it is a stupid law," I continued. "Of *course* a female could run the country as ably as any male!"

A chorus of cries broke out around me, the words indiscernible as everyone struggled to be heard over everyone else. No wonder some of the men referred to groups of women as "hens" – the cacophony sounded like nothing so much as the noise that could be heard emanating from the chicken coop.

"Lillie is right, you know," a baritone voice suddenly spoke.

The silence that followed that statement was almost deafening. All heads turned in search of the speaker. Nef was standing behind me; he was just as handsome as I remembered.

"For centuries, the Nidolan family ruled Manah and the throne passed to the eldest child – male *or* female." His gaze traveled across the faces of his audience, his eyes narrowing slightly at those who appeared ready to argue. "The country was united and, for the most part, peaceful. However, it was impossible to please everyone and some of the nobles become restless; they were dissatisfied serving as generals and advisors to the crown. Some of them decided that it was time that the Nidolans be removed from power. Fate seemed to be on their side. Manah was struck with a plague and the population, including the royal family, was devastated. The country was left in the hands of the youngest of the Nidolan sons, Lester - a weak-minded individual who cared nothing for ruling. His lack of ambition was only worsened by his propensity for drinking and whoring. He gladly left the decision-making up to his advisors, namely those very individuals who sought to overthrow his family. Over time, Lester's mental capacity was lessened even further by syphilis; his whoring finally caught up with him. Knowing his weaknesses and the fact that he had no heir except a much younger female cousin, the advisors proposed that Lester pass a decree stating that the throne could only be passed down to a male. He was easily convinced – he already believed that females were only good for the easing of his physical needs. That decree still stands today."

Tall Girl scowled; she still wasn't convinced. "Do you truly believe that a woman can rule as well as a man?"

Nef laughed. "Of course I do! If you had ever met my mother, you would have no doubt as to why I feel that way. That woman could run a country, manage the entire palace staff, *and* raise a flock of children without batting an eye. Actually, before the plague, the Nidolan throne was passed to females on several occasions; each and every queen acquitted herself ably." He glanced over his shoulder as if expecting to see someone coming down the hall. "Mama L is not happy - too many people are talking instead of working. I recommend that you return to your duties before she catches you."

The group dispersed reluctantly but not before several of the girls eyed Nef speculatively. Jealousy flared ever so briefly in my chest.

"I must return to my chores as well." I gave him a smile as I turned to walk away. "Thank you for the history lesson."

"Wait." He reached for my hand to stop me. "You're the one that I came to see." He pulled me closer, but did not release my hand. "How about joining me for the evening meal? I have something to show you that I think you will like."

I arched an eyebrow at him. "Oh, really? Something that I will like? Should I be worried for the safety of my virtue?"

He chuckled. "Your virtue is safe with me."

Damn.

"So, will you join me?"

How could I resist? "Of course, I will. And thanks - again."

I felt unaccountably shy and hurried to finish my tasks. As I worked, I wondered what had come over me. How could this man that I had only met recently make me feel so funny inside? What did he see in me? Maybe tonight I could begin to answer that question.

4

I joined the crush of servants pressing into the kitchens for the evening meal. I searched the sea of faces for Nef.

"Ah! My breakfast partner has returned." Jehrold appeared at my elbow. "Will you join me again this evening?" He hooked his arm through mine and steered me toward the long tables.

"No, she will not." Nef appeared at my other side. "Lillie already has plans."

"Oh, ho! So, the maiden has a jealous suitor, does she?" Jehrold bowed graciously and handed me off to Nef. "Never let it be said that I stood in the way of young love."

I blushed furiously. Nef simply slid his arm around my waist and steered me toward the door to the courtyard, snagging a bag from the counter as we passed.

"Where are we going?"

He nodded in the general direction of the stables, but glanced back over his shoulder at the kitchens. "How did you meet him?"

"Simple. His arrival this morning woke me up. When I went downstairs to find out what was going on, Cook pressed me into service. He insisted that I eat with him." I shrugged. "He was lonely and needed someone to talk to."

Our already slow footsteps faltered to a stop. Nef's expression had grown serious.

"Would you rather be with him?"

"Of course not. Why?" Slowly, comprehension dawned. "Wait. *Are* you a jealous suitor?"

He fingered the stray curl that had escaped my cap before speaking. "Would that be a bad thing?"

Was he kidding? I wanted to shout and dance but settled for replying, "No, I don't think that would be a bad thing at all."

His dimples blazed to life as he gave me a heart-stopping grin. "Good. Come on."

His steps quickened as he took my hand and led me into the stables, then helped me up the ladder into the loft. Even during my many excursions to the stables, I had not ventured there - climbing in a skirt was not the easiest thing in the world.

I searched the shadows unsuccessfully for anything that might be of interest. Light flared behind me as Nef lit the oil lamp that he had apparently placed there earlier. Taking my hand, he slowly led me to the far corner, ducking to avoid the rafters that slanted over our heads. He raised the lamp so that its flickering light illuminated a depression in the hay that contained a multi-colored cat nursing several babies. As we watched, she began to lick the one nearest her head. The kitten protested ineffectively, squeaking and flailing its tiny pink paws in the air.

I dropped to my knees, being careful not to get too close. "Lucy! You had your babies! I didn't know that your time was so near. Silly girl, you should have told me." I took the lamp from Nef and held it so that I could see the kittens better; there were five, all busily suckling. "You've done a good job, Mama; you have a beautiful family."

Lucy stretched out to better display her brood and squinched her golden eyes at me, purring in pleasure.

I looked up. "Oh, Nef! Thank you! I would have been so worried when Lucy didn't show up to visit me. I didn't realize that she was so near to delivering."

He looked at me, slightly stunned. "Tell you? Lucy? You gave her a name? I didn't know that you two were acquainted, but I did think that you would enjoy seeing the kittens."

"I have names for all of the cats. They know me and have learned that they can trust me – they're my friends." I cocked my head at him. "Would you like to meet them?"

Still somewhat dazed, he nodded.

I grabbed his hand and headed for the ladder. I managed to get down safely in spite of the skirt and without assistance. Nef retrieved the bundle of food he had brought and I led him to my usual spot in the hay.

"Now, let's eat. As we do, be still and watch the shadows."

He did as he was told. Within moments, my furry friends began to gather, keeping their distance, unsure of this stranger in their midst.

"It's okay," I told them. "This is Nef. He's with me. He won't hurt you."

Gradually, the cats began to inch their way closer, the bravest even came up to me to be petted.

I was handing out pieces of cheese when I realized that I was being watched. Nef lounged against the hay, his expression questioning.

"What is there between you and the animals, Lillie? The guard dogs fawn at your feet like puppies. These creatures - " he indicated the cats - "usually run at the first sign of people and yet you have them eating out of your hand - literally. Even battled-hardened Cefus acts like a colt around you."

Cefus whinnied from his stall, apparently in agreement.

I picked up a piece of hay and chewed on it absently as I considered my answer. I had only spoken of my relationship with animals once before and it hadn't gone well. I didn't expect to receive the same response from Nef, but I didn't know him very well. At least if I told him the truth, I would learn more about what kind of man he really was based on his reaction.

"I have some sort of... *connection* with animals. It's been that way as long as I can remember. We are drawn to each other. To some extent, we can communicate." I glanced up at him, trying to gauge his reaction. "The connection seems to be getting stronger as I get older."

Still no response.

"I guess that probably sounds strange," I finished lamely.

His eyes took on a distant look and he began imitating my earlier actions by tossing pieces of cheese to the strays, hoping to lure them nearer. "Maybe you're a Southron witch. I've heard that they are able to communicate with animals."

"A Southron witch?" I couldn't help but laugh. "You have seen me, right? Southroners have dark skin, hair, and eyes. I would say that I am Norte through and through – I'm so fair that I practically glow in the dark."

Nef shrugged. "Breeding can do tricky things. Look at me - I *know* my heritage. I *am* Norte through and through, yet I have traits of both Norte and Southron." He gestured at himself.

"And a striking combination it is."

He seemed pleased by the compliment.

"You don't seem very surprised by my revelation."

"I've seen you with the animals. I have to believe that there is something to what you say. Besides, what reason do you have to lie to me?"

If only he knew.

"Well, the only other time I told anyone, I was beaten."

"Beaten?" He sat up so abruptly the cats scattered. "Who would beat you for simply telling the truth?"

"My... foster-father." I pulled up my knees and wrapped my arms around them, rocking slightly as I talked. "I was young and I didn't know I was different. I thought *everyone* could understand animals the same way that I did. One day I was playing and fell asleep in the root cellar. When I woke up, I couldn't get out – the door was locked. I yelled and yelled, but no one could hear me. Finally, I became aware of the dogs. I reached out with my mind and was able to get the attention of one of them. He ran over and clawed at the door and barked until someone opened it and found me. I was fine – only a little scared by the experience. Later, my foster-father called me to his room. When I got there, he looked very serious. He asked me to explain what happened. When I did, he slapped me – hard enough to knock me down and split my lip."

Nef's eyes narrowed.

"He told me that I was a foolish child with an overactive imagination and that I was never to say such things again." I shook my head. "I thought I heard him say something about my mother, but I wasn't sure and I definitely wasn't going to ask." I raised my hand to my cheek as I remembered. "I had the imprint of his hand on my cheek for days and couldn't eat anything but broth until my lip healed."

"I don't think I like your foster-father very much."

Nef moved to my side and wiped away the tears that I had not realized were running down my cheeks. His touch was gentle and his eyes roamed my face.

"It hurts me to think of anyone treating you so." Anger suffused his voice. "Any man who raises his hand to a woman *or* a child deserves to be stripped, bound, and thrown into a den of hungry *yaren*."

My heart swelled with joy. If I had had any doubts about what kind of man Nef was, I doubted no longer.

He took my hands in his, stroking his thumbs idly across them. "What happened to your parents?"

"They sold me into service when I was only two or three. Or at least that is what my foster-father has always told me. He never lost an opportunity to tell me that they sold me because I was a bad girl and they didn't want me - that they loved the coin he could provide more than they loved me."

His grip tightened on my hands. "I *definitely* don't like your foster-father. Do you believe him?"

"I don't want to, but I have no reason not to." I dropped my gaze.

Nef put his fingers under my chin and raised my eyes to meet his. "Do you remember anything about your parents?"

"No." I shook my head. "I was too young." I hesitated before adding, "I have a few vague impressions, but I don't know if they are really memories or just wishful thinking."

"Tell me about them." He grinned as he added, "Please."

I searched for the words to describe those fleeting images. "I remember... warm hands... strong arms... the sound of laughter... and the feeling of safety."

"Then *that* is what you need to hold on to. Don't let your foster-father take that away from you. Will you do that for me?"

"I'll try."

Out of the corner of my eye, I caught movement. The cats were beginning to creep closer to us again. I took advantage of the opportunity to change the subject.

"Don't look now, but we have company."

Nef shifted, eager to see them.

"Careful. Don't make any sudden moves – you'll startle them again."

He looked so crestfallen that I couldn't help but laugh.

"Don't expect too much right away. They have to learn that you aren't going to hurt them. If you truly want them to trust you, it will take time."

We spent the rest of our time together engaging in small talk - the kind of simple nothings that people discuss when they are trying to get to know one another.

When it was time to leave, I bade the cats good night. As we walked down the aisle toward the door, a few of the horses whickered from their stalls and faces peered over the doors as they looked to see if I had treats. I petted them all, rubbed their muzzles, and promised to return with snacks as soon as I could.

Nef walked me to the kitchen door and then, in a very courtly fashion, kissed my hand. "Good night, my Lillie. It has been a pleasurable evening."

My Lillie. My goodness.

"Good night, Nef – and thank you. I enjoyed it too."

He turned and walked away, whistling. I liked his casual stride and easy confidence. I braced myself for the teasing that I was sure to face from Jehrold and stepped into the warmth of the kitchen.

5

Nef took his role as my suitor seriously; he quickly developed the habit of finding me at some point during the day for a brief chat. I looked forward to his visits more than he knew.

His timing today was perfect.

I was immersed in my least favorite chore - replacing candles. Yes, believe it or not, replacing candles was worse than emptying chamber pots – at least for me.

The walls of the long halls of the palace were lined with sconces. The candles had to be checked and replaced as needed every day. Even with a stool and stretched to my full height, I could barely reach them; I dreaded the days when this chore fell to me. I was usually able to work a trade with one of the other maids - few would refuse my offer to empty chamber pots for them if they replaced candles for me.

Today, I had not been so fortunate.

The hallway appeared to get longer as I watched. With a sigh, I lugged my stool to the first sconce, climbed up, replaced the candles, climbed back down, and then moved it to the next location. I also had to transport two bags – one containing new candles, the other the burned-down nubs. Nothing went to waste – the chandler would reuse as much of the old wax as possible.

I wasn't even halfway through and my arms were already aching from the strain; I started rushing to finish. Big mistake. Remember the problems that I mentioned with skirts and climbing? Even though I was able to climb down from the loft in the stables without assistance, I was not as lucky today. When I moved to get down from my stool, my foot tangled in my skirt; I lost my balance and began to fall. I searched desperately for something to grab in an attempt to save myself; there was nothing, not even a conveniently placed wall hanging. I let out a small scream, closed my eyes, and braced for impact on the unforgiving stone floor.

Instead of the expected bone-breaking impact, a pair of warm, strong arms enveloped me. I opened my eyes. A pair of familiar blue ones looked back at me. This close, I noticed for the first time just how long and thick Nef's dark lashes were. It seemed almost a shame that the Makers would waste such lashes on a man who would take no notice of them. Noblewomen and whores went to great trouble to make their lashes look like his did with no effort whatsoever.

Nef eased me to my feet, but kept his arms around me.

"You know, there *are* easier ways to get me to hold you." He scowled at me, but the gleam in his eyes and the dimple that flared into life were a sure sign he was teasing.

Trembling with reaction to my near miss, I leaned against him, wrapped my arms around his neck and rested my head against his muscular chest. The fabric of his shirt was rough against my cheek, but much softer than the stone I had expected. I struggled to match my ragged breathing to the steady rhythm of his heart. Once I had regained my equilibrium, I pulled back far enough to meet his eyes.

"I wish you had told me that earlier so that I could have skipped the whole *let-me-fall-and-hope-Nef-shows-up-to-rescue-me-in-time* routine."

He laughed, flashing even white teeth.

Nef never talked about his family, but I wondered about his background. Many of the servants had the missing or damaged teeth that resulted from years of improper care or poor nutrition, but his were strong and well-cared for.

"Thank you," I said and shuddered. "I don't even want to think about what might have happened if you hadn't come by when you did."

"You're welcome, little one."

He held my gaze as he reached out and gently stroked his thumb across my jaw. His touch always made me tingle from head to toe. I suspected that he was well aware of his effect on me. Once he was sure that I was all right, he settled me back on my stool, gave me a wink, and proceeded to make short work of replacing the remaining candles. When finished, he presented the bags to me with a flourish.

"There – all done." He arched a brow at me questioningly. "Will you be joining me for dinner tonight?"

"Of course."

Since our trip to the stables to visit Lucy and her kittens, we had eaten together every night.

"Good. I look forward to it." He gave me a wave as he stepped back and began to turn away.

"Wait." I laid my hand on his arm to stop him before he could leave.

He looked at me expectantly.

"You said that there were easier ways to get you to hold me." The look I gave him was equal parts question and dare. "What are they?"

"It's simple. All you have to do is ask."

Before I realized what he planned to do, he leaned over, planted a kiss on the tip of my nose then turned and walked away.

I practically floated through the rest of the day.

6

Our evenings together developed a pattern – first we ate, then we roamed the castle or its grounds. I was thrilled the first time Nef took my hand in his as we walked. Although it was now commonplace, I found it no less exciting.

I had done some exploring of the palace on my own, but I was astonished by how well Nef knew his way around – especially since he, too, had only been at the palace a few months.

One evening, our wandering led us to the great room, which was exactly what it sounded like – the largest room in the palace. At the time of our entry, its emptiness echoed our footsteps back to us. However, its barrenness was deceptive. The great room served many purposes and – with the assistance of numerous servants – changed its appearance as many times a day as any noblewoman. The king and nobles met there each morning to break their fast. Once the dishes and tables were cleared away, the room became center of activity for the king; he took his throne and held court - meeting with nobles and commoners alike – settling disputes and granting boons. Other reconfigurations occurred as needed for meals and other functions.

When the heir arrived, the Naming would take place there. Naming ceremonies were rare – most kings without heirs were killed before one could be selected. Nobility that had not set foot in Ramalda for years would put in an appearance – if only to look over the heir and determine their chances for being selected for his court should he ascend to the throne.

I groaned inwardly at the thought of the amount of work that would be required to prepare the room for the royal ball that would accompany the ceremony. I hoped that Mama L was planning to bring in temporary workers to assist. If she didn't, the rest of us would not be sleeping for several weeks.

Viewing a room that size by the light of an oil lamp left a lot to be desired – few details were visible.

With his usual uncanny sureness, Nef led me across the shadowy room and raised the lamp. The flickering rays fell across a dais and the lavish throne occupying it.

"It seems strange to me that a chair, no matter how large and ornate, symbolizes the power that one man holds over an entire country," I whispered. Somehow, it seemed inappropriate to speak louder.

An odd look flickered across his face.

"What's wrong?"

"I was just thinking about all of the people that have sat on this throne through the centuries. It must be scary." His voice was also low.

"I've never really thought about it." I shrugged. "I guess I've just always assumed that the occupants of the throne were raised to the job – that doing what they do is no harder for them than... scrubbing floors is for me."

"I can't imagine being responsible for running a country ever being an easy job." Casting one final glance at the throne, he led me from the room. "Come on, let's get out of here. This place is depressing."

By unspoken agreement, we avoided the great room from then on.

Tonight, our wanderings led us to the palace gardens. The sky was overcast; the sliver of moon cast a fitful light through tatters of clouds. A nip in the air hinted at the possibility of snow in the higher elevations. The possibility excited me – more snow would delay the arrival of the heir, giving me more time with my new family, with Nef.

Hand in hand, we strolled darkened paths lined with slumbering shrubs. Soon, they would waken, bursting with the new life of spring, but tonight they cast skeletal shadows in the erratic light.

As we walked, Nef pointed out the various features of the gardens, beginning with pedestals of gold-veined white marble quarried from mines in the Southron Mountains.

"It is said that in ages past, busts of the most famous kings and queens of Ramalda graced these stands."

"What happened to them?"

"Once Lester Nidolan turned control of Ramalda over to the nobles, they quickly removed the statuary – they wanted their takeover to be complete and wanted no reminders of the royal family visible to guests." He chuckled. "They may have planned to replace them with effigies of the new kings, but the idea was quickly discarded. The throne changed hands so often there would have been no room for plants in the garden. That's when they decided to go with the portraits that line the hallways of the palace instead. Have you seen them?"

"Oh, yes. I've dusted many of them. I noticed by the dates on them that no one seems to stay in power for long." I ran my fingers lightly over the cold, smooth stone of one of the pedestals. "So, if the statues are gone, why keep these?"

"Come spring gilded cages filled with colorful birds will be placed here - their songs will fill the gardens with music." The corners of his eyes crinkled in amusement as he continued, "I have even heard of provocatively dressed servants being whitewashed and forced to stand on them as living statues."

I stopped walking and turned to face him, placing my hand on my hips. "Surely, you are making that up!"

He laughed and held his hands up as if to ward off my disbelief. "I haven't actually seen it, but I have been told that it has happened many times – not only at the palace but also at functions put on by various members of the nobility."

He slid his arm around my waist – rather nonchalantly, I might add – and resumed walking. I suppressed a smile at his boldness.

"This is where larger cages are sometimes placed." He indicated gaps in the shrubs. "Yaren and other wild beasts are captured and put on display to reflect the hunting prowess of the king – although the actual hunting is done by others."

"How terrible!" I scowled up at him. "I hate to think of all of those poor creatures being caged like that." My appointed task would be hard enough without being able to feel their fear and anger; I hoped that I would be far enough away to not be impacted by it.

Our wanderings eventually led to the fountain in the center of the gardens. Nef led me to a nearby bench and pulled me down to sit with him. When it was warmer, water would burble from the top of the stylized sculpture in the center of the fountain, flowing into the pool at its base. Now, dead leaves blocked the flow of water, reducing it to a mere trickle; more leaves floated on the surface of the stagnant water in the pool.

I finally gave voice to the question that I had wondered so often.

"How do you know so much about the palace and the history of the royal family?"

"History has always been important to my family – especially my father. He insisted that I learn as much about Ramalda's past as possible." His eyes developed a faraway look. "He said that knowing about our past helps us to face the future."

"He sounds like a very wise man. He must be very excited about you working at the palace."

Nef's face fell and he looked away from me. After a moment, he turned back to face me, his eyes glistening with moisture.

"He doesn't know. He died several years ago."

"Oh! I'm so sorry." I reached up and cupped his face in my hand.

"Thank you." He turned his head and dropped a kiss into my palm. "My family lived in Ramalda when I was very young. I actually visited the palace when I was a child. We left the city rather... abruptly."

His memories seemed to propel him to his feet; he walked to fountain where he stood with his back to me as he stared unseeing into its depths. His sadness was almost palpable.

I hesitated to break into his reverie, but I couldn't bear to see him look so forlorn. I stepped quietly to his side and waited. After a moment, he pulled me into his arms and rested his cheek on the top of my head. We stood in silence. Finally, he sighed and lifted his head.

I looked up at him. "You don't have to talk about this if you don't want to. It's okay."

"No. I want you to know." Taking my hand in his, he led me back to the bench. "The political situation in Ramalda had become more unstable than usual and a threat of civil war hung over the town. My parents decided that it would be best to send us children away - for our own safety."

"What about your parents? Didn't they go with you?"

"My mother did. My father stayed here, working to ensure that we made it out of town safely. He planned to follow us later. Only, he never did. He was killed when the fighting broke out."

"I'm sorry." I cringed as I uttered the words. "I'm saying the same thing over and over – but I really do mean it." I looked at him, hoping that he would see the sincerity in my eyes.

"It was hard on all of us – especially my mother. She lost the love of her life *and* was left to raise us alone." Nef shrugged. "But, it has been many years and even the greatest of heartaches eases over time. Sometimes, life is hard - you can't let it get the best of you. I had a choice; I could brood, or I could be happy. I chose to be happy." Sitting up, he shook himself like a wet dog and the last vestiges of his sorrow fell away. "However, I don't really want to talk about my family any more right now if you don't mind. It's a gorgeous night, and I'm with a beautiful woman – this is not a time for sadness."

"You're such a flatterer." I ducked my head as a blush flooded my face.

"It's not flattery." He put his fingers under my chin and raised my gaze to his. "I'm serious. I think you are a beautiful woman."

Heaven help me. He *was* serious. I was in big trouble – every day I lost a little more of my heart to this man. I shouldn't let it happen, but I didn't want it to stop. How could something that felt so right be wrong?

"Lillie?"

I suddenly became aware that Nef had asked me a question.

"Um...what did you say?"

"Did I say something wrong?" The concern on his face was touching.

"Wrong? Not at all. I'm just not used to getting compliments." Feeling daring, I stretched up and kissed him on the cheek. "Thank you."

He reached out and twined one of the tendrils of hair that framed my face around his index finger. "I, uh, I hope this doesn't seem too forward... but would you let your hair down for me?" The rest of his words came out in a rush. "I mean, you don't have too, but it is such a pretty color, and I've never seen it down."

Female servants were expected to keep their heads respectfully covered while on duty, so most of us pinned our hair up so that it would fit easily under our mob caps. Now that I was off-duty, I had removed my cap, but my hair was still pinned tightly in a bun. I did not think of myself as a vain person, but I was proud of my hair - it was a deep, rich auburn; unbound it fell to my waist. In addition to fair skin and a tendency to blush, some unknown ancestor had blessed me with wonderful curls; my hair fell naturally into ringlets. Some of the other female assassins had made snide remarks about it – they seemed to be jealous. I never understood why they would hold it against me – I had had no choice in the matter.

In response to Nef's question, I reached back and pulled the pins from my hair, allowing it to fall free. He inhaled sharply and his eyes dilated.   Whatever reaction I had expected, that wasn't it.

"Makers!" He reached out and ran his fingers through my hair where it lay on my shoulders, his motions almost reverent. "I thought you were beautiful before, but now, with that hair... you are stunning."

The look that he gave me then shot arousal through my entire body. I had heard talk among the rest of the staff implying that Nef and I were a couple. Although I was skilled in many areas, relationships were not one of them. I didn't know exactly how the whole "couple" thing worked.

I ached to feel Nef's hands on me, his body against mine, but I would have been happy with a kiss – on the *lips*, not the nose. But I wasn't sure. Would it be too forward of me to kiss him? Maybe. It was probably best to let him take the lead. I didn't know how much experience he had with women and didn't want to risk scaring him off.

"I think I should walk you back to your room now." His voice was huskier than usual. "I pride myself on always being a gentleman, but I'm not having very gentlemanly thoughts right now." Standing, he took me by the hands and pulled me to my feet.

Our fingers remained entwined until we arrived at the door to my room.

"Sleep well, my Lillie." With a twinkle in his eyes, he kissed me – this time on the forehead - and walked away, whistling.

I had begun to realize that his whistling meant he was happy. Slipping into my room, I closed the door behind me and leaned against it with a blissful sigh.

"You've been with your stable boy again, haven't you?"

I jumped. I hadn't realized that Maerie was in the room. Some assassin – my powers of observation were apparently slipping.

"His name is Nef, and, yes, I have." I pushed myself away from the door and twirled, my skirts flaring out around me. I spun my way to my bed, where I collapsed on my back, my arms thrown wide.

"You've got it bad."

"Got what?"

"You're in love."

"I am? How do you know? How would *I* know?" I turned on my side to face my roommate, bending my elbow and resting my head on my hand.

"Well, you enjoy being with him, don't you? You think about him constantly when you're apart and are happiest when you're together, right?"

"Yes to all three."

"Well, it sure sounds like love to me." She studied me through narrowed eyes. "And *looks* like it – you practically glow when you have been with him." Her eyes widened suddenly in surprise. "Haven't you ever been love?"

"No. My foster-father wasn't big on relationships – courting was not encouraged." I sat up, idly swinging my feet over the edge of the bed. "I've been around a lot of men, but none that made me feel like this."

"You're lucky. I hope that I will find someone that makes me as happy as your Nef makes you."

"You will. Just give it time." I had grown to care greatly for my flighty friend, so I continued, hoping that I wouldn't hurt her feelings. "Just don't limit yourself to the lordlings. You might be pleasantly surprised if you... broaden your horizons a little."

No response.

"At least think about it – for me."

Still no response. A silence fell over the room. Maerie rolled onto her side and tugged the covers up to her nose.

"I'll think about it." Her voice was muffled, but her blue eyes were serious.

"Good." I gave her a smile.

She rolled over to face the wall. Soon, she was snoring quietly.

I stripped and bathed off, fantasizing that it was Nef's hands caressing my body instead of a washcloth. Ablutions completed, I climbed into my night clothes, and crawled into bed, but sleep wouldn't come. After tossing and turning for what seemed like hours, I pulled on my robe and tiptoed out of the room, closing the door softly behind me.

The cloud cover from earlier must have moved on - moonlight streamed through the windows, striping the hall with light. I turned in slowly in place, as though seeing my surroundings with new eyes. Usually, an assassin on a long-term mission would be required to report to Vido on a regular basis, but this time, not so. There was too great a risk that someone might see me associating with known members of the Va'Shile, which would bring me under instant suspicion. I was - for the first time in my life – completely on my own. I was free to explore my surroundings, to begin to learn who I was – even, it seemed, to make friends. Here, no masters hid in the shadows waiting to catch recruits attempting to sneak out. I was free to do what I would.

So, what did I do with my freedom? I danced, of course. With childlike abandon, I pirouetted down the hall, pausing only to curtsey to the statues and suits of armor that stood in niches along the wall. Finally, laughing and breathless, I collapsed on a seat in an alcove. Moonlight flowed down the walls like molten silver and pooled around me, making my simple garments glow as if lit from within. I leaned my head back against the wall, gazed out at the night, and sighed. Nef. Was he sleeping soundly in his bed or was he too awake, looking at the moon and thinking about me?

As I allowed my thoughts to wander, I couldn't help but wonder - what was it that made each of us who we were?

We recruits were taught that an assassin's heart must be cold - relationships were for convenience, not affection. While we were allowed to develop friendships in our early years of training, these attachments were turned against us later. As we grew older - but before our interests had turned to relationships of a more physical nature - the masters would pit us against each other. We were placed in situations where there could only be one winner - our self or our friend. It only took a few of those lessons - and the beatings that loser received - for us to learn to put ourselves before anyone else, to win at all costs. Few friendships survived these lessons, which was exactly what our masters were hoping to achieve. Most recruits, at least those who survived, became the cold-hearted loners that the Va'Shile desired.

However, I was not convinced. To the dismay of the masters, I snuck away from the guild house every chance I got to watch those who lived in the outside world – those not bound by the rules of the Va'Shile. My observations led me to believe that there was more to life than what we were taught.

I would make my way to the marketplace – and other locations trafficked by large numbers of people - and watch from the shadows. There friends openly greeted each other with smiles and handshakes, sometimes even hugs. They talked, their voices blending into the special harmony that marked them as those who knew each other well. Their laughter pealed through the air as they chortled together over a shared joke. Lovers held hands as they walked side by side – their touch was chaste and yet seemed so profound; so intent were they on one another that the world around them ceased to exist.

Then there were the parents - the type that did not sell their children into bondage – with their children, caring for them, playing with them, comforting and disciplining them as needed; their love for their offspring was obvious. Children ran together, playing and squabbling, oblivious to the fact that the ability to do so was a luxury. Childhood at the guild house was not fraught with frivolity.

The streets of Ramalda teemed with life - in all of its glory and its despair. Those with little plead for help from those with much. Those with much strove for more. Whores sold their bodies - and sometimes their souls - for money. Young women with no connections hoped for someone who would *see* them, want them, love them. Street urchins searched for dropped coins or scraps of food; sometimes they too watched from the shadows and wondered why they did not have what others had - food, clothes, a home. Some of them would become bitter and angry, always railing against the Makers for the lives that they had been given; others would remain hopeful, thankful for the little they had and ever expectant of better times ahead.

What was it that made some bitter, but others hopeful? Was it what they had learned from those that raised them? Or was there some sort of light that shined within those that hoped - something that they were born with? What was it within *me* that caused me to hope, to want something more – something *different* - when everything that I had been taught told me that it was wrong?

I had come to believe that life was sometimes beautiful, sometimes ugly, but *always* worth living. I wanted my life to be my own. Would I act on those beliefs and attempt to change my life? Or would I fall back on what I had been taught and protect myself, no matter how great the cost to others?

7

With only a matter of weeks before the Naming, the wagers began to fly. Which family would the heir come from? Some argued that the only logical choice would be a member of the highest of the noble families. Others thought that the very logic of that choice made it illogical - they believed that the heir would come from one of the families of lesser nobility. What did it matter? Our king was many things, but he wasn't stupid; he would select an heir who would satisfy the nobles. To do otherwise would merely quicken his demise.

It should not have made a difference to me - my job was simply to kill him, whoever he was, whatever family he came from. Unfortunately, the more time that went by, the harder it was for me to justify what I must do. This person had done nothing to me, nor to my knowledge, anyone else. If he had any intelligence at all, he wouldn't want the position he had been chosen for. Who in their right mind would want to be in the middle of the cesspool known as politics in Ramalda?

I chose to ignore both the politics and the wagering and focus on my work, which was just as well. Mama L was pushing us harder than ever to prepare the castle for the coming festivities. She had indeed hired temporary workers to help with some of the heavier work, of which there was plenty. Rooms that had been unused for some time would be opened to house the crowds that would be arriving for the ceremony.

Now that the days were warmer, a veritable army of servants descended on the palace, armed for battle against enemies ranging from dust and grime to overgrown shrubs. The men tasked with assisting in the cleaning of the bedchambers grumbled amongst themselves until they realized that it placed them in the perfect position to show off in front of the maids. This awareness brought on a great deal of manly grunting and flexing of muscles when in the presence of females. In spite of the posturing – or maybe because of it – the work got done. Featherbeds were carried outside to be fluffed and aired while the straw mattresses were emptied and the ticking sacks laundered. The men then removed the rush mats from the rooms and ornate woven rugs from the halls and took them outside where the housemaids beat them thoroughly to remove the dirt that had accumulated since the last cleaning.

Once the floor coverings were removed, the floors had to be scrubbed. If it was possible for stone to shine, Mama L would not be satisfied until it did so. Much to my surprise, I discovered that I *enjoyed* cleaning the floors. It was pleasant to kneel in a patch of light while the sun warmed both the stone and my back. The palace had grown stale and musty after the long winter and the windows were thrown open to allow fresh air to circulate. Gentle breezes occasionally wafted through the window, bringing with them the sounds of horses being exercised in the yard and the songs of the birds that were returning from their winter migration. Scrubbing was a task that took little concentration. As I worked, my mind was free to think of anything or nothing. That day, my thoughts flitted freely, like a butterfly drifting from flower to flower, never really settling before moving on.

"Watch it man!" Nef's voice rose above the others in the yard. "One hole in my ass is sufficient. I don't need you adding more with that pitchfork!"

The others laughed and a few ribald jokes were tossed about. Just as we household servants were cleaning the interior of the palace, they were scouring the outside. Plants were being pruned and the limbs, leaves and assorted detritus of the winter were removed. The stalls in the stable were mucked down to the floors and scrubbed before being filled with fresh straw. The ring of the farrier's hammer filled the air as he prepared to shoe the horses.

The sight of women lustily wielding rug beaters brought out the bawdiness of the men working in the yard; many expressed interest in having one - or more - of the women spank them as energetically as they were the rugs. Most of the women responded in kind. I strongly suspected that when the sun set and we were free to retire for the evening, there would be much enthusiastic coupling occurring throughout the grounds. I was beginning to feel as I did back at the guild house, when forced to sleep in a roomful of fornicating teenagers. Being a virgin did not make one immune to sexual tension – it only limited what one did about it.

Oh, did I fail to mention that I was still a virgin? It was surprising, considering my upbringing.

The Va'Shile conscripted both boys and girls, frequently purchasing their recruits from the slave markets. The younger the better. There was no allowance given for our gender; we trained together, bathed together, shared rooms and sometimes beds. Naturally, as we aged, our bodies changed and curiosity quickly followed. Sex happened. Frequently. We were thoroughly trained in the art of seduction and knew well how to pleasure. Naturally, these skills were regularly practiced on each other. Since our masters worked hard to kill any type of friendship, it was only sex, not love-making. The only allowance made for our growing sexuality was that we were also taught about the various ways to prevent conception and sexually transmitted diseases. A pregnant assassin was of no use to her guild, nor was one infected with a disease that he or she might transmit to others.

Many aspects of my life were completely beyond my control - my body was not. I determined early on that I would decide when and to whom I would give myself. I freely admit that I found kissing and touching to be pleasurable, but any attempts from another recruit to achieve something more were swiftly dissuaded. I was quick with a knife; my speed was respected even among my contemporaries.

So, though I was a virgin, I was not completely innocent. I was quite familiar with the anatomy of both aroused males *and* females. I had also pleasured myself on more than one occasion. Shocking, I know. However, I slept in a room full of hormonal teenagers, listening to the moans and cries of the twosomes and threesomes surrounding me. It was impossible not to become stimulated; there was only so much that I could take. I must say that I found orgasms to be exquisite. I looked forward to learning how much better they could be with the hardness of a man inside of me.

My reverie was broken by the sound of a horse screaming, quickly followed by complete chaos. Voices echoed around the courtyard.

"Whoa!"

"Grab him!"

"Are you crazy?"

"Look out!" This was followed by the sound of wood cracking and more screams from an obviously terrified horse.

"Lillie! Help!"

I was on my feet and running before the cry had finished echoing around the hall. I met Nef coming up the servant's staircase as I was heading down. He grabbed my arm and almost hauled me off of my feet as he turned and ran for the yard.

"It's Cefus! The farrier's apprentice put him in the travis..."

"The *what*?"

"The travis." He shook his head in frustration. "It's a wooden frame the horse stands in for shoeing. Anyway, I don't know what happened, but before Konal could do anything, Cefus went crazy, rearing and kicking. We've got to get him calmed down before he hurts himself or someone else."

"What...do...you...want...*me*...to...do?" I puffed. My teeth practically rattled together as I struggled to match Nef's much longer stride.

"I don't care. *You're* the one who communicates with animals! Do something! Anything!"

We ran through the kitchens, shoved our way through the workers who had gathered at the door to stare at the happenings outside and immediately skidded to a halt. The scene before us was utter pandemonium. Men were everywhere, yelling, waving their arms and caps, and being generally unhelpful.

Cefus had succeeded in smashing his way out of the travis — bits of wood were still tangled in his mane. He reared repeatedly, lashing out blindly with his forefeet. Warhorses were a large breed with broad chests, strong legs, and massive hooves. Even a glancing blow from one of those flailing feet could kill, which was precisely why they were used in battle. A warhorse did more than merely transport its rider into combat — it fought, its iron-shod feet felling enemies as easily as any sword.

I loved Cefus. My fear for my friend compelled me into action and I leapt into the fray, grabbing the arm of the man nearest me before he could brandish the stick in his hand again.

"Put that away, you fool! You're only making things worse! Can't you see that he's scared?"

"Get away from me, girl! This here is men's business." He shoved me - hard.

I stumbled over the uneven stones of the yard. Fortunately, the only thing injured was my pride.

Fine. Apparently we were going to have to do this the hard way.

I regained my balance and approached my adversary, who was once again waving his stick and yelling. He was so busy doing 'men's business' that he didn't even notice my approach. However, that changed when I grabbed his testicles and twisted. He hit the ground with a rather satisfying thud. I snatched the stick out of his hands and waved it under his nose.

"I *said* that you are only making things worse. Now, get out of here before I use this on you."

He glared at me through watering eyes but turned and began crawling away. The sound of choking erupted behind me and I turned. It was Nef. Amusement and astonishment warred for control of his face.

"Where in all the hells did you learn how to do that?"

I shook my head. "No time. We've got to put a stop to this before Cefus gets hurt."

I waded into the crowd putting my newly confiscated weapon to good use, rapping kneecaps, prodding ribcages, and, for the more difficult, smacking them in the head. Nef was doing his part as well, putting his elbows and fists to good use. Between the two of us, we quickly brought some semblance of order to the mob. Well, "order" might not be entirely accurate, but at least they got out of the way.

Cefus continued to rear. Poor horse – his nostrils flared and the whites of his eyes were visible as they rolled wildly. His fear was as palpable as the sweat that rolled down his sides.

"What now?" Nef whispered from his location behind me.

"I don't know. I'm making this up as I go." I struggled to remember how I had reached out to the dog when I was trapped in the root cellar. I cleared my mind and cast my thoughts toward the horse in an effort to calm him. Instead, I received his thoughts.

I got flashes of a man, an anvil, bellows – the tools of a farrier's trade. These images were the memories of a younger Cefus; the angles were different than they would be at his current size. The younger horse was nervous and tried to pull away from the man, which caused the man to get angry. Reaching behind him, he pulled a red-hot poker out of the fire and pressed it into the young horse's legs and hindquarters. The horse screamed in agony and the images faded.

"Cefus! Cefus, it's me. Lillie. Everything is okay – no one is going to hurt you." I spoke soothingly. It would have helped if I had had some idea of how this whole talking-to-animals thing worked. I tried desperately to convey calming thoughts – images of me stroking him and feeding him apples, of him safe in his warm, clean stall.

Something must have gotten through. He turned his magnificent head and seemed to see me. His sweat-soaked sides continued to heave, but he stopped rearing. I stepped closer. He shied away, but with a little more coaxing, allowed me to take his head in my hands and pull it down to my level.

"There, there, big guy. Everything is fine. I'm not going to let anyone hurt you." Without changing my tone of voice, I tossed a glance at Nef over my shoulder. "Please get me some apples. I'm sure Cook will be willing to spare a few if you explain the situation."

He headed back to the kitchens at a run.

While he was gone, I continued to stroke Cefus and talk calmly. He slowly relaxed. Now that the danger was past, I was able to look around and check on the others who were involved in the melee. I was the recipient of many angry looks from the injured men lingering in the yard. They nursed a variety of wounds – bloody noses, blackened eyes, and an assortment of rapidly darkening bruises. It was plain that they would not be forgiving me anytime soon.

When Nef returned, Mama L accompanied him. She walked slowly, her violet eyes sweeping the scene in front of her, not missing a single detail. She stopped frequently to speak to the battered men. Her demeanor was as calm as ever, but her brows rose a little higher after each conversation. I suspected that by the time she arrived at my location, they would have disappeared into her hairline completely.

I had no intention of denying my role in the chaos, and so, I waited.

"Ah, Lillie. I thought you were safely tucked away scrubbing floors. Instead, I am told that you rushed out here and molested these poor, innocent men with no provocation whatsoever." Her voice smiled; her eyes did not. "What do you have to say for yourself?"

"Mama L, I can explain," Nef interrupted before I could respond. "Cefus went berserk when the farrier tried to shoe him and I asked Lillie to help calm him. She... is good with animals." He suddenly recalled the apple that he was practically crushing in his nervousness and handed it to me.

"Thank you, Nef." Mama L turned her full attention to me. "And so, you felt that the best way to calm the horse was to beat up the other laborers?"

"Not at all." I shook my head emphatically. "Their yelling and carrying on was only making the situation worse. I asked them to stop, but they wouldn't." I met her gaze without flinching. "Cefus was a danger to himself and everyone around him. The fools were lucky that no one was killed. They weren't willing to cooperate, so I chose to make them."

"And you?" This question was directed at Nef.

"I helped." He stepped to my side and placed his hand on my shoulder to show his support.

I smiled up at him.

"I see." Her gaze flickered from me to Nef and back.

I suspected that she saw a great deal indeed.

"Konal?" She raised her voice. "What do you have to say for yourself?"

An extremely muscular young man, looking rather pale under his tan, stepped out of the shadows to stand beside us. He wrung his hands nervously. "This is the first time that Master Gren has allowed me to shoe the horses on my own." He hung his head. "I forgot that Cefus was to be blindfolded before I began work."

"A rather serious mistake, young man."

Konal flinched at the tone of Mama L's voice.

"Cefus could easily have injured or killed himself or someone else. You are lucky that Lillie was here to help." She looked him over carefully. "Please send Master Gren to me. I will inform him that he is not to fire you. However -" she raised a hand in caution as Konal's shoulders sagged in relief - "he will be in charge of your punishment. Such a grievous error cannot go without reprimand."

"Yes, ma'am. Thank you, ma'am." Konal bowed deeply.

"Lillie, I will excuse you from your regular duties for the rest of the day. The remaining horses will have been spooked by all of the commotion. I want you to stay here and help with them until the shoeing is complete."

"Yes, ma'am."

"Now, I must go and see to those who are injured." Giving us a slight nod, she turned with a swirl of skirts, then hesitated and looked back over her shoulder. "Please try to avoid hurting any more of my workers. We have too much to do; I can't afford to be short-handed."

"Yes, Mama." I had the decency to blush at the rebuke, gentle though it was.

As she walked away, Cefus became impatient with the delay and nudged my shoulder so hard he almost knocked me off of my feet. I laughed and without thinking, pulled out my knife, sliced the apple, and began feeding pieces to him.

"A knife? You carry a knife?" Nef's voice had risen a good octave in surprise. "First, you single-handedly brought grown men to their knees, some crying in pain, and now I learn that you carry a knife?"

I was forced to respond with a partial truth.

"My foster father may not be the nicest man, but he did make sure that we all learned how to defend ourselves." I used the blade to motion at myself. "It was especially important for me. There were many in The Narrows who might try to, shall we say, 'take advantage' of a female of my size."

"True enough, I suppose." A slow grin spread across his face. "You are just full of surprises."

"You have no idea." I grinned back. And this time I was being completely honest.

"Thank you." Konal stepped forward and offered his hand to each of us in turn. "Both of you." He shook his head. "I've been around horses all my life and I've never seen one respond like that. What in the name of the Abyss happened?"

I nodded toward Cefus' right side as I fed him more slices of fruit.

"If you look carefully, I think that you will find scars on his legs and hindquarters. When he was much younger, and nervous, an impatient farrier burned him with a hot poker."

With exclamations of surprise, both men disappeared around the far side of the horse. They returned moments later, scowling.

"You're right." The young farrier cocked his head as he looked at me with a mixture of respect and disbelief. "How did you know?"

I sighed and stroked the white blaze on Cefus' nose. "He told me."

"Ah."

I looked at Nef helplessly. As always, he came to my rescue.

"I don't know how to explain it – and neither does she – but Lillie is able to communicate with animals on some level. I've seen her do it before. It's why I asked her to help."

I snorted.

"Bellowing my name at the top of your lungs is how you *ask*? I'll try to remember that." My eyes were dancing in merriment – and challenge.

Nef was equal to the task.

"You aren't the only one with a few surprises up their sleeve." He whispered the words, his lips brushing my ear.

I broke out in gooseflesh in response. He stepped back with a chuckle.

I fed Cefus the last of the apple, wiped the blade of the knife on my skirt, and then slid it back through the slit in my pocket and into the sheath on my thigh. Nef watched, a bemused expression on his face. I suspected that he was trying to visualize exactly where the knife was going. He blushed when I caught him looking.

"Shouldn't you be getting back to work? I'm sure that Konal could use your assistance with *something*."

"As you say, madam." He clicked his heels together and gave me a formal bow. However, all formality was lost when he gave me a playful swat on the rear as he walked by.

Cefus and I watched with interest as the two men searched through the scattered remains of the travis for pieces of usable wood. In less than an hour they had cobbled together a new frame and a much calmer – and blindfolded – Cefus was shoed without further incident.

As instructed by Mama L, I stayed with Konal the rest of the day. The remaining horses had indeed been spooked by the earlier cacophony, so I doled out doses of comfort and fruit as needed.

My initial impression of Konal had been impaired by his dangerous oversight, but first impressions could be wrong. My respect for him grew as I watched him work. He moved smoothly from one task to the next. One moment he pumped bellows that were as big as I was; the next he hammered red hot metal into shape, every move confident and sure. He was always gentle with the horses, stroking them, talking to them, even calling them by name – he never once raised his voice, even when some of the more skittish creatures put his skills to the test with their constant movement.

He, too, seemed to have a soft spot for Elah, the aging mare. She trotted happily at the end of the lead when he led her from the stable, tossing her head in pleasure. She stepped into the travis without hesitation, her bearing regal and dignified. If Cefus was the king of the stable, Elah was definitely the queen.

Konal apparently felt the same way. Once Elah was in position, he bowed to her good-naturedly.

"Welcome, milady. I am honored to have you at my humble forge." Standing, he eyed her hooves carefully. "It is my understanding that you are here for new shoes."

Elah whickered in response.

"Ah, my thoughts exactly. Every woman should have new shoes for a ball. I'll be sure to put a little extra shine on yours." With that, he bowed again and disappeared into the forge.

When he returned, the horseshoes that he carried were indeed shinier than the others that I had seen. He immediately got to work putting them on.

I distracted Elah with snacks while Konal worked on her hooves. She was perfectly happy with the arrangement.

"There, all done." Konal hammered in the last nail and stood, stretching to ease his back. He had removed his shirt sometime earlier and his rather gorgeous torso glistened with sweat.

I was covered in sweat as well, but I definitely wasn't glistening. My clothes and skin were flecked with pieces of hay, horse hair, and a fairly significant amount of drying drool - horses were not exactly the neatest of eaters. I needed a meal and a bath, not necessarily in that order.

"Thank you, Lillie." White teeth flashed against dark skin as Konal gave me a smile. "I don't even want to think about what might have happened if you and Nef had not come to my aid."

"You are most welcome. After I take Elah back to her stall I am going to find something to eat. Why don't you do the same? You must be starving."

"No. No." He waved me away. "I need to clean up around here first." He brushed strands of golden brown hair out of his eyes. "I'm in enough trouble without leaving the area in a mess."

In the stable, I made sure that Elah had more hay and fresh water. I spent a quiet few moments with her, my arms wrapped around her neck, my face pressed against her warm hide. My stomach growled, breaking the silence and ending the moment.

"Okay, okay." I gave Elah a final pat and left her stall. "Good evening, old lady. Behave – you don't want to mess up your new shoes."

I stopped by each of the occupied stalls and gave each of the horses a final pat for the day. I took a couple of extra minutes with Cefus – he had had a rough day and I wanted to make sure that he was all right.

"How's my big man? Are you okay?"

In response, he laid his massive head on my shoulder and whickered softly in my ear. I felt certain that he was thanking me for helping him.

"You're welcome." I gave his nose a final scratch. Many people were afraid of the warhorse due to his sheer size. I was not, in spite of the fact that the top of my head did not even reach his shoulders. You see, I knew the truth. Cefus was a gentle giant; off of the battlefield, he wouldn't intentionally hurt a fly.

As I stepped back into the courtyard, the scent of food permeated the air causing my stomach to growl again, almost angrily. I had not eaten since morning. I stopped by the nearest rain barrel, splashed water on my face and rinsed my arms and hands as best I could, then went in search of the source of the smells.

"Lille!" Just as I reached the door to the kitchens, Maerie darted across the yard and grabbed my still damp arm.

I braced for a lecture on my appearance – and smell. I was pleasantly surprised when it wasn't forthcoming.

"Have you seen?" She pulled me across the grounds to the gardens, which had changed greatly since my nighttime visit with Nef.

The kitchen staff had converted the gardens into a picnic area, complete with blankets to sit on and baskets of food. Maerie led me to a convenient spot where I collapsed gratefully. She rummaged in the basket, pulling out a variety of foods. As she arranged the delicacies to her liking, I had an idea.

"Maerie? Have you ever met Konal?"

Her brow furrowed as she thought.

"Konal? I don't think so, why?"

"You should. He's rather handsome. I think you would approve."

"Is he a noble?"

"Not exactly. He is the apprentice farrier."

"Farrier? But... that means that he is a servant."

"*Yes*, he is a servant. Just. Like. You." Sitting up, I reached over and shook my friend. "Maerie, you could try the patience of the Makers themselves. *Listen to me*. You are a beautiful girl, but you are a *commoner*. Few lords will marry someone of common birth; however, many of them would be more than willing to bed you. You might even find one willing to bed you more than once - but he would never take you home to meet his family. Take a chance – at least *meet* the man. You might find out that he is even better than all of the lordlings that you have been mooning over." I couldn't help but give her a wicked grin before continuing. "Besides, he's the farrier's apprentice – he's very muscular. Just think of all of those lovely muscles and what those strong arms would feel like as they pulled you against his wide, rippling chest for your first kiss."

"Well..." Maerie's eyes grew wide as she did just that. "Since you put it that way, I guess that meeting him is the least I can do."

"Can we join you?" Nef didn't wait for a response; he simply dropped to the blanket beside me and waggled his eyebrows at me. He was obviously up to something.

"We?" Maerie and I replied in unison.

Nef motioned to someone hesitating at the entrance to the gardens. I glanced up. Konal nodded and began working his way through the crowd to us. He had obviously taken the time to clean himself up as well his work area.

"Oh, my," Maerie murmured when she saw him.

Konal was indeed a sight to behold. He was a strapping young man with golden blond hair and brown eyes flecked with gold. His skin was burnished from his time in the sun, the hairs on his arms bleached to a pale blond. His wide shoulders tapered to a narrow waist and his muscles flexed easily as he moved. Many of the women that he passed eyed him speculatively. I suspected that they would be willing to give him more than a chance if Maerie wasn't interested. He stood awkwardly by our blanket until Nef motioned for him to sit down. The sight of his thigh muscles bunching and flexing beneath the fabric of his breeches was not lost on my roommate. Once Konal was seated, introductions were made all around.

"Maerie? That's a beautiful name."

"Thank you." The rosy glow that rose in her cheeks only enhanced Maerie's beauty.

Konal seemed quite smitten already.

As we ate, Nef, Konal and I took turns filling Maerie in on the events of the day.

"Lillie, I'm shocked! I can't believe that you would do such a thing!" She looked at me, her blue eyes round with astonishment.

"I would do it again in a heartbeat to protect Cefus. I can't bear to see an innocent animal hurt."

"Just be glad that Lillie is on your side." Nef laughed as he stood up and stretched and then reached down to pull me up beside him. "Now, if you will excuse us, there is something that I would like to show her."

"Oh really? More kittens?" I smiled to let him know that I was teasing.

"Not this time." He gestured at the sky. "It is going to be a beautiful night. It will be the perfect time to show you my favorite part of the castle."

I glanced at Maerie and Konal. Was it safe to leave them? After all, they had just met. My concern was unfounded; they were completely absorbed in each other.

"All right. But I will need time to bathe and change. I'm covered in bits of hay and it's making me itch like crazy."

Nef laughed. "I understand. I'll come to your room in an hour."

8

I rushed inside with every intention of going to my room and taking a quick sponge bath. Halfway up the staircase, I changed my mind. I was so grimy there was no way that I was going to be able to get clean enough using a bowl of lukewarm water and a small cloth. Only a full bath would be able to do the job - even if it had to be quick. Fortunately, the palace had access to hot springs and the servants were allowed to use the bath on the lowest level, so I reversed direction and ran back down the stairs.

When I reached the bathing room, I was pleased to find it unoccupied; after years of forced communal bathing, I had learned to appreciate my privacy. A natural opening in the rock floor had been enlarged at some point over the centuries forming a pool large enough for several people. I stripped out of my filthy clothes and lowered myself into the steaming water, sighing with bliss. I anchored my toes in the sandy bottom and leaned back against the side wall until the water lapped at my chin. The gentle current of the unseen stream that supplied the water brushed against me in a warm caress.

I allowed myself to soak for a few minutes, reveling in the heat of the water as it soothed away the aches of the day. Mama L ensured that there was always an ample supply of soap on hand; I grabbed the nearest bar and inhaled its delicate scent. The soap that we used was not of the same quality as that provided to the nobles, but it was heaven compared to what the Va'Shile had given us. I had always wondered if bathing with soap harsh enough to practically remove skin was part of our training. Perhaps some sadistic master felt that would be a test of our mettle – more likely, they just didn't care.

It was delightful to smooth the fragrant soap over my body, letting the lather remove the bits of hay and dirt that clung to my skin. After a quick debate, I ducked under the water and wet my hair. Surfacing, I rubbed more soap into it and scrubbed vigorously, hoping to get it at least somewhat clean in the limited amount of time available. Once satisfied that I had most of the grunge removed, I submerged again, working my fingers furiously through my hair to remove the suds. I thought my lungs were going to burst before I finished.

Reluctantly I climbed out, grabbed a clean towel from the pile and rubbed it through my dripping curls in order to remove as much water as possible; a second towel was required to dry my body. It was at this point that I recognized the flaw in my plan. Since I had not gone to my quarters first, I did not have any clean clothes to put on. The thought of putting my sweat-soaked undergarments back on my clean body made my skin crawl.

I did the only thing that I could do; I threw on my soiled dress, grabbed the aforementioned undergarments and made a dash for my room. I made it safely to my floor without encountering anyone else, but when I rounded the corner closest to my room, I found Nef standing outside the door, his hand raised to knock.

"I guess I'm late," I said to his back.

He jumped and whirled around. I couldn't help but giggle. The laughter died in my throat at his expression; I could only describe it as *greedy*. Following his gaze, I glanced down. The water from my hair had soaked into my dress; the damp grey fabric clung to my breasts as if painted on and my nipples shone through pinkly. My face, hot with embarrassment, no doubt turned a similar rosy shade.

"No... uh... no. I'm, um, I'm a little early. I apologize." Nef cleared his throat and manfully pulled his gaze back to my face. "I'll just, um, wait out here while you finish getting ready." He stepped slightly to the side so that I could go through the door, but not quite far enough away so that I could do so without brushing against him.

I suspected that I wasn't the only one who was feeling a little... amorous.

"I'll be right back," I promised, as I gently closed the door in his face.

When the latch clicked into place, I rested my head against the age-darkened wood while giving myself a stern lecture. *No. You cannot yank him into the room and have your way with him.* However, that was exactly what I wanted to do. Movement. I needed to get ready; perhaps the activity would keep me focused on the tasks at hand and off of my growing desire. I could only hope.

Again I glanced down. Crap. Hopefully the sight of my perky breasts prevented Nef from noticing the dirty undergarments that I still clutched tightly in one hand; I tossed them into a pile in the corner and struggled to remove my dress. Of course. I had already taken this same garment off and put it back on within the past hour and *now* it decided to be difficult. The buttons suddenly developed a mind of their own and gleefully refused to cooperate. I gritted my teeth and slowly worked my way down the row, resisting the urge to simply rip open the dress and let the obnoxious little orbs fend for themselves. However, giving in to that impulse would not be worth the tongue-lashing that I would receive from the laundress.

Finally freed from the stubborn garment, I tossed it the general vicinity of the others and rushed to the dresser that Maerie and I shared. Snatching out clean underclothes I pulled them on as quickly as possible, cursing softly as the fabric caught on my damp skin. Locating what I hoped was a clean towel, I gave my hair another thorough rubbing to remove any remaining water before putting on a clean gown - no need to repeat the transparent dress issue unnecessarily. Back at the dresser I adjusted the looking glass and began roughly pulling my comb through my hair as I shoved my feet into my shoes. Painful tangles quickly brought an end to the yanking.

I forced myself to relax. Rushing was achieving nothing except frustration on my part. I slowed down enough to treat my hair properly, removing the tangles gently. I fumbled in the drawer for some cologne that Maerie kept hidden away, then, at the last moment, changed my mind; I'd rather smell like myself. After one final glance in the mirror, I went to find Nef.

He had apparently been pacing the corridor while I dressed. He turned at the sound of the door opening and smiled when he saw me. I realized for the first time that he had apparently bathed as well. His hair, like mine, was unbound; his dark hair fell in shimmering waves to his shoulders. My fingertips suddenly ached to reach out and touch it; I felt sure that it would feel like silk. That desire drew me to him like a magnet.

"So, where are we going? Back to the stables?" I smiled and slid my hands into my pockets so that they couldn't do anything without checking with the rest of me first.

"No, not tonight. Which is a good thing, actually. The return of spring seems to have everyone feeling a bit randy. Once the sun sets, I suspect that it will be hard to find a stall or bush unoccupied by an amorous couple. We, however, will be staying within the confines of the castle." He held his hand out to me and I took it with only the slightest hesitation. Surely my fingers would behave if secure in his grasp.

We strolled through several corridors with which I was not yet familiar. This section of the castle was largely unused and had only recently been reopened in preparation for the Naming. Nef pointed out the pictures of previous rulers that lined the walls and supplied bits of information about their reigns. He was also familiar with the different time periods represented by the suits of armor that watched us like silent sentinels.

A door at the end of the last corridor opened into a tower with steps leading to both the floors above and those below. We went up – and up, and up, and up. I was beginning to get winded when we stopped before another door; it seemed to me to be rather average, with nothing to distinguish it from the countless others that we had passed. Nef, however, seemed excited to see it. He ran his hand lightly over the scarred wood.

"I haven't been here in far too long." He seemed to be talking mostly to himself, but the slight smile on his lips spoke softly of fond memories.

After a moment, he shook his head slightly, bringing himself back to the present – and me. He pulled a key from his pocket and unlocked the door; the hinges squealed in protest as he pushed it open. I clapped my hands over my ears.

"From the noise, I'd wager that no one has been here in quite a while." The shrill sound had seared a path from my ears to my toes and made my teeth hurt in the process. I looked at him curiously as I pried my fingers cautiously away from my ears. "How, pray tell, is it that you just happen to have the key to this particular door?"

"Well, I can't very well take you to our destination if the door is locked now, can I?" He gave me a heart-stopping grin. "Besides, I can't tell you *all* of my secrets. You might get bored with me if I did."

I snorted. "I seriously doubt that."

One short flight of stairs and another locked, squeaky door found us at the top of the tower; its edges were surrounded by a battlemented parapet.

"Ah! Perfect timing - the light is just right." Nef led me to the wall and helped me step up on the ledge that ran around the base.

The whole of Ramalda lay sprawled below us, lit only by the lingering rays of sunlight that stretched from the setting sun. In the fading light, the differences between the wealth of MidTown and the squalor of The Narrows ceased to exist; everything was covered in a diffuse beauty. Candlelight twinkled from windows giving the appearance that stars had fallen from the sky to lend their glow to the land. Even the river flowing past the island on which the palace stood seemed to glow with an inner beauty of its own. I turned to find Nef watching me, a smile on his face.

"Oh, Nef!" I cried in delight. "It's beautiful."

"I'm glad you like it." He joined me in looking out over the city, still smiling. "This is where I always feel at peace. No matter what is going on, coming here brings solace to my soul."

We stood side-by-side in silence, watching as darkness slowly covered the town. A stiff breeze swirled up from the water below, lifted my curls and rippled them out behind me. Nef watched me out of the corner of his eye and I felt like the beautiful, romantic heroine in the stories that other recruits occasionally smuggled into our quarters. At least until the wind suddenly changed direction, whipping my hair into my face and tangling my skirts around my legs.

Nef struggled unsuccessfully to contain his laughter as I fought to get the long strands out of my eyes and into some semblance of order. It was a losing battle. The wind took a seemingly perverse delight in changing directions just as I seemed to be getting wind-tossed mass under control. I stuck out my tongue as he leaned against the parapet, practically doubled over with mirth.

Gasping for air and wiping his eyes, Nef took my hand to help me from the ledge. Once I was safely down, he pulled me to him and held me there while he went off into fresh gales of laughter. After pouting for a few seconds I had to admit to myself, albeit reluctantly, that the situation was pretty funny and joined him in laughter, sliding my arms around his waist and resting my head on his chest. His mirth rumbled pleasantly against my ear and I felt warm and safe in his embrace.

Once his merriment subsided, he led me to a seat on the far side of the tower. I had not even realized that it was there; it was nearly invisible in the fading light. He sat and pulled me down next to him as he leaned back comfortably against the wall and stretched his long legs out in front of him. I imitated him. Well, sort of. My feet barely touched the ground so I couldn't stretch them out. I settled for resting my back against the wall while resisting the urge to swing my feet like a child.

"I've always loved coming here in the evening to watch the stars come out." His blue eyes surveyed the heavens as he spoke.

We watched the darkening sky in silence for a few minutes.

"You talk like you have been doing this for years." I broke the silence, turning to look at him. "I didn't think that you had been here that long."

"Don't forget, I spent a lot of time here as a child." He shrugged. "I have always watched the stars, wherever I was, but it was never as nice as here." He waved his hand at the expanse above us. "Here, on this tower, it feels as if I am a part of the heavens – and they are a part of me."

When the sun set, the temperature dropped. A cool breeze whispered through the evening air. I shivered; I should have brought a cloak. Nef noticed my discomfort, leaned over, and pulled a blanket out of the shadows. I cocked an eyebrow at him.

"You certainly came prepared. What exactly did you have in mind?"

His low chuckle made me quiver with anticipation.

"I was planning to bring you up here for a picnic. I didn't realize that Mama L would beat me to the punch." As he spoke, he shook the folds from the blanket. "No picnic would be complete without a blanket." He wrapped the heavy fabric around both of us, using the action as an excuse to put his arm around my shoulder.

I didn't complain.

"Now," he ordered, "watch the sky."

Obediently, I snuggled against his side, leaned my head back against his arm and watched as the last hints of sunlight faded from the horizon. One by one, the stars began to appear. It was incredible; I never knew so many stars existed! Suddenly, a flash of white streaked across the sky. I sat up so quickly that both the blanket and Nef's arm slipped off my shoulder.

"What was that?" I whispered excitedly, turning to look at him.

"It was a falling star." He grinned at my delight and then looked at me curiously. "Have you never seen one before?"

I shook my head as I eagerly scanned the heavens, looking for more. He wrapped the blanket around me again, pulling me closer as he lowered his head.

"Some people say that when you make a wish upon a falling star, it will come true."

His breath was warm against my ear. My body broke out in gooseflesh in response. I pulled the blanket tighter against me as if the night air was responsible for my shivers. It wasn't.

"Really? I *definitely* need to find another one!"

Nef smiled as I resumed my search in earnest. As I watched the stars, he watched me. I finally gave up and turned to face him.

"You know, it's really hard to concentrate on the stars when *you* are so focused on *me*."

In answer, he reached out and ran his fingers through my hair. I closed my eyes while my heart tried to beat its way out of my chest. This time, I made no attempt to hide the fact that it was his touch that made me shiver.

"I just can't get over your hair. It's magnificent." His voice caressed my skin as he wound a curl around his finger and held it to his nose, inhaling deeply. "It smells like you."

My eyes flew open as I thanked the Makers that I had washed my hair. I shuddered to think what it would have smelled like if I hadn't.

"Don't be silly. It smells like soap."

"Yes, it smells slightly of soap." His eyes locked onto mine. "But mostly, it just smells like you. And *that* is my favorite fragrance."

I realized that I was holding my breath and forced myself to let it out. I didn't move as I waited to see what would happen next. As I searched Nef's face, movement caught my eye; another falling star flew through the sky behind him. I made my wish.

Nef ran his thumb gently over my cheekbone before sliding his hand to the nape of my neck and leaning toward me, his gaze intense. Our lips met with the lightest of touches. I sighed and closed my eyes. His lips curled into a smile against mine at the sound. Keeping his hand on my neck, he deepened the kiss. I slipped my arms around his waist and reveled in the feel of his muscles as they moved and flexed beneath his shirt. As our bodies pressed together, I offered myself to him freely. My mouth opened slightly; he accepted the invitation and explored its depths tentatively with his tongue. My back arched in pleasure and my chest pressed against his, my nipples hard with desire. He ended the kiss and pulled away slowly.

"*That*," he said huskily, "was what I wished for."

"Me too," I told him with a grin. "You didn't see the shooting star behind you."

He planted tender kisses on my forehead, my eyelids, and the tip of my nose before twining his fingers firmly in mine. We then returned to our stargazing, frequently pausing for more kisses. I can safely say that it was the happiest night of my life.

I would have been content to stay with Nef on top of that tower for the rest of the night, but he finally insisted that we go back inside before we froze to death and so that we could get at least a few hours' sleep before we would be required to return to our duties.

Our return journey was very slow; neither of us really wanted the evening to come to an end. As we wandered down one of the vacant corridors, Nef guided me into the stream of moonlight flooding through a window. He drew me into his arms for a kiss that left me tingling all the way to the soles of my feet. Pulling away, he tucked my hair behind my ears and ran his fingertips softly across my face as if memorizing it; an odd mixture of happiness and sadness played across his face.

"Nef, what's wrong?"

"I'm just trying to remember every detail about tonight, about you. I want to always remember how you look right here, right now, in the moonlight." He took both of my hands in his and pressed a kiss on to each one. "Lillie," he whispered, "you are so beautiful."

My face flushed with pleasure and words failed me - a very rare occurrence indeed. I stood on my tiptoes and kissed his cheek.

"Thank you," I whispered back. Probably not exactly what he wanted to hear.

As he turned to continue down the hall, I stopped him and shook my head.

"Not yet. It's my turn."

I pulled him back into the light and studied his face as carefully as he had mine. The beams of moonlight dusted his dark hair with silver, giving me a glimpse of how it might look in a few decades when it had been touched by the fingers of time. The slightest of creases framed the corners of his eyes; they could have been the result of the amount of time he spent in the sun or sheer good humor. I suspected a little of both. I loved everything about his face – and the man that it was attached to.

Feeling brave, I finally gave my fingers permission to do what they had been aching to do all night. I ran my thumbs over the arch of his eyebrows and then slid my hands across his cheeks, the coarseness of the stubble that was beginning to cast a slight shadow there rough beneath my fingertips. Nef closed his eyes, leaning ever so slightly into my touch as I explored. I traced the outline of his ears, which seemed incongruously delicate in the moonlight. Finally, I slid my fingers into his hair; it was every bit as silky as I had expected it to be. Nef sighed in pleasure – a simple sound with a profound effect. Arousal shot through me as I had visions of that silken hair sliding across my bare breasts as he showered them with kisses.

It was time to find something else to do with my hands before things got really, well, out of hand.

We walked the rest of the way to my room in silence, fingers entwined. At the door, Nef gave me one final kiss, squeezed my hand and turned to walk away. I found my voice just before he disappeared around the corner.

"Nef." I managed to keep my voice from quivering too much. "I think you're beautiful too. Inside and out."

The joy that swept over his features was something amazing to behold. It was one of those sights that I would always hold close to my heart.

I opened the door to my room and peered into the darkness. Maerie had obviously not returned; she would have lit a candle while she waited for me. Obviously, she and Konal were getting along. I just couldn't force myself to step over the threshold. The room was cold and I was still chilled from my time in the night air. "Reluctant" doesn't even begin to describe how I felt about putting on my night shift and sliding in between the covers. Even with a quilt on the bed, the sheets beneath would be like ice. If I didn't find a way to warm up, it would take me forever to fall asleep. My current state of stimulation would make sleep difficult enough; the last thing that I needed was chattering teeth and cold feet to make it worse. I needed a nice cup of tea to warm me up and make sleep come easier.

The kitchens were empty with the exception of a lone male seated before one of the massive fires, his shoulders slumped dejectedly.

"Jehrold? Is that you?"

He looked up. It was indeed Jehrold. The man that usually had a smile and a smart remark for every occasion looked haggard and his hair stood on end as if he had run his fingers through it repeatedly. I had never seen him so morose.

"Are you all right?" I stepped close enough to press my hand against his forehead. No fever – whatever was wrong, it wasn't illness. "What's the matter?" I motioned toward the courtyard just a few feet away. "Why aren't you out, um... enjoying yourself with everyone else?"

"If by 'enjoying' you mean 'screwing,' how can I do that when the only woman I want won't have anything to do with me?"

"I came down here for some tea, but I think that you may need something a little stronger." I patted him on the leg. "I'll be right back."

Serious talk required serious measures; it was the work of only a few minutes to prepare two cups of tea.

As Nef had done on the night that we met, I added a hefty splash of whiskey to Jehrold's.

"Here. Drink up." I pressed the spiked beverage into his hands and guided them to his mouth.

His eyes widened when the smell of the alcohol hit his nostrils. He took a large gulp and winced. Whether his pain was from the heat – which was just short of boiling – or the whiskey, I wasn't sure.

"Thanks," he gasped, his eyes watering.

I sat down beside him and tucked my skirts around my legs. We stared into the flames, each lost in our own thoughts. I reveled in the heat that quickly began to dissipate the chill that had driven me downstairs. After he had polished off most of his drink, I broke the silence.

"I thought that you and Mama L... I mean Mistress Lalane, were a couple."

"Ah, young Lillie. I don't own much, but I would gladly give everything that I have to make it so." He scrubbed his hand over his face before running his fingers through his hair again.

"But, I don't understand. I saw the two of you together the day that you arrived. It seemed obvious that you knew each other. Your actions – and hers – spoke of a more intimate relationship. That's why I put you in a room close to hers."

"So, I have you to thank for that, do I?" He gave me a nod of gratitude. "Cissy and I have a long and confusing relationship." He glanced forlornly into his now empty cup and gave me a pleading look.

How could I resist such puppy-dog eyes? I laughed and stepped away long enough to prepare refills for the both of us. When I returned, he seemed far more composed.

"I have been enamored of her for many years." He shook his head, continuing his story without any prompting from me. "There are times when I think that she may return my feelings, but I just don't know." He looked at me, his dark eyes filled with pain. "My duties frequently keep me away from the palace for extended periods. When I'm here, she seems reluctant to allow me to get close."

"I'm probably the last person in Ramalda to discuss relationship problems with." I stifled a sudden yawn. "I'm still trying to figure out how the whole 'couple' thing works myself. I'm pretty new to all of this."

"I don't know." He cocked an eyebrow at me knowingly. "That handsome young stable hand seems quite smitten with you." The eyebrow was joined by a somewhat evil grin. "And, if I'm not mistaken, you are equally taken with him."

"It's one thing to be 'smitten' with someone as you say, but it's quite another to know what in all the hells you are supposed to be doing." I hoped that he would assume the firelight was responsible for the sudden flush of color in my cheeks.

"See? You do understand! *That* is my point exactly. I don't know what I am supposed to do to get through to her."

"What are you doing now?" I swirled the liquid in my cup as I thought. "Whatever it is, it apparently isn't working, so you obviously need to do something else."

Jehrold snorted. "I had pretty much figured that out for myself. I just don't know what the 'something else' is."

"Well, let's look at this logically. You aren't traveling now. You're going to be at the palace at least until the Naming, if not longer, correct?"

He nodded.

"So, now that you have more time on your hands, what are you doing differently?"

"Nothing." His dark brows furrowed in concentration. "We talk occasionally. I flirt and she lets me."

"That's it? You flirt? How is she supposed to take that seriously? She's just going to assume that you are flirting with her the same way you flirt with countless other women during your travels. Why should she assume that you are interested in anything more than a casual fling?" I gave him a scowl. "After all, the morning that we met, you made a toast to 'the best piece of ass' that you had had in quite a while."

"That was just talk." He jumped to his feet and began pacing, waving his hands as he explained. "That's the sort of thing that people *expect* me to say.

I'm the light-hearted ladies' man that never takes life seriously – or at least that's what everyone thinks."

"I'd say that you have played your role well. Perhaps *too* well, for obviously that's what Mama L thinks of you as well. Why would she want to risk getting involved with someone who would just break her heart by sleeping with the Makers only know how many women every time he is away?"

"I hadn't looked at it like that." He stopped walking and dropped like a rock, landing at my feet. "I would never hurt Cissy. I'm no saint, but I haven't even looked at another woman in ages." A sheepish look crossed his face. "Well, that's not exactly true. I *have* looked, but I haven't touched and I definitely haven't... well, you know."

"Really? You care for her that much?"

"Absolutely. I'm miserable without her. If she would just give me a chance, I know that I could make her happy." His shoulders slumped and he seemed to pull into himself once again; the light that had flared in his eyes as he spoke faded.

"Well, I think the solution is fairly simple." I placed my hand on his knee to get his attention and waited until he looked up. "*Tell* her how you feel. Don't leave her to guess and wonder."

"So, I should just go find her – wherever she is - and tell her that I love her. Just like that?"

"I think you might want to get her alone somewhere, not just blurt it out in front of everyone. She does have a certain reputation that she needs to uphold." I smiled to let him know that I wasn't fussing. "Besides, you just told me, so why shouldn't you tell her? She's the one that needs to know."

Jehrold leapt to his feet with a whoop and I suddenly found myself in a crushing bear hug that literally swept me off of my seat.

"Thank you, lass!" He set me gently on my feet, then reached out and mussed my hair genially. "I'm glad you showed up tonight. I'm going to find Cissy right now." He gave me a wink as he headed to the door. "If this works out, we'll name our firstborn after you."

"I hope it's not a boy!"

He was still chortling as he walked into the night, shutting the door behind him.

I quickly finished off the remainder of my tea and cleaned up all signs of my visit, shaking my head as I worked. Some people said that the Makers had no sense of humor. I knew better. I had spent part of my night dispensing relationship advice to both Maerie and Jehrold, yet I had no idea how to proceed with my own. I could almost hear the laughter drifting down from the heavens.

9

It was my favorite time of year. Spring now held sway over the days, with just enough of a nip in the air to require a light cloak if the wind was blowing – as it was today. Winter had not completely loosened its hold on the nights – it was wise to have a blanket on one's bed or a heavy cloak if going out after dark. The drabness of winter was gradually being replaced by the greens of spring; trees and bushes sported new coats of tiny leaves while grass struggled valiantly to gain a foothold in the crevices of the stones in the courtyard.

Mama L still worked us hard, but at a slightly less frenzied pace than before. Word had come that there had indeed been late snows in the mountains which would delay the return of the royal entourage charged with the safe transport of the heir. Morale among the staff had improved greatly at the slight reprieve.

We servants got one day out of seven off. It was my habit to leave the palace grounds and venture into MidTown on my free days; I didn't want my activities to seem suspicious when the time came to begin my preparations for the assassination. That time had arrived.

Much to the dismay of Maerie, I began the day by sleeping until after sunrise – a rare treat. Our off days did not coincide and she took special pains to make extra noise while washing and dressing. Her feelings would have been hurt had I not acknowledged her in some way, so I waited until both of her hands were occupied with getting her hair into an appropriately modest bun before I threw my pillow at her. My aim was true and the attack caught her completely off guard. However, her retribution was swift and I quickly found myself being pummeled with my own pillow. I was obviously not the best tactician when half asleep.

Once up, I dressed in one of the two well-worn but serviceable dresses that I could call my own. It would not do for someone in the uniform of the palace staff to be seen in the area of The Narrows that was the goal of my excursion. The cloak necessitated by the slight breeze would allow me to cover my hair without raising any eyebrows and a basket to carry over my arm would complete my ensemble. A casual observer would assume that I was just another female of the not-so-well-to-do variety out taking advantage of the weather to do some shopping.

As I crossed the courtyard, two of the younger lurchers ran up to me, their rear ends wagging in their eagerness to be petted and scratched. They knew that I was always good for a few minutes of attention, but they also had ulterior motives. In response to the change of seasons, they were beginning to lose their shaggy winter coats and were always looking for extra hands to assist with the process. I was glad to oblige but when I finished, my skirts were covered in what appeared to be most of the fur that they had lost.

"Just look this mess!" I admonished the dogs as I attempted to brush off the coarse strands. My efforts were in vain as they refused to budge. "Thanks to you scruffy hoodlums, I've got to go back and change." I scowled.

The lurchers just grinned at me before trotting off in search of a new victim, their collars jingling in time with their footsteps. They knew instinctively that my bark was worse than my bite - pun intended.

"C'mere, lass." The gate guard waved me over, chuckling at my predicament.

When I stopped at his station, he grabbed a small hand-held broom before holding me at arm's length as he swiped at my skirts. Once finished, he motioned for me turn in a circle as he eyed his work critically; he gave a satisfied grunt.

"The missus insists that I keep this with me." He waved his hand at the broom that he had tossed back into the guard shack. "She gets tired of me coming home covered with hair." He gave me a wink. "She says that if she wanted to sleep with a dog, she would have married one."

"Oh, thank you! You're a life-saver. Well, a time-saver at least. I wasn't looking forward to having to change before I left."

"I'd wager that you've got a bit of shopping in mind." He nodded at the basket on my arm.

"Probably more looking than buying, but I don't mind." I gave him a wave as I stepped out onto the wooden bridge that led from the palace to MidTown. "Thanks again!"

The gentle murmurs from the muddy waters of the Ocoee River muffled my footsteps as I crossed the span to its western bank.

The royal palace was the crowning jewel - no pun intended - of Ramalda. Located on a peninsula that jutted out from the cliffs lining the eastern bank of the river, it was surrounded on three sides by water. The bridge that I was on was the only connection to the mainland. A simple tug on the lever in the guard shack would operate a system of ropes and pulleys causing sections of the bridge to collapse against their stone supports thereby dumping anyone on them into the water.

At first glimpse, the cliff behind the castle would appear to be a weakness in its defenses; in many cases, that would be so. But not this time. The cliffs were made of razor rock which, as the name implied, was extremely sharp. The rock would easily cut through any ropes used in an attempt to descend the cliffs, leaving the unfortunate individuals holding them to fall to a rather unpleasant death on the knife-edged rubble littering the ground below. The rear of the castle was easily defensible against all but enemy archers. Of course, any archers close enough to fire on the castle would also be in range of the royal archers basically negating any advantage to their attack.

The western bank of the river was lined with the large manses belonging to the nobles and the rich. As usual, the owners of these residences were busily trying to out-do each other with their extravagant displays of wealth. My route was blocked by a large wagon containing wooden crates and a variety of plants and stone brought in from the arid regions far to the south. Unlike the green, graceful plants native to Ramalda, the specimens on board the cart were as unyielding as the environment in which they grew – they were tough and gnarled with long thorns that caught at the skin and clothes of the men moving them. I had to step off of the path to avoid two men struggling to move a plant that was almost round, which gave them nowhere to place their hands without injury.

"Damn it, man! Be careful! I've got enough holes in my shirt. I'll catch hell from the missus tonight."

"Your shirt, is it? These 'ere plants have stabbed me arms so many times I feel like I'm bein' stung by bees."

"I wonder what sort of monsters live in the desert? Even the damn plants are wearing armor."

"We'll find out soon enough. I heard somethin' movin' around in one of them boxes."

I cast an eye at the containers as I passed. Several sported what appeared to be air holes near the tops; malevolent thoughts rolled forth from the occupants. I shuddered at the thought of dangerous animals being brought in simply to satisfy the perverse whims of the prosperous.

I developed a spring in my steps as I approached the outskirts of MidTown proper, the domain of the middle class and a glorious mixture of homes, markets, and shops. This was where I came when, as a child, I would sneak out of the guild house to watch people. I had scouted out several vantage points around the marketplace from which I could watch others without them seeing me. It was during those illicit visits, for which I was invariably beaten when I was caught, that I first felt the longing to be a part of a family. To belong.

I tugged on the hood of my cloak to ensure that my hair was fully covered. Being both a redhead and an assassin was not an impossible combination; those of us with red hair were less in number than those with hair of other shades, but were not so rare as to attract undue attention. However, this close to my old home, there weren't too many individuals with both my hair and stature. I didn't want to risk being recognized – especially by someone who would know of my involvement with the Va'Shile.

Secure in the limited disguise provided by my cloak, I became just another shopper meandering through the market where I was immersed in a sea of sound – voices rose and fell in greeting, negotiations, and occasionally even arguments while laughter lapped at the shores. And the smells. Oh, the smells! There were some that were less than pleasant, of course, and I had to watch my footing to avoid stepping in animal dung. But my nose pulled me toward the food vendors and my only extravagance – fruit pasties. I would be expected to turn over most of my pay to the Va'Shile upon my return, but I was willing to live dangerously and spent a few coppers on myself.

I walked as I munched, stopping at various stalls and shops to peruse the items on display. This also gave me a chance to use the windows to observe the streets behind me so that I could make sure that I wasn't being followed.

A small crowd, made up mostly of couples, had gathered outside of one particular shop. Many whispered conversations took place as they jostled amiably to view the contents of the window. I stepped closer. What was so interesting? Bonding bracelets.

The ultimate symbol of belonging. No wonder the crowd was made up of couples. I suddenly felt very out of place, yet couldn't help looking wistfully at the items on display.

Bonding bracelets were sold in pairs and were the symbol of a committed, monogamous relationship. For a man to present a woman with a bonding bracelet was more than just a declaration of love. It was just one very small step short of an actual marriage. The design was simple; a braid of three strands represented the man, the woman, and the Makers that had brought them together. Where the strands overlapped, they were bound together to symbolize that the union could not be broken.

While the symbolism was all well and good, there was nothing magical about the bracelets, in spite of what some craftsmen said. If a man - or woman – were going to cheat on his or her "beloved," no sort of mystical alarms would go off to warn the soon to be victim. However, most people who entered into a bonded relationship took their promises very seriously.

The proprietor of this particular shop was smart indeed. The wares in his window were made of a variety of materials, making them accessible to those of varying income levels. Those at the lower end of the price range were simple braids of leather with brass studs fastening the strands together. They only increased in value from there. The most expensive were braids of gold encrusted with gems. My gaze was drawn to an unusual pair where the strands were of different materials – one of gold, one of silver, and one of copper. I thought it was perfect. No two people were alike, so why should the strands that represent them be the same?

The whispers being exchanged by those around me seemed to indicate an event of some import. I quickly finished the last of my pastie and wiped the crumbs off of my face.

"What's going on?" I asked the young woman closest to me.

"Oh, miss! Me and - " the woman blushed slightly as she nodded to the young man beside her - "my... friend were looking at the bracelets when a man came up and starting asking us questions about them."

"What kind of questions?"

"He asked us which ones we liked best and why. He said that he was interested in buying a pair, but said that he didn't know nothing much about what a woman might like and needed some opinions. So, as other couples came by, he started asking them the same things." She nodded to an empty slot on the display case. "After a while he made his choice. He's inside now, bargaining with the owner."

"Are the bracelets arranged by cost? If so, he must have picked out some pretty nice ones."

"Indeed. The braid is made of gold strands fastened with red stones. His lady is sure to be thrilled by them."

"Well, I wish him the best of luck then." Just before stepping back into the flow of people passing by, I turned back and added, "And to you and your 'friend' as well."

"Thank you, miss." She smiled shyly, a dimple forming at the corner of her mouth.

The bell on the shop door jingled and I glanced up to see Jehrold stepping out, sliding a small package into his pocket. My, my. Either things were going *very* well with Mama L or he was very much an optimist. Smiling, I slipped into the crowd and moved away before he could see me. Oh, well. It was time to get serious.

I wended my way to The Narrows, which were both adjacent to and nothing like MidTown. The Narrows had earned their name from the narrow streets and twisting alleys that ran through the area like game trails. It was the dwelling place of the poorest of the poor. It was my home. At first glimpse, The Narrows bore many similarities to MidTown – there was a marketplace, there were homes, and families. But here, a veneer of despair coated everything. The goods in the market were usually second-hand; the foodstuffs would be considered unfit for use in most households. Homes were frequently marked by extremes of violence or apathy. Families – even those that truly loved each other – struggled to get by. Far too many people here grew old before their time, their lives cut short by lack of food or back-breaking labor.

Below the despair lurked the vermin that both fed on it and cultivated it. These were the creatures that ran the other markets; the ones that no one talked about. The ones where people were bought and sold like livestock.

Treating any person like cattle was bad enough, but it was the children that affected me the most. The fortunate ones would become servants in a household where they would at least have food and clothing; some might even be lucky enough to be respected and treated as members of the family. The less fortunate would be forced to work endless hours in the blackrock mines. Dangerous, back-breaking labor. The mine owners used children because they did not have to pay them the wages that they would pay an adult; frequently, they paid them nothing at all. They did not worry about the working conditions or how many children were injured or even killed - they didn't see them as people at all, just a commodity easily replaced.

However, there were fates far worse than working in the mines. Some children would become slaves, sold to be used and abused by those with perverse desires, both sexual and otherwise. The most fortunate of them - if such a word could even be used - would be abandoned by their owners once they grew too old to be considered exciting. They would be free to begin new lives for themselves if they could; far too many would turn into copies of the monsters that they had dreamed of escaping for so long. Some of the children had no hopes of escape; the fiends that owned them enjoyed causing fear and pain. Those children would have agony and abuses too horrible to describe heaped upon them; death, when it came, would be their only release. Those owners, predators really, were the ones that I had preyed upon. As I said before, I felt no remorse for their deaths.

The most lucrative businesses in The Narrows were the brothels. These facilities ranged from filthy bug-infested hovels where customers could ease their needs for a few coppers to higher-end facilities that catered to any whim imaginable – as long as there was coin to back it up. I always found it amusing that the upper classes of Ramalda barely acknowledged the existence of those that they considered to be beneath them, yet they were frequent patrons of these establishments. Apparently, it was all right to be below them as long as your legs were spread.

The headquarters of the Va'Shile were in The Narrows. The aristocrats would rather not acknowledge the existence of an assassin's guild; as long as it was tucked away in the warrens of The Narrows, they could deny its existence while still paying for its services.

While most of the citizens of the region struggled to survive from day to day, those of us "fortunate" enough to belong to the Va'Shile lived lives of virtual splendor. An assassin had to be healthy, so we were given food of the highest quality on a regular basis. While most residents of The Narrows rarely washed, we were expected to bathe daily as well as clean our teeth. We couldn't be expected to pass as a member of the nobility if half of our teeth were missing.

Many people assumed that being an assassin simply involved killing people. They were wrong. My training began at age five and I was just one of many children. We were taught to read and write along with rudimentary mathematics. Those lessons were interspersed with others on hand-to-hand combat. Yes, where the more fortunate might have been playing with dolls at age six, I was learning how to fight.

We were given detailed lessons on anatomy. An assassin must be able to kill quickly and efficiently; therefore, it was important that we know where the major organs and vessels of the bodies were located and the most precise locations to strike in order to inflict damage on them. Of course, our lessons on anatomy were not restricted to the inner workings of the body and the quickest way to bring about death. As I mentioned previously, we were also taught the art of seduction. After all, an assassin must get close to his or her victim in order to kill them. It was hard to get much closer than sex. I could make any man want me, like he had wanted no other. I could bring him greater pleasure than he had known with any other. I could make him scream with desire, even as his life's blood covered my hands. I could be very, very scary.

I chose not to be.

There were also ways to kill that did not involve weapons. We were taught about poisons and the antidotes for those that have them. Due to my size, I could easily be outmatched in a knife fight - I did not have a long reach. However, I wouldn't recommend that anyone take me on in a fight unless they were *very* sure of themself and their ability. I may not have had reach, but I had speed and *I* most definitely knew what I was doing. Alas, I digress. Poisons were time-consuming to prepare and required painstaking attention to detail, both of which I exceled at. Sorry. Modesty was not among the training that I received nor did it come to me naturally.

A side effect of learning to kill was learning to heal. The Va'Shile were cruel taskmasters. When we received wounds during training, our masters did not treat them; they were left to fester. They did, however, leave us the supplies necessary for the care of our injuries. We learned through trial and error which of the materials provided were beneficial and which were not. It only took one incident of treating a wound with acid rather than antiseptic for us to learn the characteristics of each so that we did not make the same mistake again.

Most of the plants from which poisons were made were also used by healers. Frequently, only a few small drops meant the difference in life or death. We used our newfound knowledge of herb lore to create concoctions for the wounded to use in an attempt to fight off infection. If they died, we were forced to watch as the surgeon opened up the body to determine the cause – traumatic injury, widespread infection, or botched healing potion. There was nothing quite like watching someone who one had grown up with be dissected to get one's attention. I was determined that such a fate would not befall me.

I was sure that I had not been followed, nor had I seen any familiar faces. So, after a few more twists and turns, just in case, I arrived at my destination - a squalid little hovel that looked like any other in any of the many unnamed alleys. The Va'Shile had several safe houses scattered throughout the town where we could take refuge before or after a hit to avoid capture - provided, of course, we could get there without being seen. But this place was mine alone.

The door to my hideaway was disguised to look like a continuation of the wall of the adjoining building. The latch was hidden in what, to the casual observer, was a knot hole in the wood. After a quick glance to make sure that no one was watching and a firm press on the latch, I was inside, closing the door behind me. There was a trick to getting it to close properly – I had to lift up on the door while simultaneously pulling it slightly toward me in order for the latch to engage properly. Failure to do so would make the presence of the door evident to any passersby.

It was the failure of the previous inhabitant to close the door correctly that had allowed me to find it. Being the curious sort, I wondered what could possibly be so important that it required such elaborate precautions to protect it. However, when I entered the room, it seemed obvious that no one had been there in some time. A fine coating of dust covered everything, including the floor and there were no footprints to indicate that the owner was simply a messy housekeeper. So, I claimed it for my own and established it as a base for brewing my poisons.

It was here that I maintained a supply of the varied plants, herbs, and a few slightly more exotic ingredients required for my brews. I had built my supply painstakingly over an extended period of time. Many of the items had been supplied by the guild house, although their generosity was unintentional. I guess some – including the masters - would call it theft. If my thievery were discovered, my punishment would be severe; the loss of a hand would be the best that I could hope for. Fortunately, the other ingredients were those that I could obtain from any herbalist, meaning that I was only dependent upon the Va'Shile for the more under the table, black market types of items.

I knew this place like the back of my hand. Even though it was dark, I moved unerringly to the cabinet and pulled out several candles and a tinder box. Within moments a gentle, flickering light filled the room. I did a slow walkthrough, surveying the ingredients on hand and determining which should be replaced. Some items could be stored indefinitely, but others deteriorated over time. Not knowing exactly how much time I had to work, I decided to go with some of the poisons that I had already prepared; I chose a couple of alternatives and the appropriate antidotes. I couldn't help myself; after so much time, it was ingrained into my psyche. I would no more poison someone without having the antidote with me than I would run through the streets of Ramalda naked.

Most of my pedophile hits entailed poisoning the wine of my target, which was simple enough. However, I never knew when I might be required to drink some of that same wine - some abusers prefer to lull their prey into insensibility. I always carried a vial of antidote, just in case. On more than one occasion I found myself puking up my guts as my body struggled to purge itself of the poison it had ingested.

My selections complete, I doused the lights, put the candles back in the cabinet and prepared to leave. Sliding open the peephole, I carefully checked the surrounding area. My field of vision was limited, but I saw no immediate danger. I slipped through the door, latched it properly behind me and turned to walk away. The hairs on the back of my neck prickled and my eyes narrowed as I surveyed the shadows before me. Something wasn't right. My hand fell to my dagger as a large shadow pulled itself away from the others and blocked my way down the alley. I recovered my composure quickly – or at least pretended to.

"Master Jaidon. I see that you haven't lost your touch." My voice was a tad higher than I would have liked.

The Va'Shile Master of Disguise stared down at me from his good eye. A patch covered the scarred remains of his other eye – thankfully. Few recruits were ever brave enough to ask the master how he lost his eye, and those that did simply received a withering stare in response. The most common theory was that he had obtained the injury when wrestling a yaren for its mate. If any man would have been capable of mating with a yaren, it would have been Master Jaidon. He stood well over six feet and was built like a stone wall. Even the slight hunch on his back did nothing to reduce the air of intimidation that rolled off of him. I personally thought the eye patch gave him a rather piratical air, but there was no way in the many hells that I would have ever admitted it.

"Aye, girl. There is still no one better than me at moving in the shadows. I tracked you here from the palace."

"How? I was careful and I wasn't followed." I bit my lip in frustration. "I would have staked my life on it."

"Well then, it's a good thing that you didn't, isn't it?" He cocked his head as if to get a better look at me. There seemed to be a twinkle in his eye.

Surely not. Master Jaidon would not, under any circumstances, *twinkle*.

"You did good, girl. But, I am better." He drew himself back up to his full height. "After all, I taught you everything you know – about disguises and remaining hidden, at least." In a lower voice he added, "Vido wants an update."

"An update? Now?" I reached up to push back the hood of my cloak, but stopped myself just in time. Standing in the presence of a known member of the Va'Shile was not the time to remove my meager disguise. "He knows as well as I that the heir is not yet at the palace. Therefore, I cannot do anything to him." I pulled myself to my full height and continued haughtily, "I have fully integrated myself into the staff; no one will suspect me. On that note, once the deed is done, I cannot flee the palace at once; to do so would appear suspicious. I must stay there long enough to allay any misgivings once I announce that I must leave."

Master Jaidon looked as though he would like to argue with me, but he knew that my logic was sound. He grunted - a smooth talker, as always. "I will report your plans to the Master. But do not tarry long. Vido does not like to be kept waiting when there is coin to be made."

"Coin to be made?" My surprise colored my voice. "Does this mean that he is already lining up additional hits for me? It's not like Vido to make such plans before he even knows that I will acquit myself ably of this one."

"You are a killer, girl. That is what you do, and you do it well. Of course, he is lining up more jobs for you. Any number of assassins can be used for the quick and dirty hack jobs. He only has a few, like you, that can be used in delicate situations. After all, who would suspect such a dainty young thing of being a cold-blooded assassin? Now, get back to work. Don't make us look bad."

I laughed as I pushed by him. "Master Jaidon, I cannot possibly make you look any worse than you already do!"

He huffed out a sound. I wasn't sure if it was laughter or displeasure and I didn't wait around to find out.

I returned to the palace by a different, but no less circuitous route. Nef was waiting for me at the end of the bridge. He slid his arm around my waist as we walked slowly back to the palace.

"I was getting worried. You've been gone a long time."

"Well, I'm back now." I stopped and stood on tiptoe to give him a kiss on the cheek. "As soon as I put my things away, I'm all yours."

"Well, then." He swept me off of my feet and into his arms before proceeding to jog the rest of the way across. Only when he had reached the kitchen door did he put me down and give me a rather friendly pat on the rear. "Hurry back."

Once safely back in my quarters, I hid the vials where they would not be found – at least not by accident. My preparations, such as they were, could proceed no further until the heir arrived.

10

Nef cupped my face in his hand, his gaze devouring me hungrily. He pushed back my hair, exposing my neck; his fingers took advantage of the exposed flesh and began lightly tracing lazy circles there. Gooseflesh pebbled my skin. His blue eyes were dark with desire as he lowered his head to press his lips gently to mine. I melted against him, opening my lips slightly in invitation. Accepting the offer, he slid his tongue into my mouth, where it parried briefly with mine. He was all warmth and sweetness.

I pressed myself against him eagerly, wanting to be closer. Wanting him. I flattened my hands against his back, eager to feel his muscles flex as he moved. One of his hands dropped to cup my buttock as the other traced its way down my spine before moving to the curve of my hip. My nipples tingled in anticipation as his hand began to move upward. He stopped just shy of my breast. I ached for him to move those last few inches.

Bam. Bam. Bam.

"What was that?" I asked against his lips, not opening my eyes. I shifted slightly in his arms so that his thumb was just grazing the side of my breast.

"Only the pounding of my heart," he replied, then deepened the kiss. He kissed me until my head spun, then dropped his lips to where my pulse fluttered in my throat. I gasped and arched my back as he nibbled his way down my neck, using his teeth and tongue to fan the flames of my desire.

Bam. Bam. Bam.

This time I opened my eyes and found myself in a passionate embrace - with my pillow. It was only a dream. But it had been so real! I closed my eyes and clung desperately to the fading tendrils of my fantasy, begging it to come back.

Bam. Bam. Bam.

Someone was pounding on my door. The pieces fell into place with an almost audible snap. It was my day off and someone had taken it upon themselves to ruin my reverie. The knocking continued as I struggled to untangle myself from the covers.

"I'm coming," I snarled. *This better be good.* I grabbed my robe as I staggered across the room, but didn't bother to put it on; I simply held it in front of me as I snatched the door open. "What?" I asked grumpily.

My cheeks flamed when Nef grinned back at me. Had my lust been strong enough to call him to me?

"Good morning to you too." He paused briefly as he took in my dishevelment then continued determinedly, "Get dressed. I've got a surprise for you."

"Again? You never give a girl a chance to plan ahead do you? You're always springing things on me at the last minute." I had never been a morning person.

"That's why it's called a *surprise*. C'mon," he wheedled. "I had to pull a lot of strings to get today off and we have a full day ahead of us. Get dressed."

Who was I to resist well-intentioned wheedling?

"Fine. Have it your way." I smiled to take the sting from my words. "Stay there. I'll be out in a few minutes." Closing the door, I stripped off my night clothes, took a quick, cold, sponge bath, brushed my teeth and threw on my dress before dragging a comb through my hair. Finally giving up any attempt to get the unruly mass to cooperate, I pulled it into a long tail on the back of my head. *That will have to do.* I was still somewhat grumpy. Truth be told, I would rather have been getting *un*dressed and inviting him into my bed. However, I was relatively sure that that wouldn't be proper. After one last splash of cold water in my face, I shoved my feet into my shoes and stepped into the hall, eager to find out what sort of adventure Nef had planned for us today. Well, maybe "eager" was an overstatement; "ready" was about the best I could do right then.

"Where are we going?" I asked, trying to sound a little perkier than I felt.

"You'll see."

He had apparently been up for a while – busy with preparations, no doubt – and had already eaten. I had not and my stomach was beginning to protest. Loudly. We detoured through the kitchens where he snagged cider and a sweet roll for me to munch on as we walked.

Our footsteps led us to the docks and a boat that was already stocked with what looked suspiciously like a picnic basket and blankets. He stepped into the boat, balancing easily as it swayed under his weight. He placed one hand on the mooring post to hold the vessel steady and held out the other to me. I placed my hand in his then froze.

"What's wrong?" Nef's concern was obvious in both his voice and the way he tightened his grip on my fingers.

"I don't know how to swim." I swallowed rapidly, praying that my breakfast would stay down. "I'm scared."

"Do you trust me?"

Trust. That was really the question, wasn't it? My gaze traveled over his face and he returned my look calmly, not rushing me. Less than an hour before I had dreamed of offering this man my body – something that I had never trusted anyone else enough to do. It came to me in a rush that the answer to his question was simple.

"Yes." Taking a deep breath, I stepped into the boat and took my seat.

Nef sat across from me, facing me. Giving a satisfied nod, he cast off the rope that secured us to the dock, picked up the oars, and pulled us into the current. I immediately panicked and grabbed the edge of the boat, gripping until my knuckles turned white.

"Relax, Lillie. It's okay. I know this river; I won't let anything happen to you." He gave me a rather wicked grin, dimples flashing. "If it will make you feel better, the pad that you are sitting on will float; if you decide that you simply *must* fall out of the boat, be sure to take it with you and hold on tight."

Damn it. His dimples always made me go weak in the knees. Of course, I wasn't about to admit that to him. At least not right then.

"If I weren't so terrified, I would *hit* you with this pad," I growled through gritted teeth. "Of course, that would mean loosening my death grip, so I guess you're safe."

Nef chuckled, never losing his pace. He moved easily, his body flowing smoothly from one stroke to the next. I found the rhythm relaxing – until I noticed his arms. His shirt sleeves were pushed up, exposing his forearms. The light furring of dark hairs there only served to accent his muscles as they moved under his skin. My throat grew dry – and other parts of me wet – as I thought about those arms and all of the times that they had held me. I was eager for them to do even more. I groaned inwardly. Our outing was only just beginning and I was getting aroused by the sight of his *arms*. It was going to be a long day.

A few miles downriver, Nef grounded the boat on the sandy shore of a small island. "We should have the island to ourselves," he assured me as he helped me out of the boat. "Most people don't come here because of the yaren."

"But you aren't concerned?" I cocked an eyebrow at him.

"Not really." The dimples flashed again. "There are a few yaren here, but not as many as most people think. I spent my younger years spreading the rumor that the island was overrun by the creatures. That way, I could have it to myself when I needed to get away from everyone for a while." He glanced at the trees lining the beach. "Hopefully, my tall tales have become local legend - at least strong enough to keep most people away."

"I never knew that you were such a sneak." I grinned up at him. "I'm proud of you."

Giving me a wink, Nef shoved the blanket into my arms, then he snagged the picnic basket in one hand; his free arm slid around my waist. After looking around quickly to get his bearings, he led me away from the shore along a faint trail that made its way through the tall grass and into the forest. The shade of the woods provided a welcome respite from the heat. Beyond the trees lay a small clearing, perfect for a cozy meal. Nef spread the blanket on the grass while I inspected the contents of the basket. I was impressed; there was a selection of bread, soft cheese, fruit, and even some assorted sweets for dessert.

Once our meal was completed and the leftovers packed away, we stretched out side by side on the blanket to watch the clouds that drifted by overhead. Ribbons of birds streamed across the turquoise sky as they returned from their winter migration. I closed my eyes, basking in the warmth of the day and the man beside me. My reverie was disturbed when a bug chose to wend its way across my nose, which I wriggled in an effort to dislodge it; it returned in a matter of seconds.

I opened my eyes to find that it wasn't a bug - Nef had plucked a blade of grass and begun trailing it down my nose. I grabbed his wrist, planning to wrest the grass away from him and failed. Sort of. My attempt resulted in a rather pleasant wrestling match, which was definitely a plus, in my opinion. He won handily, kissing me into submission. I surrendered willingly; after all, I would have hated to be a poor loser. Giving me one last kiss, he rolled over on his side, facing me.

"Tell me, Lillie. What were you like as a child?" He pushed himself up on one elbow and rested his head on his hand. "Were you in as much trouble as I suspect that you were?" He tugged gently on one of the curls that had escaped its binding during our tussle.

A sudden restlessness overwhelmed me; I needed to move. But, I couldn't run away from my past, so I settled for sitting up, drawing my legs up under my skirt, and resting my chin on my knees. I stared intently at my fingers as they traced idle patterns on the blanket.

"Probably." I finally looked up at Nef. "I told you that my foster-father frequently reminded me that my parents didn't want me because I was a 'bad girl.'"

He scowled and nodded.

"I decided that if he was convinced that I was a bad girl, I may as well *be* one." I attempted to smile, but it felt more like a grimace. "I would sneak out of the house every chance I got and go to the MidTown markets. There, I could watch real families and dream of what it would be like be a part of one – to belong and be loved. To be more than a convenient business transaction."

"What happened?"

"It didn't take long for my foster-father's cronies to learn all of my hiding places, so I would be found, taken back, and beaten. But somehow, each beating made me that much more determined to do it again."

"A true redhead statement if I've ever heard one." Nef laughed, but sobered quickly. He sat up and faced me. "I'm sorry that your life has been so hard." He placed his finger under my chin and raised my head until our eyes met. "But, whatever you've been through, I like the way you turned out."

"Thanks." I flushed with pleasure. "It wasn't all bad," I explained, changing the subject. "One of my caretakers when I was very young was full of stories of the Va'Kyrian. During my forays into the marketplace, I was always on the lookout for their crimson and gold cloaks. I just *knew* that if they ever met me, they would realize that I was the recruit that the order had been waiting for since its inception." I chuckled. "It was several years before I understood that they were just stories – no Va'Kyrian were going to be coming to my rescue."

Nef scooted closer and pulled me to him, settling me between his legs with my back pressed against his chest. He wrapped his arms around me, resting his chin on top of my head.

"Most legends have their roots in truth. The Va'Kyrian *were* real – they were an offshoot of the Va'Shile."

"Really?"

He nodded, which made his chin bang against my head. He shifted slightly, so that his lips were just inches from my ear.

"The Va'Shile is a foul organization, willing to do anything, kill anyone for coin." His disgust was evident in his voice. "Some members of the group were not willing to live like that and rebelled. They took the skills that they had learned and put them to use helping and protecting others rather than harming them."

Nef's tone cut me to the quick. He would be devastated when he learned that *I* belonged to the institution that he felt such antipathy for. I was sure that he would speak of me the same way. The only good thing was that I wouldn't be around to hear it.

"How did they get away with that? I can't imagine the Va'Shile just letting them walk away." Actually, I *could* envision the Va'Shile's reaction – quite well.

"Nor did they. However, the dissidents had been among the best of the Va'Shile. There were brutal attacks and ambushes and lives were lost – but only by the Va'Shile. Eventually, they decided that it was wiser just to let the Va'Kyrian be. The Va'Kyrian served nobly as protectors of the royal family for centuries."

"What happened to them?"

"When the royal family lost the throne, the Va'Kyrian faded into obscurity as well. A shame really, if they hadn't, perhaps the Va'Shile wouldn't have risen to such a position of power." Tightening his arms around me, he rolled and shifted until we were once again laying side-by-side on the blanket. "Now, enough talk of assassins and heroes. It's time for a post-lunch nap."

Within minutes, Nef's breathing had taken on the slow regularity of sleep. I could have slept as well, but preferred to stay awake and bask in the sensation of safety his arms afforded with his warm, hard body pressed against mine.

Now that it was quiet, I became aware of a low noise that I had not been able to hear earlier. I raised my head, turning it from side to side as I tried to determine where it was coming from.

"What is that sound?" I spoke softly, hoping that I wouldn't startle Nef.

"That's the waterfall," he replied sleepily, trying to pull me back down on the blanket.

"A waterfall? Are you serious? I've never seen one." I shook him awake and gave him my best doe-eyes, fluttering my lashes with nauseating sweetness. "Show me, please?"

He fell for it.

Sighing, Nef stretched, stood, and pulled me to my feet. "I was *trying* to take a nap."

"Later," I promised him.

He led me to the far side of the clearing and back into the forest, once again following a winding game trail. As we drew closer to the sound, the temperature of the air dropped and the vegetation grew thicker. More than once, my skirts snagged on thorny vines - sometimes to the point that Nef had to help me extricate myself from their clutches. My frustration level grew with each prickly encounter and I grew more than a little grumpy until we finally shoved our way through waist high shrubs and stepped onto a narrow, rocky shore lining the edge of a lake.

It was the most beautiful sight that I had ever seen.

The crystal waters reflected the spring sky perfectly. I felt that if I stepped onto that shimmering surface, I would find myself walking on clouds. A rocky cliff rose from the far side of the lake; a torrent of water cascaded from its crest, striking the water below with a roar. The air sparkled with tiny rainbows where the sunlight struck the mist that rose from the union of the waters.

I turned to Nef, speechless. He smiled at the look on my face. Slipping my shoes off, I stepped toward the lake. He put his hand out to stop me.

"What are you doing? The water will be like ice!"

"That's okay. I just need to feel it."

I hiked my skirt up around my knees, eased into the water and yelped. He was right. I turned to find Nef, arms crossed, giving me a rather smug I-told-you-so look. Right or not, I couldn't have that. I cupped my hand and swept it through the water, splashing him neatly.

"Why, you..." he sputtered as the cold water struck him. Wading in, he splashed me back. It was a declaration of war.

In a matter of minutes we were both panting, soaked to the skin, and freezing.

"C'mon." Nef grabbed my hand and pulled me out of the water. "Let's go back to the clearing and dry out in the sun. I could use something else to eat too. I've worked up an appetite." His wet clothes hugged his body, from broad shoulders to powerful thighs.

"I was thinking the same thing." Of course, I wasn't sure that we were discussing the same sort of appetite.

When we reached the edge of the clearing, Nef stopped so quickly that I almost crashed into him.

"Don't move," he whispered.

"W-w-why not?" I whispered back through chattering teeth; standing in the shade was definitely not doing anything to warm me up.

Without taking his eyes off of whatever lay in front of us, he reached back, drew me up beside him and pointed to the clearing.

A yaren was rummaging through the remains of our lunch.

"Be still. If it sees us, it may attack."

The yaren was on all fours, its golden brown fur glistening in the sun. It used its nimble front paws - which were very similar to a human's hands - to sort through the leftovers, occasionally sniffing or tasting a particular morsel. The tidbits that met with its approval went into the pouch located on its abdomen. Yaren were curious creatures and avid collectors of items that struck their fancy. Their multi-purpose pouches could be used for transporting young or, as in this case, food or other items of interest.

"She isn't going to hurt us." I watched her carefully as I spoke. "It hasn't been long since she came out of her winter sleep. She's hungry and may have young to feed. The smell of our food lured her in; once she has taken what she wants, she'll leave. We're in no danger."

Nef gave me an odd look. "You can communicate with yaren too?"

"Apparently." I shrugged. "This is the first time that I've been this close to one."

As we watched, the yaren gathered up her final selections and placed them in her pouch with the others. Sitting back on her haunches, she looked directly at us and huffed out a sound that was almost a greeting of sorts. She then turned away and lumbered off into the forest without looking back.

Nef gave me that look again. "Sometimes, you're scary."

I just rolled my eyes at him, took his hand in mine, and led him back to our blanket in the clearing. The sunshine felt wonderful, but my teeth wouldn't stop chattering. Nef wasn't much better off. As I watched, he stripped out of his shirt and spread it on the grass to dry. His chest was beautiful - it was leanly muscled, with a faint furring of dark hair in the center. I shoved my hands in my pockets to keep from reaching out to touch it. As he reached up to release his hair from its bindings, he motioned toward me.

"Why don't you take off your dress? It will dry faster on the grass and you'll warm up quicker in just your shift."

"There's just one problem with that." Remember when I said that I 'threw on my dress'? Well, that was *all* that I threw on. No shift, no undergarments of any sort. Damned if he hadn't called my bluff — even though he hadn't known about it. I struggled to give him a winsome-yet-wicked grin as I began to unbutton my dress. I almost hurt myself.

"What would that be?" Nef watched me with casual interest.

I let my gown fall to the ground, revealing me in all of my pale, freckled glory.

"I'm not wearing a shift." I hoped that I hadn't just made a mortally stupid mistake in judgment.

Nef's eyebrows shot up higher than I thought possible. This time, it was *his* breath that caught. Based on the, uh, *reaction* in the area of his groin, I suspected that he was not too displeased. I stepped close enough to reach out and stroke the silky down on his chest as I had ached to earlier.

"Lillie," he croaked. He cleared his throat and tried again. "Lillie, did you plan this?"

"No. But, I have thought about it."

"You have?" Stepping closer, he reached behind me and deftly removed the tie from my hair. "Should I be concerned that my sweet, innocent little Lillie thinks of such things?" A smile colored his voice as he ran his fingers through my hair, loosening the strands.

I shivered where the damp curls touched my skin but burned where his fingers brushed against me. I ran my fingers across his chest and abdomen, tracing the striations of his muscles. His flesh pebbled in the wake of my touch.

"Nef, I am many things, but 'innocent' is not one of them."

His hands - which had been caressing my shoulders – froze.

"What, exactly, do you mean?"

"Not what you are probably thinking." I felt, rather than saw, him relax imperceptibly. I hung my head; for the first time I was ashamed of my upbringing. Ashamed that I truly wasn't innocent. "I have been kissed and touched, although I have never... Well, you know. I'm well acquainted with what goes where. I've just never actually *experienced* it." I suddenly felt extremely vulnerable and crossed my arms over my chest, covering my breasts. It wasn't much, but it was the best I could do.

"Are you trying to tell me that you're a virgin?"

I nodded. "There have been many things in my life that I have been unable to control, but to whom I give my body – my*self* - is not one of them." I met his blue eyes directly. "I have never felt this way about anyone until now. Until you." I was beginning to feel a little awkward, but at least everything was out in the open.

"Lillie, I don't know what to say. I'm honored - and flattered. But..."

Honored. Flattered. Not exactly the words that I had been longing to hear. I tried to figure out how I was going to get back into my wet dress and act like nothing had happened.

"...do you think you could lose the knife?" he continued. "It's not exactly conducive to romance."

Startled, I glanced down and realized that although I had skipped donning undergarments, my sheathed dagger was firmly strapped in its usual location on my thigh. It was such a part of me that I didn't even remember putting it on. I burst out laughing at the image I must present – stark naked except for a knife.

"My pleasure." Divesting myself of the blade was but the work of a moment.

"Much better." He swept his eyes slowly from my forehead to my toes, the intensity of his gaze almost tangible. "You're not the only one that has thought about this, you know."

"Oh, really? Tell me more."

He ran one finger lightly down my nose and then began tracing the outline of my lips. Opening my mouth slightly, I grasped the tip of his finger gently with my teeth, stroking it with my tongue. Nef groaned then replaced his finger with his lips, brushing them softly across mine, teasing me with his tongue.

"A gentleman," he said, then kissed me, "*never kisses and tells.*"

I twined my fingers into his dark hair urging him closer, engaging his lips and tongue fully. His chest grazed my breasts; my nipples hardening instantly. Warmth pooled briefly in my belly before spreading to my extremities. I broke away long enough to issue a challenge.

"Well, then maybe he should *demonstrate*. It isn't polite to keep a lady waiting."

His answering chuckle was the most erotic sound that I had ever heard. Desire shot through me.

Nef quite literally swept me off of my feet and dropped to a sitting position on the blanket; I was firmly positioned in his lap, with my head cradled in the crook of his arm. As he bent his head to kiss me, his free hand trailed down my side, his thumb just inches from my breast. As in my dream, I shifted slightly so that my nipple grazed his thumb. The intensity of the slight touch left me gasping.

"This... is... what... I... was... dreaming... of... when... you... woke... me... this... morning," I panted.

"Oh?" He pulled back his head and looked at me with interest; his blue eyes were dark with desire, but a smile played at the corner of his lips. "What were we doing?"

"Basically, the same thing that we are doing now – you were caressing me and I was 'encouraging' you to put your hand on my breast."

"Mmm." He shifted his hand to cup my breast and began stroking my nipple with his thumb. "Like this?"

"Yes," I gasped, arching my back and closing my eyes. My hips moved slightly of their own accord, a glorious ache spreading between my thighs.

I was well aware of Nef's erection. It was hard not to be with it pressed against my leg; it responded with enthusiasm to my undulations, quivering as it strained to be free of the constraints of his breeches, marking the coarse fabric with a slight dampness. My awareness of his desire heightened my own.

He moved his hand from my breast, only to replace it with his mouth, his lips and tongue closing on its sensitive peak. I cried out wordlessly, twining my fingers in his hair, pressing him to me. He teased my nipple with his tongue; the sensation that shot from that point through the rest of my body was almost unbearable. I wanted more.

I shifted in his arms, urging him toward my other breast - it was beginning to feel left out since its partner was getting all of the attention. He lifted me smoothly, laying me on my back on the blanket, which freed him to put both hands to use; he did so rather skillfully. As he turned his attentions to the virgin breast, one hand moved lower, trailing lightly over my stomach before coming to rest on the auburn curls between my thighs. His long fingers twined briefly in the locks before sliding even lower to tease the mound of sensitive flesh that throbbed there. I gasped, my hips arching up to meet his touch.

With a groan, Nef slid himself between my legs, grinding himself against me. My entire body hummed with tension; the coarseness of his breeches against the sensitive skin of my thighs was sweet torture. I sat up, reaching to undo the buttons of his pants.

"Lillie, are you sure you want to do this?" He grabbed my hands before they could come into contact with his crotch.

"I've never been so sure of anything before."

Within seconds, he had freed himself from his trousers and was once again positioned between my legs, his cock quivering against me. He pressed into me and stopped, poised on the edge of penetration.

"I've heard that the first time can be painful." His eyes were sincere, but the words ground out through gritted teeth. "I don't want to hurt you."

I appreciated his concern, but it was time for less talk and more action. I wrapped my legs around his waist and arched my back, pressing him into me. I gasped as sensation flooded through me. If there was any pain, it was lost in the flood of emotion that threatened to overwhelm me. Yes, he filled me physically, but also emotionally. For the first time in my life, I was complete. I belonged.

"Are you all right?" Nef's hips began a rhythmic thrusting, seemingly of their own accord.

"Better than all right." I met his gaze, fighting the sudden urge to burst into tears of sheer joy. I was pretty sure that crying, no matter what the reason, would bring a rapid end to our coupling. I moved my hips tentatively, encouragingly.

Nef actually *growled*, low in his chest, and his thrusts became more urgent. At first, I struggled to match his rhythm, but once I finally did... Having pleasured myself more than once, I was familiar with orgasm, but the feeling that suffused me each time he sheathed himself fully was amazing. I felt as though I was reaching the crest of a precipice and longed to plunge over the other side. However, before I could, Nef cried out.

"Lillie," he gasped; the cords in his neck stood out as his thrusts reached a frantic crescendo. He grabbed my hips blindly, his fingers digging into my flesh as the essence of his completion filled me. He collapsed against me, his chest heaving.

I wrapped myself around him as I waited for his breathing to return to normal, desperately wishing for a way to stop time. I wanted that moment, that day to last forever.

"I'm sorry," Nef panted.

"Sorry! For what?" I gave him a smirk. "I don't have anything to compare it to, but I think that you acquitted yourself admirably."

"Thank you." A faint blush touched his cheeks – the ones on his face, anyway. "But you didn't get to... finish."

I rose up and gave him a shove on the shoulder, following his body with mine as he rolled. I ended up lying on top of him – a position that I was willing to get used to. "Correction. I didn't get to finish *that* time. Who said that we're done?"

"You said that I could take a nap later." He chuckled.

"Nap if you want. I'm going exploring."

"Exploring what?"

"You."

I learned many things during my explorations – that Nef's sides were ticklish, that licking the soft skin just behind his earlobes brought him to instant arousal, and that there was a difference between knowing what to do and actually doing it. Most importantly, I learned that there was a difference between having sex and making love. Anyone could have sex; it was purely physical. Making love, however, involved the heart. We were making love.

When the sun dropped lower in the sky, we reluctantly dressed and prepared to return to the castle. I was pretty sure that I was going to be sunburned in some interesting locations, but it was worth it. We were silent on the trip back although many satisfied smiles and playful glances were exchanged.

Back on the docks, Nef pulled me into the shadows, and cupped my face in his hands.

"Thank you, Lillie. No one has ever given me such a precious gift. I will treasure it always." He smiled. "I hope I responded with proper gratitude."

"You were everything I hoped for." I pressed myself against him and stretched up to nibble on his neck.

"However, I hope we will be able to 'thank' each other again sometime soon."

"You can count on it." He slid his hands to my buttocks and his fingers began plucking at the fabric of my skirts, gradually raising them higher. He had once again grown hard.

Was he going to take me right here where someone might find us at any moment? I was surprised to realize that I was completely fine with that idea. Just as I was preparing to undo his breeches, voices approached; their tones had an air of urgency. We quickly moved away from each other, straightened our clothes, and stepped out to greet them.

"What's going on?" Nef asked.

"The king has received word that his advisor is en route with the heir. They should arrive in about two weeks. Mama L is fit to be tied. There is still so much to do."

I really didn't see how that was possible. The entire castle had been swept, polished and mopped within an inch of its life. Little did I know.

11

The royal entourage did *not* arrive in two weeks as expected. Their ranks were hit with dysentery, bringing their progress to a temporary halt. I sometimes wondered if they actually existed since one problem after another prevented their arrival, but I didn't really mind the delays. Nor did Nef – he seemed both astounded and pleased to discover that I was as enthusiastic about the physical aspect of our relationship as he was.

Mama L kept everyone busy, but we made opportunities to be together as often as possible. Although, in our lust, we sometimes took chances that we shouldn't have. It was a miracle that we didn't get caught in the act – on more than one occasion.

One of my duties was dusting the obligatory suits of armor and busts of long-dead ancestors situated in alcoves lining the halls. Some of the niches were bare stone, others were backed with a floor to ceiling tapestry. My earlier explorations had shown that the tapestries simply hid a continuation of the niche. I found the configuration odd, but never questioned the reason for it – if there even was one. One afternoon I was working away, lost in my own thoughts when Nef's arms suddenly slid around my waist from behind as he dropped his lips to graze on my exposed neck.

"Nef!" My voice was husky. "What are you doing? We'll both be fired if we get caught." However, my actions spoke louder than my startled whisper as I leaned into his embrace, angling my neck for easier access.

"I know just the way to avoid being seen." Giving me a wink, he quickly checked for onlookers, scooped me into his arms, and stepped behind the tapestry lining the nearest niche. "I do believe that it is time for another history lesson, little one. You see, our forefathers – and many of our foremothers – were a randy bunch. The palace is rife with secret passages – some, of course, to allow individuals to escape in the event of an attack, but most simply connect the many bedchambers. It was much easier to deny allegations of impropriety if the accusers never actually caught anyone en route to an illicit liaison." As he spoke, he sat me on the narrow ledge that ran around the back wall of the niche. "However, there were those that found the risk of capture titillating. They would use these lovely little nooks for quick... meetings."

I cocked an eyebrow at him. "I think you're making that up." My attempt at sounding stern didn't fool either of us.

Nef suddenly seemed to have several extra hands and they were all doing delicious things to my body.

"You'll just have to take my word for it." One of his many hands was doing interesting things between my thighs. "Unless you would like for me stop so you can check with one of the oldsters?"

"No, no. That's all right. I'll...uh...I'll...*ah!*...take your word for it."

He chuckled at my reaction and proceeded to demonstrate how the ledge placed me at just the right height for... other things to pick up where his hands left off. We acquitted ourselves both thoroughly and quickly, although it would be sometime before Nef would be able to remove his shirt while working. His shoulders bore the brunt of my efforts to muffle my cries; the resulting bite marks were quite evident against his fair skin. However, I wouldn't have been surprised to learn that he flaunted them to his fellow stable hands as sort of a "badge of honor." Although, the term "*dis*honor" might have been more appropriate.

We also attempted to use the loft in the stables for a more leisurely rendezvous. And it would have been – except for Lucy's kittens. The kittens were now weaned, fully mobile, and very rambunctious; they were delighted to have new playmates enter their territory. Nef found it very disconcerting to look up from our amorous activities to find several small pairs of eyes watching our every move intently. However, he found it even more distressing when they decided to demonstrate their burgeoning skills as hunters – using the enticingly dangly bits of his anatomy as prey. The fact that I dissolved into laughter at his repeated attempts to dodge the frequent assaults on his testicles didn't help. It was a revelation to learn that lovers can laugh together even when at their most vulnerable, if their relationship is more than merely physical. I had half expected my mirth to result in not being spoken to for several days. I should have known better.

On a positive note, I did learn that in the right circumstances and with the right person, communal bathing can actually be quite pleasant. Each time we were together, I drank in every nuance of Nef's body – the warmth of his skin, the way his hair curled when damp with sweat from his exertions, the noises that he made when in the throes of passion. It was going to break my heart when I had to leave - and I could honestly say that I thought it would break Nef's as well - an unintended consequence. I never intended to hurt him. I had allowed myself to get so wrapped up in my own feelings and desires that I failed to fully consider what would happen in the long run and how it might affect him. And now it was too late to change it. I could only hope that once his initial anger faded, that he would be able to look back on our time together with at least a touch of fondness.

However, the delays eventually ended and the royal entourage arrived with much pomp and circumstance bringing an end to our idyllic journey of discovery. In the days leading up to the formal acknowledgment of the heir, the king would be hosting several large parties, culminating with a grand ball the night of the Naming. Nobles began pouring into the castle from far and wide to be present for the festivities; every room in the castle was full. The entire palace staff was stretched thin keeping everything running smoothly and maintained up to the standards expected. During those days, Nef and I barely had a chance to speak, much less anything more.

12

It was here - the night that I had dreaded for so long. My preparations had long been complete; now, all I had to do was wait a little longer until I could implement them. Unfortunately, waiting was never one of my strong points. The ball was underway and I was temporarily off-duty; I roamed the hallways restlessly. As I paced, I became aware of an odd sound that was growing steadily closer. Before I could determine its source, a river of grey swept around the nearest corner and flowed toward me, its relentless progress overcoming all but the sturdiest of objects in its path. I didn't stand a chance. Just as the leading edge reached me, a hand darted out of the mass, grabbed my wrist and pulled me into the midst of the stream of servants.

"Can you believe it?" Maerie's face was alight with excitement and her words tumbled over themselves in her enthusiasm. "A ball! And the prince is here – a real prince! And we might actually get to see him!"

I couldn't help but smile at her ebullience even if I didn't feel it myself.

I allowed myself to be swept along by the crowd of off-duty servants pouring into the service passage that led to the ballroom. Everyone wanted a chance to peek at the happenings on the other side of the doorway; the Naming of an heir to the throne was an event that few, if any, of us would have the opportunity to see again. With so many people crowded into such a small space, it would have been easy for violence to erupt as everyone vied for their opportunity to look. Fortunately, the manners that Mama L expected from those in her employ held true and resulted in a minimum of pushing and shoving, although numerous toes were unavoidably stepped on during the jostling.

I was near the front of the crowd and didn't have to wait long for my turn. I had no preconceived notions of what to expect, but what I saw was amazing. Magnificent tapestries covered the walls of the great room; the scenes depicted ranged from warriors engaged in battle to nubile females involved in pursuits of a more erotic nature. A raised dais sat at the far end of the room, an ornate gilded throne at its center; the king, of course, would sit there. A smaller, less elaborate chair sat at its right hand for his soon-to-be-named successor. At the opposite end of the room a troupe of musicians performed on a smaller platform. A small cadre of servants, hand-picked by Mama L, worked their way through the crowded room bearing trays laden with food and drink. Tables were located strategically around the edge of the room, each topped with a glorious floral centerpiece. The center of the room was reserved for dancing.

The men and women crowding the room were dressed in their finest, and occasionally, most outrageous clothing; tastes ranged from simple and elegant to over-worked and ridiculous. Mama L was allowed to attend the ball in her capacity as head of the household staff; her white hair stood out among the crowd like a beacon in the night. She was striking in a dress of crimson silk, a matching feather in her hair; accents of gold gleamed against her dress and ears.

Crimson and gold - something about those colors teased at my memory. Before I could remember what it was, movement caught my eye.

Jehrold approached Mama L with a purposeful step, his dark eyes intense. Simply put, he was stunning. Gone was the easy-going stubble-faced man that I knew. This man was clean-shaven with a strong jaw that was set in determination. As was the style of most men at the palace, his dark hair was pulled back in a tail that was almost lost against his equally dark cape. Yes, he wore a cape – and he knew how to use it. He stopped in front of Mama L and bowed with a flourish of fabric. Somehow, a cloak could make the simplest of movements grand. I hoped that she was suitably impressed; I certainly was.

Without waiting for her response, Jehrold slid his arm around Mama L's waist and guided her onto the dance floor. His movements were sure – and possessive - as he took her in his arms and joined the dance in progress. Mama L seemed surprised at his boldness but followed his lead skillfully. They side-stepped neatly as another less dexterous couple almost crashed into them.

The flow of the dance brought the other couple closer – it was Lord Narvel and Lady Adele. Lord Narvel appeared to be more than a little inebriated. His wife appeared to be mortified – and with good reason. Lady Adele was several inches taller than her husband; her low-cut, corseted gown displayed her modest bosom to great effect. Lord Narvel couldn't keep his eyes, or his hands off of it. It was quite obvious that he intended to take her as soon as he could get her alone. At least, I hoped he would wait that long and not embarrass her any further in public.

Neither Lady Adele nor I had had any choice in the lives that were thrust upon us. As distraught as I was by the actions that lay ahead of me that night, at that moment I wouldn't have changed places with her for the world. I wasn't overly religious, but I offered a brief prayer of thanks to anyone that might be listening that I had not been born a female noble.

"Get movin', you. Let someone else have a turn."

I could take a not-so-subtle hint. Leaving the opulent sights behind, I pushed my way through the crowd until I reached the main hallway where I reveled in the cooler air. It was a welcome relief from the stifling atmosphere that I had left behind. I picked a direction at random and began to walk.

"Lillie, wait."

It was Nef. I turned to greet him, but could only stare. He was dressed in the royal livery for the occasion as were all of the stable hands, but I was sure that none of the others looked as grand. The dark blue of the coat brought out the color of his eyes and the gold trim complimented his skin tone. His black hair had been brushed until it shone and then pulled into a tail that fell below his shoulders. When he reached me, he simply held out his hand. I took it without hesitation. Neither of us spoke.

Grasping my hand firmly, he led me down the hall to a locked door to which he once again mysteriously possessed the key. Yet again, I wondered how a stable boy came by the keys to locked doors throughout the palace, but did not ask. After securing the entrance behind us, he led me up a narrow flight of stairs to a large room with a balcony overlooking the ballroom. The musicians were directly below us; their music floated into the room and fluttered around us on invisible wings.

He extended one leg in a courtly bow and then opened his arms in invitation. "May I have this dance?"

I curtseyed in acceptance, a smile spreading across my face.

He placed his hands firmly on my waist and led me into the dance. He was an excellent dancer and seemed slightly surprised to find that I was too. Dancing was part of the training we were expected to master in order to pass ourselves off as members of the nobility. When the music changed and slowed our steps did as well. As we moved, I laid my head on his chest and inhaled the combined scents of horses and hay tinged with masculine sweat; the scent that was uniquely Nef.

We wrapped ourselves in a cocoon of music. Our world began and ended in each other's arms. Even when the performers took a brief break we continued to move to a melody that only we could hear. At last, we stopped and Nef lowered his head, pressing his lips to mine. It was a kiss not only of passion, but of promise – a promise of a future, of a life together. Of course, those promises could never be, yet I returned the kiss, wanting them with all my heart.

He ended the kiss and pulled away, his blue eyes searching my face seriously. He tucked a loose strand of hair behind my ear and cupped my cheek in his work-roughened hand. "I have a surprise for you. Close your eyes."

"Another surprise?" I arched a brow at him playfully. "Mmmm. I hope it's as nice as the last one."

"You'll never know if you don't close your eyes."

"All right, all right." I closed my eyes like the good girl that I was not.

There was a brief rustle of fabric and the warmth of Nef's skin against mine as his hands grasped my left forearm. The heat of his touch faded quickly as he moved his hands away.

"You can look now."

I opened my eyes, my gaze falling to the slight weight on my wrist.

"Oh, Nef!" My free hand flew to my mouth and tears filled my eyes. Thin strands of gold, silver, and copper gleamed in the light from the room below. It was a bonding bracelet. But not just any bonding bracelet; it was the one that I had seen in the jeweler's window in MidTown. The one that I thought was perfect. And now it was on my wrist. I couldn't speak.

"Change is coming. After tonight, things may never be the same. Can you feel it?"

I nodded mutely. If only he knew just how acutely I *did* feel it; I had been carrying the weight of this change on my shoulders for months.

"We will be together, no matter what - no matter how much things change. I promise. This bracelet is a symbol of my promise. Will you wear it?"

I nodded, still searching for my voice.

Nef rummaged in his pocket once again and held out the matching bracelet. "Will you do me the honor…?" He held out his bare wrist to me.

I took the bracelet, fumbling with the clasp to cover my uncertainty. Oh, how I wanted to be with him! Yet how could I? Damn my parents, damn Vido, damn… *everything!* Tears blurred my vision; I swiped my arm across my eyes, drying them on my sleeve before returning to the oh-so-important task at hand. My decision made, it was the work of but a moment to secure the bracelet to his arm. I raised his wrist to my lips and pressed a kiss against the clasp, sealing it not just with metal, but with affection. We would be a bonded couple, if only for one night.

I raised my eyes to meet Nef's gaze; his blue eyes were solemn. To my surprise, tears glistened on his dark lashes.

"I love you, Lillie."

How I had longed to hear those words! "I love you, too." I should not have said it, but it was true. And I wanted him to know – he deserved at least that much honesty from me.

His face lit up, the dimples that I adored blazing to life. After a flurry of murmured endearments punctuated with kisses, he led me back to the main corridor and squeezed my hand gently in farewell.

"It's a busy night," he whispered, giving me a quick hug. "I'll see you as soon as I can."

As he walked away, I sighed. How had I gotten myself into this situation? I had always wanted to know love, and to be loved, but the lifestyle into which I had been raised did not allow for such. Now that I had been blessed with my heart's deepest desire, I had to turn my back on it and walk away. I did not think that I could, even though I had no other choice.

I roamed the halls aimlessly, avoiding others as much as possible. I did not wish to be around people, but I had to stay close enough to hear what was going on in the ballroom. Although I couldn't distinguish voices, I could hear enough to know when the heir had been introduced and acknowledged; the crowd burst into applause. That was my signal; it was time for me to go back to work.

I went to the kitchen and found Cook waiting, her foot tapping rapidly and her arms crossed over her abundant belly.

"Where is that girl?" She glanced at the staircase behind me as if expecting someone.

"Which girl?" I was all innocence even though I knew exactly who she was waiting for – and that she had suddenly taken ill. It was funny how that sort of thing happened to those who got in my way.

"Lev. She is supposed to get the heir's room ready for his arrival."

"I saw her upstairs earlier. She wasn't feeling well – she was pale and sweating something awful. She said something about her monthly flow. Do you want me to go check on her?"

"No time!" She pressed a platter into my hands. "You must hurry if you are to get the heir's room ready in time." She gave me a gentle push toward the servant's staircase. "Be careful not to spill! I prepared that food personally and I'm quite proud of it."

I could only nod as I moved carefully up the stairs, my attention focused on the tray.

"Don't forget to have a little fun tonight," Cook called, just before I disappeared from her sight.

I paused and looked over my shoulder.

"That handsome fella of yours has been hard pressed all day, feeding, watering, and caring for the horses that have borne the crowds to the castle. He might need a good 'rub down' hisself after all his hard work."

Her gap-toothed grin helped to lighten my mood, if only temporarily.

I made it safely to the new prince's room, the contents of the tray still intact. Apparently the king was taking no chances with his protégé; a guard slouched outside the door. He straightened at my approach, holding up a cautionary hand.

"Here now, miss. What do you have there?"

"A gift from Cook for His Highness." I offered him the tray. "Would you like something? I'm sure she wouldn't mind."

He surveyed the selections, chose a sweetmeat and bit into it. "Delicious." He sighed. "Let's keep this just between us. I doubt that Cook would appreciate any of her delicacies going to the likes of me." He gave me a wink and a swat on the rear before opening the door.

Once inside, I placed the tray on a small table before lighting the fire and turning down the bed clothes. Finally, I pulled a small vial from my pocket and surveyed its contents; the liquid glistened in the firelight. It was strange how something so seemingly insignificant held such power. I removed the cork and slowly poured the contents into the decanter; the liquid was colorless and its slight taste would be hidden by the spices in the wine. I placed the empty bottle in my pocket where it clinked softly against the container of antidote that I had placed there out of habit. The poor man would never know what happened; he would drink his wine and drift into a pleasant sleep – one from which he would not awaken. I saw no need to make him suffer unnecessarily; none of this was of his choosing – or mine.

As I left the room the guard stopped me again, his eyes roaming over my body speculatively.

"My shift ends soon." He reached out and stroked my cheek. "How's about you and I get together and have a little celebration of our own?"

"Sorry, sir, but my evening is already spoken for." I giggled and batted my eyes at him. "But don't you worry none - I'm sure a handsome fellow like you won't be alone for long."

He laughed. While his teeth were crooked, they were all accounted for. He really wasn't a bad looking man. I doubted that he was truly in danger of spending the evening alone.

I worked my way back to my quarters by a circuitous route in an effort to avoid running into anyone else. I just wanted to be alone with my thoughts - which primarily consisted of *I will be glad when this night is over.*

Fortunately, I had the room to myself – Maerie had not yet returned. I ripped off my cap and threw myself onto my bed, fighting nausea. The rolling of my stomach came with a sense of *déjà vu*. I had battled sickness the night of my first kill as well – and lost. I had vomited on Lord Landry's corpse, soiling my clothes in the process. When I returned to the guild house, I burned my dress then went to the bath house and scrubbed my skin until it bled. When Vido learned about the garments, I was beaten. He wasn't worried about me, but clothing designed to catch the eye of a perverse nobleman was not cheap and was not to be treated as disposable.

My nerves had added something new to their repertoire this time – the constant urge to piss. Some days seemed like nothing more than a journey from one chamber pot to another. I forced away the memories as I emptied my bladder – again – and imagined what would happen when the prince finally retired to his room. First, his manservant would help him undress and prepare for bed, fussing over every detail. Then, once he was left to his own devices, he would sit in the chair by the fire to think over all of the recent changes to his life; as he thought, he would sip the wine that I had left for him, not realizing that it would cause the biggest change yet - his death.

This was why I was here - the *only* reason that I was here. It was my job to kill this man. As I straightened my clothes, my resolve hardened; I had made my decision. I knew what I must do. I had to dispose of the wine before the heir got to his room. Yes, I was a killer. But I could not - *would not* - murder an innocent man.

I retraced my steps through the maze of corridors as quickly as I dared. As I stepped into the passage that led to the heir's room, I froze. In my haste, I had forgotten about the guard; fortunately, he was looking the other direction, so I was able to dart back around the corner without being seen. I shook my head, fluffing my curls to their full advantage, loosened the top buttons on my dress, and pinched my cheeks to bring some color to them. I then stepped back into the hallway and approached the guard, swaying my hips as I walked. When I glanced up through my lashes, I realized that it was not the same man that I met earlier.

The new sentry turned at my approach and leered at me.

"Well, well. What have we here? A little something for His Highness, I presume?" He chortled at his unintentional pun when he noticed my size.

However, his laughter died away quickly and with a speed that I would not have believed him capable of, he shoved me against the wall and wedged one knee between my legs. He lowered his scarred face to mine, scraping his whiskers against my cheek.

"I'm thinking that I should try you on for size – I can teach you a few things to use on the princeling." He dropped his mouth to my neck and began kissing me roughly.

My first impulse was to go for my dagger in its ever-present sheath on my thigh. However, if he realized that I was armed, he would raise an alarm and I would never get past him. I decided to let him think that I was receptive to his advances and ran my hands slowly down his chest to his waist before proceeding lower to grapple with the front of his breeches.

He was indeed ready for action, but my target was softer flesh. He groaned in ecstasy as I grasped his testicles; the groan turned into a yowl of pain as I twisted them.

"Stand back and let me be on my way." I gave an extra turn of my wrist for emphasis. "If you touch me again, I will rip your bollocks off. Do you understand?"

He nodded, cursing fluently. Stepping back, he dropped his hands protectively over his crotch as he nodded at the door. "I reckon you won't try that with *him.*" Sneering, he added, "Try to be loud, little one. If I can't take part, I'd at least like to listen."

I slipped through the doorway. Only flickering firelight lit the room. When my eyes adjusted, I froze. I was too late. The new prince, dressed only in his nightshirt, stood in front of the fireplace, his back to me. My heart went out to him; an aura of despair surrounded him. He leaned against the mantelpiece, his head resting on his arm in an attitude of hopelessness. With one smooth movement, he drained the last of the wine from the goblet in his free hand. I must have made a sound for he turned with a start.

In that moment, I realized that I knew him.

"Nef!" his name tore from my throat. "What are *you* doing here?"

13

"Lillie?" Nef's face paled as he stepped toward me, his confusion evident. "Why are you here? This..." He gulped. "This isn't how you were supposed to find out." He dropped his gaze, no longer able to look me in the eye.

"You can fill me in on the details later." My voice was steady, not betraying the turmoil that I felt. There was no time for subtlety; I nodded toward the glass in his hand. "The wine is poisoned – I was coming to dispose of it."

"Poisoned?" The goblet slipped from his suddenly nerveless fingers and shattered, the shards of glass sparkling in the light of the fire. "How... do you know?"

"It's a long story - which will have to wait." Pulling the vial of antidote out of my pocket, I thanked the

Makers for the long-standing practice that had caused me to put it there and held it out to Nef. "Right now you need to drink this."

He threw his hands up as if to ward off an attack, uncertainty clouding his face.

"Do you trust me?" I struggled not to scream in my fear and frustration.

"Yes," he whispered.

"Then *drink this*. It will save your life."

His hand shook as he reached for the vial and his eyes locked on mine. His gaze never wavered as he thumbed open the container, downed the contents, and then threw it to the ground where it splintered, the pieces blending with those of the wineglass.

Once I was sure that he had swallowed, I ran to the corner and grabbed the chamber pot. Returning, I thrust it into his hands.

"What is this for?"

"You'll find out soon enough."

Guiding him to the nearest chair, I forced him to sit and knelt beside him. Soon, sweat beaded on his brow and upper lip. Good. The antidote was working. The next phase would be abdominal cramps. Almost as if he heard my thoughts, Nef doubled over, groaning. The last, and most important step, was the vomiting. Understanding flooded his face as he clutched the chamber pot tighter and regurgitated the contents of his stomach into it. He heaved until there was nothing left, then heaved some more. Each wave tore at his throat and my heart.

I moved to the dresser and the pitcher that resided on top of it, sloshing water into the basin and wetting a cloth. I had to fight the urge to stop and clean up the water that had spilled. It was amazing how quickly my new duties had become ingrained.

Nef slouched miserably in his chair. I applied the cloth to his face and throat, wiping away the vileness that had spattered there. I waited until the spasms had subsided before speaking.

"We have to get out of here." Yes, I know. I was a master of the obvious.

"I can't." He pushed at me weakly.

"You must." Standing, I pulled at his arm – to no avail. "If we remain here, we will both be killed."

There was no time to waste. Releasing his arm, I searched the room, opening closets and drawers until I located his clothes. Flinging them over my shoulder, I returned to Nef, grabbed his arms and attempted to work them out of his nightshirt.

"Stop that!" he grumbled irritably. "I can dress myself."

"Then stop whining and prove it." I threw his clothes at him unceremoniously before starting to pace. "As soon as whoever hired the Va'Shile to kill you discovers that you are still alive, another attempt will be made on your life. And then another, and another. The attempts will continue until you are dead. I won't

be here to protect you because *I* will be dead. The Va'Shile do not look kindly on those that interfere with their assassination attempts." *Especially when the one interfering is the assassin.* Time enough to explain that fascinating little tidbit later – if we lived that long.

Unable to bear his slowness any longer, I snatched the remaining clothes away from him and began to dress him - as I would a rather large, extremely reluctant child.

"We've got to get out here - and soon. The antidote has purged your system of most of the poison, but there is still some left in your bloodstream. You are going to feel very bad, very soon. We have to get you somewhere safe, and we have to do it *now*." I shoved his shoes onto his feet, grabbed the coat of ornate livery that he had worn earlier and then flung it to the floor. "This won't do at all. Everyone knows that is what you were wearing. We need to find something else." Grabbing his hand, I tugged him toward the door. "Come on, we'll find something on our way out."

"Not that way." He shook his head, resting one hand on the back of a chair for support. He was pale and sweating, but mobile. For the time being, at least. "There are guards in the hall."

"I can handle the guard." My dagger appeared in my hand with the ease of long practice.

"No. There's a better way. Come with me." Turning, he led me to the alcove in the corner of the room where he ran his fingers lightly over the wall until he found what he was looking for. A press of his fingers on one of the stones caused a hidden panel to swing open. Giving a satisfied grunt, he twisted the handle that had been revealed.

The entire back wall of the alcove swung into the shadows with a small squeal. The darkness before us was complete.

"Stay here." It was only a few short steps to the fireplace where I grabbed two candles from the mantle – one for each of us.

Once we were safely in the passageway, Nef swung the wall shut behind us. The latch caught with a click.

"I did tell you that I spent a lot of time here as a child and that the palace is riddled with hidden passages." He leaned against the wall, his face once again sheened with sweat, but he managed to give me a somewhat sickly grin. "I haven't been here in years, but I think I can still get us out of the castle."

"I believe in you." I stood on tiptoe and kissed him on the cheek, his skin cool against my lips.

He was starting to feel the effects of the remaining poison; it wouldn't be long before he felt like hell.

"Let's get moving." I slipped my hand into his and let him lead the way.

He moved slowly but surely, pausing occasionally to get his bearings – or to wait out a wave of cramps. My sense of direction was never great and with the

constant twists and turns, I was soon hopelessly lost. I could only hope that Nef's memory served him well.

Even as we fled for our lives, I reveled in the feel of my hand in his. His touch, although a bit clammy, was a comfort. I had come so close to losing him that I didn't want to ever let go. I held my emotions in check by sheer force of will. I couldn't afford to fall apart or start bawling like a baby – no matter how badly I wanted to.

Just as I was beginning to wonder how much farther we had to go, Nef stopped and pointed at a section of the wall.

"There." The sound came through gritted teeth. Shoving his candle into my hand, he leaned against the stone with a groan and wrapped his arms around his abdomen in a desperate attempt to contain the pain that was growing there. "The latch should be somewhere over there."

Several frustrating minutes went by before I located the handle and shoved open the panel. We stepped into a small room, crowded with heavily laden shelves – the pantry. Relief surged through me - the kitchens should be empty by now. I blew out the candles and hid them amongst the crockery. I knew the layout of the room well and the banked fires would provide enough light for us to make good our escape. I closed the panel behind us before slightly cracking open the door in order to give our eyes a chance to adjust – and to give Nef a moment to rest. He was fading rapidly and I was getting desperate. If he collapsed I would not be able to carry him.

"We're almost free. I need for you to hold on just a little longer. Can you do that?" I wished that I could see his face.

He gave me a noncommittal grunt that I chose to take as an affirmative.

"Come on."

Once again we joined hands, but this time I was in front.

We stepped out of the pantry, shutting the door quietly behind us. The exit to the courtyard was on the far side of the room. I could tell from Nef's labored breathing that even that short journey was going to be a trial. I slipped under his arm, draping it across my shoulder to give him some measure of support; he leaned on me gratefully. The difference in our heights – and the darkness of the room – meant that we moved slowly and somewhat awkwardly. We had only managed a few steps when the shadows ahead of us shifted and separated, a dark figure moving between us and our goal. Metal sang softly as a sword was unsheathed.

Damn. I guided Nef to a nearby table and pushed him down onto the bench. "Wait here," I cautioned. Without waiting for a response, I advanced on the mysterious figure – dagger in hand. "Show yourself!" I hissed.

Light flared as a lantern was uncovered. Mama L, still dressed in her beautiful crimson gown, stood before me, her violet eyes blazing and a short sword held in her right hand; both her grip and her stance indicated that she knew how to use it.

Crimson and gold.

The sword.

The pieces finally fell into place.

"Va'Kyrian? But... they aren't... I mean, I thought they were a myth."

"I assure you that we are very real. When the Nidolans lost the throne, we followed them into obscurity. Their family is constantly under our watchful eyes – as is the throne." A grim smile crossed her face. "The palace head of household is always a member of the Va'Kyrian. Not all of the kings that have died in... untimely fashions have been the results of political machinations. Some have died at our hands. We will not let anyone harm this country or its rightful rulers." The tip of her sword flashed dangerously close to my face. "And that includes you. I know what you are."

What I was, not *who*.

"Vido convinced me to hire you. He said that you had washed out as an assassin, but that for personal reasons, he did not wish to see you die." Her voice dripped with venom. "I know Vido; he cares for no one. No life makes a difference to him. If he wanted you here, it had to be for a reason. Everyone knew that the king was searching for a new heir. The most likely reason for your presence would be that you were sent to kill either the king or the heir. I have been waiting for you to make your attempt and tonight seemed to be the most logical choice for the hit. It seems that I was correct."

"*No.* Nef lives." I gestured at the shadows behind me. "See for yourself."

Keeping one eye on me, she raised the lantern – its glow revealed the new prince, slumped over the table where I had left him. She inhaled sharply in recognition.

"You know what Vido *wants* me to be, what I refuse to become." I motioned to Nef, whose condition was continuing to deteriorate. "Yes, I was sent here to kill the king's heir. Yes, I poisoned the wine. But, I couldn't go through with it; I could not kill an innocent man. I went to the prince's room to get rid of the wine, but it was too late." I let my despair show on my face. "I *didn't know* that Nef is the heir. I would never do anything to hurt him. I love him."

I slipped my knife back into its sheath and stepped closer to Mama L, raising my hands to show that they were empty. She grabbed my arm, glaring at the bonding bracelet that glittered in the lantern light. Her gaze shifted to my face and I nodded in response to her unspoken question.

"I've given him the antidote to the poison. He will live, but he will be very sick for a while." I jabbed a finger in his direction. "Look at him! *Please*, you have to help me get him out of here. He - *we* – can't stay. He is still in danger - others will come to do what I did not. I will do everything in my power to protect him, but I can't do that here."

Another figure stepped out of the gloom to join us.

Maker's teeth! I glared into the darkness wondering how many more people were hiding there.

"Let them go, Cissy." Jehrold laid his hand on Mama L's arm; his calm, steady gaze never left hers.

Time slowed to a crawl as they stared at each other. Finally, Mama L nodded and sheathed her sword.

"Thank you." I gripped Jehrold's arm briefly in gratitude before running to Nef.

"Nef!" I shook his shoulder, gently at first, then harder. "Nef, you must get up. We have to get out of here."

He struggled to his feet, sweat dripping down his face. He took one step and his knees buckled. There was no way that I could prevent his collapse; all I could do was try to keep his head from hitting anything on his way down. Tears of frustration and fear threatened to blind me. We had come so close.

"C'mon, lad. Up you go." Jehrold strode to our side, pulled Nef to his feet then bent and draped him across his shoulder.

I could have hugged him.

"Come with me." Standing, Jehrold tossed his head in the direction of the door to the courtyard and headed off at a brisk pace.

As I moved to follow, Mama L's hand snaked out and grabbed my arm; her grip was like steel. When I looked at her, indecision warred in her eyes.

"Let go!" I struggled vainly to break free.

"There is more."

"What are you talking about?" I was getting frantic.

Jehrold was already out the door and headed across the courtyard. Maybe this had just been an elaborate ploy to separate us. Maybe Jehrold was planning to kill Nef himself. Even in my panic that thought didn't ring true.

"There is more... about you."

I ripped desperately at her fingers. I had to get to Nef. Mama L pulled me closer, leaning forward.

"Child," she whispered in my ear, "the things that you have been told about your past – your parents - are lies. There is more to you than you know. Seek the truth. Become what you were *truly* born to be." Releasing me and stepping away, she added, "Take care of Nef." She then snapped closed the cover of the lantern and moved away into the darkness.

I hesitated for only a moment before running after Jehrold. I caught up with him halfway across the courtyard.

"Where are you taking him?" My whisper was shriller than I would have liked.

Jehrold chuckled. "To the stables, of course, lass." The corners of his eyes crinkled in amusement when he looked at me. "If you are going to escape, you're probably going to need a horse." His teeth flashed briefly. "Or were you planning on walking and dragging him behind you?"

I bit back the sharp retort that rose to my tongue, but he must have seen something in my face.

"It's all right, child. I know that you are worried for him – and yourself. You don't have to put up a front with me. I'm on your side."

He shoved open the door to the stables and stopped, staring that the stalls that lined the aisle. Equine faces, many of them unfamiliar, stared at us over the half-doors.

"Well, hells. I forgot that half of the horses in Ramalda are here tonight." He grunted as he shifted Nef's weight to a more comfortable position. "We need one that won't be missed for a while."

"Elah." Nef's voice grated painfully from his raw throat.

"At the end, on the left." I both pointed and grabbed Jehrold's arm to lead him.

As we staggered to a stop in front of her stall, Elah stepped to the door and whickered quietly. Jehrold slid Nef to the ground, leaning him against the stall door.

"Good girl, Elah." Nef managed to reach up and stroke her muzzle in greeting. "Elah has been my companion since birth. She would have been put down long ago, but I used my position to secure her safety. She will take us where we need to go. If anyone even notices that she is gone, they will not waste any time looking for her."

Closing my eyes, I could feel the love and trust that the old mare had for Nef. She thought of him as a friend, almost as a child. She would give her life for him if necessary. Stepping closer, I held out my hand; Elah's soft lips searched my palm for snacks.

"I'm sorry, girl. I don't have anything for you now. Once we're safe, I will make sure that you have treats on a regular basis." I opened my mind to her so she could feel my love and fear for her master in addition to my need to get us to safety. "Will you help us?"

She blew softly against my cheek and tossed her head in agreement.

"Thank you." I patted her flank affectionately as I moved into the stall to saddle her.

"Stay with him." Jehrold stepped into the stall, motioning for me to join Nef at the door. He then proceeded to saddle the mare with practiced ease. He frequently cast a thoughtful gaze in my direction but never spoke, simply shook his head before returning to his endeavors. When he led Elah from the stall, he apparently couldn't take it any longer.

"Did you just... talk to the horse? With your mind?" He pressed his fingers against his own head as if to ensure that I understood his meaning. "And she talked back?" His eyes grew wider with each question.

"'Talk' isn't necessarily the right word. But, yes, we communicated."

"How..."

"Don't ask." Nef gave what seemed to be a laugh. "She doesn't know how it works; only that it does. I've seen it more than once."

"Amazing." Jehrold shook his head once again, then led Nef to the horse and helped him into the saddle. Grabbing two blankets from the nearby pile, he draped them over us like cloaks and placed Elah's reins in my hand. "I will stay here until the two of you are safely gone." He arched a brow at me. "You're on your own with the gate guard. Do you think you can come up with a convincing story?"

"Of course." Fidgeting with the reins, I finally asked the one question that was nagging at me. "Why did you help us?"

"There are obviously things that I don't know about you lass." He smiled as he stroked my cheek with one work-roughened thumb. "I do know you have a good heart. No matter what your original motives were, you made the right decision in the end." He gave me a wink and a gentle shove toward the door. "A friend helped me to see that we all deserve a second chance."

"Thank you!" Dropping the reins, I threw my arms around him in a hug. Before he could respond, I spun on my heel, grabbed the bridle and led Elah and her precious cargo into the night.

I jumped when the sentry stepped in front of us.

"Halt!" His voice changed to one of concern when he saw the figure slumped in the saddle. "Is everything all right?"

"Please, sir, my master over indulged tonight." I disguised my voice as I pulled the hood of my "cloak" forward to hide my face. "He is feeling poorly; I need to get him home. The mistress is going to have a fit when she sees the state that he is in."

"Proceed then, lass." He chuckled and stepped aside. "If a good tongue lashing is all he gets, he'll be lucky."

"Thank you, sir." *You don't know the half of it.* I dropped a curtsey and clucked to Elah while tugging gently on the reins. She followed me obediently through the gate and onto the drawbridge across the Ocoee. Now that we were free of the palace, there was still one major obstacle to overcome.

I had no idea where we were going.

I had access to a couple of tiny hideouts, but they would no longer be safe. No matter - they had never been intended for long-term use anyway. We needed a place to stay for several days as Nef recuperated and I figured out what in all the hells to do next. In a flash of inspiration, I smiled. A brothel in The Narrows. Perfect.

14

We reached the brothel, a rather non-descript little place in a back alley of The Narrows, in safety. I had taken as indirect a route as I dared and was as certain as I could be that we had not been followed. This bordello was not generally of the sort to attract the attention of the nobles, nor were the workers or their clients the type to attend the night's festivities at the palace, so Nef should not be recognized.

"Thank you," I whispered to Elah, rubbing her muzzle briefly in gratitude.

"Kin I help yer?" The night watchman sat on a stool at the front door, cleaning under his nails with the tip of a rather wicked looking dagger; the remains of his evening meal clung to his shirt front and breeches. He studied us with an experienced eye. "Brava's girls don't service your type," he indicated me with a jerk of his chin. Turning his attention to Nef he added, "And he don't look like he could get it up even if'n he wanted ter."

"We aren't clients," I fumed. This close to safety, my redheaded obstinacy was operating at full capacity and I was not about to get pushed around by a flunky. "Brava is my friend. I need to see her immediately."

"Now, don't yer go gittin' uppity with me!" He stabbed his knife into the wooden bench as he levered himself to his feet. Obviously, he didn't consider either of us a threat.

I narrowed the distance between us and used his precarious position – no longer sitting and not yet fully standing – to overbalance him and shove him against the wall. The knee thrust firmly into his meaty nether regions and the dagger pressed against his throat finally convinced him that I was serious.

"Hey, now..." he squeaked, sweat beading his brow. "Don't be gettin' hasty. I was just havin' a little sport." He smiled nervously, displaying badly rotted teeth. Turning his head, he bellowed, "Boy! Get yerself over here – and no lollygaggin'."

"What 'er ya carryin' on about at this hour?" A young boy with sleep tousled hair rounded the corner and skidded to a stop, his eyes widening at the scene.

"Would you like to earn some extra coin?" I gave the boy my best smile, while applying extra pressure with my knee – just in case my new acquaintance was getting any ideas.

The boy nodded while the bouncer hissed in pain.

"Very well. Please step inside and tell the girls that Lillie is here with a friend and needs help. Then, I want you to take my horse to the stables, remove her saddle and make sure that she has food and water." Narrowing my eyes, I warned him, "Elah is a magic horse – she can talk. I will check on her in the morning; if she tells me that she was mistreated in any way, you get nothing. Understand?"

"Yes, miss." The boy's voice was a whisper and he gulped loudly as he moved past me to put action to my orders.

"I'm going to let you go now," I told the bouncer, "and I don't want any trouble. I promise that I know how to use this." My dagger glinted in the lantern light as I waved it in front of his face. Stepping back, I made good on my word.

"Yer coulda killed me!" He glared at me through narrowed eyes as he rubbed his throat.

"Yes, I could have," I assured him. "But I didn't."

The door was thrown open and a swarm of Brava's girls – dressed in an interesting variety of titillating costumes – descended upon me and Nef. Their cries of concerned tumbled over one another as they took in the situation.

"Lillie!"

"Who is this?"

"Help him down."

"Oooh, he's handsome!"

"I get him first!"

Time for me to step in.

"Sorry, girls – he's mine. Help me get him to Brava's quarters." As the chattering flood carried us inside I called to the boy, "Thank you. Don't forget what I said about the horse!"

The girls and I half-carried, half-dragged Nef to Brava's parlor.

"Brava is with a client," one of the senior girls warned; her status automatically made her the spokesperson for the group. "Normally, we wouldn't dare bring anyone here when she is occupied, but since it's you…"

"I understand; I'll tell her that I gave you no choice." We laid Nef on the couch – after moving the fluffy white cat snoozing contentedly on the cushions - and I collapsed onto the floor next to him, murmuring my thanks to everyone as they left.

The building, while well cared for, was old and the walls were thin. As quiet descended, I became aware of the sounds issuing from Brava's boudoir as she completed her current business transaction. It sounded as if things were going well. Perhaps I should have been embarrassed by my inadvertent voyeurism, but raised as I was, I was not. Nef was too unconscious to care. Finally, the door opened and the client left, looking quite satisfied and somewhat smug. I suspected that his skills in the bedroom were not nearly as good as he thought they were - Brava did not become the madam by being average at what she did.

Shortly after her gentleman caller left, Brava herself joined us. She was a handsome woman of Southron heritage; her skin was the color of coffee with cream while her hair was black with a streak of grey framing her face. The effect was striking. She was aging, her face beginning to show the slightest of wrinkles at the corners of her eyes and mouth. Her body was visible through her sheer dressing gown; her breasts were still full although perhaps not as perky as they must have been in her youth, her belly not quite as flat. Unlike many of the girls in her employ, Brava did not remove her body hair and many, mostly men, considered the nest of dark curls between her legs to be her crowning glory. I had heard men speak of an hour with Brava in hushed, almost reverent terms. I was in the presence of whorehouse royalty; I was honored to call her my friend.

"It has been a while since I have seen you, little one." Brava's voice was low and husky. "And this time you are not alone." She stepped closer, studying Nef. "He is a handsome one. What is the problem?"

"He is my friend. He has been poisoned - we need a place to stay while he heals."

"Who poisoned him?"

"I did." I help up one hand to forestall any additional questions. "It's a long story."

"I offer you the hospitality of my home." Brava nodded, taking everything in stride - as usual. "The price will be the story of how you came to poison one that you call friend. However, that can wait until he is better. For now, let's get you settled." Stepping forward, she helped me get Nef to his feet.

"Just a little more," I assured him when he stirred and moaned.

We struggled through the halls until we reached a door that opened into a small closet, the back of which opened to reveal a staircase. I groaned. The thought of trying to get Nef up the steps was almost enough to make me cry. However, he seemed to sense that safety was near and rallied briefly, enough so that he was able to do most of the work of climbing the stairs.

The small room at the top of the stairs was just as I remembered it. It contained a bed, just large enough for two people, one chair, a night stand and a small dresser. The bed was made with clean linens and the pitcher on the dresser contained fresh water. Brava kept this room ready for me at all times; there was no way I could even begin to repay her efforts.

Once Nef was safely on the bed, I turned to thank Brava. She pulled me into her arms, brushing my sweat soaked hair away from my face. Was this what it would be like to have a mother?

"Hush, little one. Help your friend. Sleep." She patted my cheek gently. "I will check on you in the morning." She left, closing the door quietly behind her.

Nef had faded back into unconsciousness. While I would have loved nothing more than to do the same, I needed to attend to him first. I stripped him and washed his face with cool, clean water before pulling the covers over him. Then, *finally*, it was my turn. I peeled off my filthy clothes and washed myself with the remaining water. Joining Nef under the covers, I was asleep as soon as my head hit the pillow.

15

An insistent sound gradually worked its way into my subconscious. Someone was retching. *Maerie?* No, that wasn't right. My dry, gritty eyes stubbornly refused to open. As I battled with them, memories of the previous night returned in a rush. *Nef!*

I struggled to free myself from slumber, but it pulled at me, beckoning, promising sweet oblivion if only I would surrender to its siren call. The offer was tempting, but I had to help Nef - he needed me.

"There, there. Be strong, this will pass soon enough." The voice was low and soothing and accompanied by the gentle splashing of water. "You owe your life to Lillie," it continued. "You will do well to remember that in the days to come."

Nef groaned, his misery evident.

I finally succeeded in pushing myself upright, still wiping sleep from my eyes. Brava sat on a chair next to the bed, surveying me with a smile.

"Good morning. You must have been exhausted to sleep through the noises being made by your handsome young friend here." She looked me over appraisingly. "On a different note, should you desire to give up your current profession, you can always come and work for me. You are not as well-endowed as most of my girls, but many men would find you exciting. You have the look of... 'forbidden fruit' shall we say. Many men would pay well for the chance to screw one with the look of a young maiden without actually being in danger of arrest – or worse." She arched a well-groomed brow in acknowledgement of what I had done to those who chose to molest children.

I glanced down. The sheet was crumpled around my waist. I quickly pulled it up over the small swell of my breasts. I had forgotten that I was naked.

"Nudity is nothing to be ashamed of, child," Brava remonstrated gently. "All bodies are beautiful in their own way." She smiled as her eyes took on the distant look of one lost in memories. "A man came in many years ago, insisting that he would bed no one but me. He was a sight - buck teeth, pock-marked face, slightly hunched back - not to mention *filthy*. I made a sponge bath part of the foreplay." She threw back her head and laughed. "That miserable looking man had the most glorious cock that I have ever seen - or felt." She leaned forward conspiratorially, "And he knew how to use it." She writhed slightly on her chair as she reminisced. "He brought me to climax many times." Her eyes returned to the present, her voice husky with remembered desire. "I have never seen him again. If he were to return, I would bed him again gladly, for free."

Shaking her head briskly, Brava shoved away the last of her memories. "I brought food and clothes for both of you." She waved a hand at the covered tray on the small table. "You should get your young man to attempt to eat something soon - he is growing weaker. I will check on you later." She stood and moved the chair back to its proper location, then, with a swish of skirts swept from the room to begin her day.

I slid out from under the covers and made my way to the dresser and the clothes waiting there. Knowing me as she did, Brava had selected items that fit me well. They were worn, but serviceable; nothing about them would call attention to me should I need to venture into The Narrows. I felt sure that the garments for Nef would be equally satisfactory. However, it would be a while yet before he needed them.

My stomach growled in response to the aromas rising from the tray. Removing the cover, I found eggs, bread, cheese, and a pot containing fragrant, blissfully hot tea – there was even honey to sweeten it with. Sitting down, I made short work of the meal and immediately began to feel better. I had learned over the years that the world always looked brighter on a full stomach.

Nef grew restless, tossing his head on his pillow. I moved to sit beside him, speaking soothingly in an effort to quiet him. His forehead was slightly warm, but not alarmingly so. I moistened the cloth that Brava used earlier and wiped the sweat from his face and chest. His eyes flickered open in response to my touch.

"Where are we?" His voice was a painful whisper, his lips dry and cracked.

"Somewhere safe. I'll tell you everything when you are better but right now you need to eat. Brava sent some broth; it will be easy on your stomach. Here, I'll help you sit up." Putting my words into action, I pulled him upright and shoved the pillows behind his back to help him stay that way. Once I was certain that he wasn't going to faint, I uncovered the container of broth and spooned some up.

Nef turned away.

"You have to eat, or at least try," I said in my sternest voice. "Your body has been weakened by the vomiting and residual poison; it can't begin to heal until you give it nourishment. Now, either you eat willingly or I'll hold your nose until you open your mouth and force it down. It's your choice."

"You wouldn't dare." He attempted a weak smile.

"Try me."

He must have heard the steel in my voice because he rolled his eyes but opened his mouth obediently. I gave him a little broth and waited to see if he could keep it down. He couldn't and soon began heaving violently again. When he was finished, I cleaned him up, laid him back on the pillows and searched the tray; Brava was too familiar with this process not to.... *There* - a small cloth pouch filled with herbs.

I dropped the pouch into the teapot and let it steep for several minutes, then poured a cup of the infusion and woke Nef, holding the cup as he sipped. The herbs did indeed have the desired effect; he kept down the tea. Over the course of the next several minutes, I got the rest of the cup into him and then let him sleep. After he had rested for a few minutes, I poured more tea, woke him, and helped him drink. The cycle continued until the tea was gone and I was exhausted. I crawled into bed next to him and joined him in slumber.

I awoke slowly, aware of a heavy weight lying on me. It took me a moment to figure out that it was Nef's arm. I smiled; I could get used to waking up like this. The smile quickly faded. I'd best not get ahead of myself. Once he learned the truth of what had happened and who I was, I would be lucky if he ever spoke to me again, much less anything else.

Nef's breathing changed as he too began to awaken. He tightened his arms around me reflexively, pulling me close.

"Lillie?" He sounded lost, almost like a child. "What's going on?"

I turned in his arms to face him. His hair was lank and hung over his eyes; I brushed it gently away, pleased to see that his color was better and he was no longer sweating. The stubble of his beard was rough against the palm of my hand. Thank the Makers – it seemed as though the worst was past.

"How much do you remember?"

"I remember you coming into my room and telling me that the wine was poisoned and making me drink the antidote." He wrinkled his forehead in concentration as he continued, "After that, it becomes a blur of pain and vomiting until I woke up here." He lifted his head slightly to survey his surroundings. "Wherever 'here' is."

"We're in The Narrows, in a place of safety. We have a lot to talk about, but I think it should wait until you regain your strength. You've been very sick." That was me - queen of the understatement.

"I remember you telling me that I would be. How did you know?"

I sighed. "That is one of the things that we need to talk about."

Once again, the smell of food was in the air. I pushed myself up onto my elbow. The tray from the morning had been removed and replaced with a new one. I dropped a kiss onto Nef's forehead and crawled out of bed.

"Let me see what we have to eat."

There was bread, cheese, and fruit for me and more broth for Nef. I carried the tray to the bed where he was already sitting up, waiting. Definitely a good sign. We both ate eagerly and, this time, he kept down the broth. He was doing so well, I even let him have a tiny piece of bread to sop up the remains of his soup.

"Excellent! If you keep all of that down, I'll see about getting you something more substantial for your next meal." I wrinkled my nose at him, only half in jest. "Now, you *really* need a bath. You're getting a bit ripe."

A quick glance showed that the water in the wash basin had been replaced and a bar of scented soap brought in. I soaked the rag, lathered it up and approached Nef with purpose.

"This will help, if you don't mind smelling a bit like a whore." I gave him a wicked grin.

He protested profusely as I scrubbed his face, chest, and arms vigorously.

"Oh, quit being such a baby." After I rinsed and dried his upper body, I threw back the sheet in preparation for applying the same treatment to his nether regions.

A large, work-roughened hand reached out to stop me. "That's okay. I think I can do the rest myself." He struggled to his feet, grabbed the cloth from my hand and shuffled to stand next to the dresser within easy reach of the basin. After a brief hesitation, he moved the chair closer so that he could use it for support. He then turned his back on me and resumed his ablutions with as much dignity as he could muster.

"I don't know why you're being so modest," I sniffed. "I've seen you naked – or have you forgotten?"

"I remember." He snorted. "However, there is a big difference in seeing me naked and washing my ass. No one has done that for me since I was a child, and I don't intend to change that now."

There was nothing for me to do except lean back on my elbows and enjoy the show. I had seen many naked males during my time in the guild house, but Nef was different - he was the most beautiful man that I had ever seen. His movements were mesmerizing. The muscles in his shoulders and arms rippled under his skin as he moved. My eyes followed the motion of the cloth; the water on his skin gleamed, highlighting the line of his spine and the curve of his buttocks. Warmth blossomed in my belly and slowly worked its way outward. His illness had certainly done nothing to affect *my* libido.

I cleared my throat before attempting to speak. "There are...uh..." I closed my eyes so that maybe I could remember how to speak in complete sentences; it helped a little. "There are clothes on the top of the dresser for you. I don't know if they will fit or not. But -" I opened my eyes and waggled my eyebrows suggestively "- you don't have to worry about getting dressed on my behalf."

He turned as he examined the garments, giving me an opportunity to admire his front as thoroughly as I had his back. He was lean, his shoulders not as broad as those of some men, but every inch of him was hard with muscle. The skin on his face, neck and forearms was noticeably darker than the rest of him due to his time in the sun. My fingers ached to touch the patch of dark hair in the center of his chest – and its twin at the apex of his thighs.

Completely ignoring my attempts at lechery, he dressed quickly – or as quickly as he could manage. The clothes fit well enough, with the exception of the pants which stopped several inches above his ankles. He scowled at me when I giggled.

"Don't worry about it. You won't be going out in public any time soon and I'll make sure to get you proper trousers before you do." I patted the mattress next to me. "Now, come and get back in bed for a while. You need to conserve your energy."

Nef did as ordered then looked at me seriously. "Start talking. I need to understand what is going on."

I sighed. I really wanted to wait until he was stronger - and perhaps several years older - but the telling would not get easier with time. I sat facing him with my chin on my knees and my arms wrapped around my legs feeling smaller than ever. "Before I start, did you mean it when you told me that you love me?"

"Yes, absolutely." He reached for my hand, taking it in his own.

I welcomed his grasp; it was the only lifeline in my sea of despair. "Try to remember that when you hear what I have to say. What do you want to know first?"

"How did you know about the wine?"

I closed my eyes unable to meet his gaze. "I poisoned it."

Nef dropped my hand as if burned; the hurt in his eyes was almost unbearable. My heart broke.

"*You* poisoned me? Why? You said that you love me. Was that a lie?"

I longed to reach for him, but didn't dare. "No, it wasn't a lie. I *do* love you." My eyes burned with unshed tears. "I didn't know it was *you*. I would never do anything to hurt you." Sobs threatened to burst from my chest as I hung my head, allowing my hair to fall in a curtain around me. "I am – *was* - an assassin. I was sent to the palace to kill the heir to the throne."

"An assassin?" He practically spat the words at me. "I thought I knew you!"

"You do know me - better than anyone!"

He turned away.

"Nef, don't! Please, listen to me. I need to explain."

He stopped in the act of getting out of the bed and nodded, but kept his back to me.

I moved to sit next to him – close, but not touching - and told him the whole story. "My parents sold me to the Va'Shile when I was three; I was raised to be an assassin. My guild master used me to target child molesters; the king's heir was to be my first 'normal' hit." My voice broke. "But I couldn't go through with it; I couldn't kill an innocent man. I went back to dispose of the wine, but it was too late; you had already finished it. I gave you the antidote and brought you here, where you will be safe."

He still refused to look at me. I understood his anger; I didn't blame him. I waited in silence, feeling as weak as if I were the one that had been sick.

Finally, he turned to look at me, his face expressionless. "Where are we?"

"We're in a brothel in The Narrows; the madam, Brava, is my friend. She allows me to use this room as a… hiding place when I need it."

"A brothel!" His eyes narrowed in suspicion. "Are you a whore as well?"

I leapt to my feet, anger quickly replacing my sadness. "How *dare* you!" I slapped him hard enough to leave the imprint of my hand on his cheek. "It seems to me that I'm not the only one in this room with secrets, *Your Highness*."

He flinched at my use of the title.

I dropped into a curtsey, as was proper when addressing a member of the royal family. However, I did *not* bow my head. Instead, I leaned forward until our noses were almost touching. "And, I seem to recall that *I saved your royal ass*." I punctuated each word with a jab of my forefinger. After giving him one last glare, I turned to storm out of the room.

"Lillie, wait," he said softly.

I didn't. I left, slamming the door behind me with enough force to crack the frame.

I made it all the way to Brava's parlor before bursting into tears.

There was more to running a whorehouse than simply spreading one's legs - there was also paperwork. The madam was responsible for the care and feeding of her staff and the maintenance of her facility. Most of Brava's time was taken up in mundane tasks such as paying bills, settling disputes between the girls and making sure that her customers were satisfied. Brava's personal services only went to the select few that could afford her fee, or those on whom her favor rested. Her favor rested on me, but I had no desire for her services. I simply needed her friendship – and her advice.

After one look at my tear-stained face, Brava closed her ledger, pushed to her feet and enveloped me in her arms. "Shhhh," she stroked my hair and murmured soothingly until my tears subsided into muffled sniffling. "Is it safe to assume that your young man now knows the truth of your actions?"

I nodded against her bosom.

Brava pulled away and led me to the couch, shooing away the cats that seem to have taken permanent residence there. In addition to the fluffy white one from the night before, there was also a battle-scarred tabby tom. She loved cats and the feeling seemed to be mutual. It seemed as though virtually every stray in The Narrows knew to come to her establishment for food, and occasionally, a home. Her affinity for all things feline led to her establishment being known as "The Cat's House" to the locals. She appreciated the humor – and the double-entendre – and did nothing to discourage the use of the name.

Once we were seated, she pulled the bell cord twice, notifying the kitchen staff to provide refreshments for two.

"I take it that your news didn't go over very well?" she asked as we waited.

"No." I searched my pockets in vain for something to wipe my nose on before giving up and using my sleeve. "But, I guess he took it as well as could be expected. He is still too weak to attempt to leave, so I did – after slapping him."

Brava's well-groomed brows arched questioningly as she offered me her personal handkerchief.

"He practically accused me of being a whore!" I accepted the square of cloth gratefully, wiping away the last of my tears and blowing my nose. My face reddened as I realized my faux pas. "Sorry," I added sheepishly.

"Quite all right." Brava waved one slender hand in the air dismissively.

There was a knock at the door.

"Enter!" she called, motioning for the serving girl to place the heavily laden tray on the low table in front of the couch.

When the girl moved to serve us, Brava dismissed her, indicating that she would pour the tea. I was honored.

"The first fight with a lover is always the worst." Her movements were sure as she filled my cup and added a heaping spoonful of sweetener before handing it to me.

"How did you know that this was our first fight?" I closed my eyes, inhaling the delicate aroma rising from the tea and sipped carefully, relaxing somewhat as the warmth began to spread through my body. A slight weight filled my lap. I opened my eyes to find a small plate laden with snacks – all sweet. I had quite a sweet tooth and had not been able to indulge my cravings at the castle. Here, I stuffed myself shamelessly.

"It is a safe assumption." She shrugged, her expression shrewd. "You can't have known each other long and when love is new, everything is wonderful." She smiled. "The arguments come later – when you realize that your lover is not perfect."

"Does it get easier?" Maker's Teeth, I certainly hoped so. If it didn't, it was a miracle that any relationships survived.

She chuckled. "It doesn't necessarily get easier – but it does become less traumatic."

I wondered about Brava's own relationships; she had never talked about her past.

"It will be all right, child." Brava's dark eyes studied me over the rim of her cup. "Your young man has secrets as well. He will calm down and when he does, he will be ashamed of his actions." She nodded at my plate, "When you finish here, you are going back to your room; you both have apologies and explanations to make."

"I don't know *how!*" I wailed through a mouthful of cake, spraying crumbs with each word. I stopped to wash everything down with another swallow of tea before continuing. "I'm an assassin – we solve problems with weapons, not *words*." Fresh tears ran down my cheeks. "Besides, he hates me."

"Really? And you know this how, exactly? Did he tell you?"

"No..." I was in no mood for logic. "How could he not? I poisoned him!"

"You *saved* him." Brava's voice had taken on the patient tone usually reserved for one of her girls that was being exceptionally difficult. "Did he throw you out?"

"No, I left. He..." My words faded into a stunned silence as I realized what had happened. "He tried to stop me."

"See? He doesn't hate you. You just caught him off-guard. His world has been turned upside down too, remember." Brava patted my knee consolingly as she stood and returned to her desk. "Now, I must return to my duties. As much as I would like to visit, I have responsibilities." She smiled as she added, "As do you."

I lingered, pouring myself another cup of tea and nibbling - very slowly - on another cookie. However, Brava was not one to tolerate dawdling; her patience would soon wear thin. Finishing, I thanked her for her courtesy and left.

Still not brave enough to face Nef, I went to the stables to check on Elah. I could feel her anxiety before I even entered the building. She stood at the half-door to her stall, staring at the entrance, and waiting.

"Hello, old girl." I rubbed her muzzle in greeting while mentally sending her reassurances. "Are they taking good care of you?" A quick check of her surroundings showed that the boy had done well – she had plenty of fresh straw and clean water. "Nef is much better – he will come see you as soon as he can."

Relaxed, now that she knew her master was well, Elah nudged my hand, her lips fluttering over my fingers.

"You're incorrigible!" I laughed. "I don't have anything for you now, but I'll try to bring you something soon. Right now, I have to go talk to your master." I hesitated, stroking her forelock. "I'm glad your stall is clean – if things don't go well, I may be spending the night with you."

Elah whickered and nudged me again – this time pushing me away from the stall and toward the door.

"Okay, okay, I'm going." Great. Even the horse was pushing me around.

Reluctantly, I returned to the brothel and made my way back to my room with the sort of enthusiasm usually reserved for prisoners on the way to their execution. I steeled myself for what lay ahead and began to climb the stairs; the staircase seemed to have grown in length and the treads creaked loudly beneath my feet. So much for subtlety. As I reached for the handle of the door, it was snatched open from the other side and Nef stood silhouetted in the opening.

"Lillie?"

"Of course, it's me," I grumbled as I pushed past him. "Who else would it be?"

"Oh, I don't know." He slammed the door in frustration. "Maybe a horde of assassins sent to finish me off?" His eyes flashed, the muscles in his jaws clenching as he bit back his next retort.

I finally looked at him – really *saw* him. What I thought was anger was actually fear. While I was off pouting over our fight, Nef had been left alone – and afraid – in a strange place. This was probably the first time that anyone had tried to kill him and he was handling the situation as best he could. My hurt feelings seemed kind of petty when I looked at things from his perspective. Too bad I hadn't done that earlier.

"Not a horde." I shook my head as I dropped into the chair. "Just one fairly small assassin and she isn't here to harm you." I rubbed a hand across my eyes, suddenly exhausted.

We stared at each other, neither of us having the faintest idea as to how to proceed. We were never going to get anywhere at this rate, so I threw myself into the abyss that lay between us.

"Look, I know that this is awkward, but we are going to have to come to some sort of... something. A truce, maybe? By all the hells, I don't even know what to call it!" I jumped to my feet but immediately sat back down. With Nef standing between me and the door, there was no room for pacing. "As I said earlier, Brava lets me use this room, but she's a business woman; she isn't going to give us another one. At least, not unless one of us begins accepting clients." I glared at Nef. "Contrary to what you may think, I'm not ready to do that yet. However, if you would like to give it a try, feel free." I gestured toward the much abused door behind him. "Plenty of the girls would be willing to show you the ropes – some of them literally."

The briefest flicker of a dimple creased his cheek as he moved to sit on the edge of the bed across from me. He fidgeted, plucking nervously at the covers and occasionally drawing in breath as if to speak. I bit my lip and waited.

"I'm sorry." He glanced up at me through his lashes. "I can't take back what I said, but I didn't mean it. I just..." He shrugged helplessly.

"You've been through a lot in the past couple of days."

"That's an understatement if I've ever heard one." This time there was no mistaking the smile that crossed his face briefly before he turned a serious blue-eyed gaze on me. "Where do we go from here?

"I really wish people would stop asking me for relationship advice." I sighed and then I shrugged. "I'm making things up as I go."

Everything in me was screaming for me to run, but I had done enough of that. I settled for pacing, now that I could. For several minutes the room was silent with the exception of my footsteps. Once I thought that I could sit without fidgeting, I returned to the chair and perched on the edge of the seat, my knees almost brushing Nef's.

"I guess the first thing we have to do is decide if we trust each other."

We stared at each other for the space of a few heartbeats and then Nef held out his hand. I took it gladly.

"I do."

"Me too."

"So, what comes next?"

I rolled my eyes. "If we are going to work this out there can't be anymore secrets between us. Agreed?"

He nodded and tugged on my hand, pulling me to sit beside him on the bed. "I was the one asking all of the questions earlier, but you probably have a few of your own."

"I do." I twined my fingers in his, using my free hand to stroke the pulse that beat strongly in his wrist. "Why didn't you tell me that you were the heir to the throne?"

"I couldn't. Not then - I needed to wait until after the official ceremony." He gave a bitter laugh, "And until I had figured out *how* to tell you − it's not the sort of thing that I could just casually bring up."

"Well, at least that explains why you had the keys to so many doors." I smiled in a futile attempt to lighten the mood. "Why were you posing as a servant?"

"That was one of my conditions to agreeing to become the heir. The king and his nobles are too far removed from the people that they rule. I don't want to be like them." He idly stroked his thumb across mine, a faraway look in his eyes. "I believe that a good ruler is actually a servant to his people. How better to learn a servant's role than to be one?" He shrugged. "I insisted that I be allowed to live as a servant for several months before accepting my new position. The whole 'hunt for the heir' was a ruse to throw off anyone who might want to hurt me."

"It worked." I couldn't help but laugh. "My masters, or rather, my *former* masters had no idea that you were already there." My laughter faded as I continued. "Ramalda is now in turmoil. The new heir is missing and the Va'Shile know that I am missing as well. It will not take them long to realize that we're together. By failing to complete my assigned task, I have signed my own death warrant. They will not rest until I am dead." I swallowed, my throat suddenly dry. "Until *we* are dead."

The silence stretched out for several minutes.

"Any ideas?" Nef asked quietly.

"No..." I yawned suddenly, my eyes watering from the effort. "But don't worry, I'll come up with something."

Night had fallen as we talked and the room was now lit only by the moonlight filtering in through the window. Nef shifted to the far side of the bed and pulled me down beside him, wrapping his arms around me and burying his face in my hair.

"Correction," he whispered, his breath warm against my scalp. "First, *we* will get some sleep and then *we* will come up with something."

For once in my life, I didn't argue.

16

Nef slept soundly.

I did not. My thoughts jumbled themselves into one giant, panic-inducing knot as I struggled to decide what we should do next. I came up with exactly nothing. My biggest concern was money; we left the castle with nothing but Elah and the clothes on our back. I felt sure that any plans we could devise would require some sort of funds. As a servant, I had very little coin to call my own. As an assassin, I had small amounts squirreled away in a few safe places. The Va'Shile may not have succeeded in turning me into a murderer, but they did succeed in making me paranoid.

I hadn't yet learned anything about Nef's family and how he came to be selected as the heir. Hopefully, he had money. But, even if he did, the difficulty would be getting to it. He couldn't exactly wander back to his rooms at the palace to reclaim his possessions. He was a marked man – even if the target was invisible. For him to set foot outside would be to proclaim that he was no longer interested in living.

I was obviously missing something and needed to know more. Why would someone want to kill Nef? Politics had never been of interest to me. It was a shame, considering that both my life and the life of the man that I loved now hung by what I suspected was a political thread.

I desperately needed sleep. Surely, I would be able to think more clearly if I were better rested. I closed my eyes, willing sleep to come. It refused. I couldn't get up and pace the small room as was becoming my habit; to do so would disturb Nef and he needed his rest even more than I did.

Deciding to experiment with my ability to communicate with animals, I stilled my thoughts and reached out with my mind. At first, I sensed only the colony of mice that lived in the walls as they made their nightly forays for food. As I reached farther, I became aware of the pigeons roosting under the eaves, cooing softly even as they slept.

Testing my reach, I searched for the stables and Elah. She roused as she sensed my mental touch but exuded no fear, only curiosity; I could almost feel her welcoming whicker. I sent her thoughts of love and reassurance; she understood. She was warm and comfortable and her presence was reassuring. Our minds still touching lightly, we drifted into dreams together.

The next morning, Nef was much better, but still somewhat weak; the days of vomiting and limited food had taken its toll on him. Brava had nursed enough sick people, including me, to know the proper steps to take. Today, she had provided more than just broth for Nef, but nothing that would put a strain on his still recovering digestive system.

He studied me thoughtfully as we ate.

"You look tired."

Apparently I wasn't the only one who excelled at the art of the understatement.

"I am. Fearing for my – *our* – lives tends to have that effect."

"So, did you come up with any masterful plans during the night?"

"No," I told him truthfully. Snagging a pillow, I placed it behind me and leaned back on the foot of the bed facing him as he did the same at the other end. "Tell me more about yourself, how you were selected to be heir. Maybe it will help us figure out what to do next."

"I was the only logical choice." Nef shrugged. "The king is no fool. I am the *last* person that the nobles would want to assume the throne, so he believed that selecting me made him safe from their machinations – at least for a time. Apparently he didn't think that anyone would act to remove me from the position so quickly."

His explanation did nothing to clarify the situation.

"I don't understand..."

"My last name is Nidolan." He smirked as he waited for me to figure it out.

"Nef... Nidolan?" I pulled the pillow from behind me and threw it at him, my emotions in turmoil. "You jerk! You really *are* a prince? I mean, even before... without..." Words failed and I waved my hands in an attempt to encompass everything that had happened.

Nef nodded - and grinned as he placed the extra pillow behind his back smugly.

The nerve! I searched in vain for something else to throw at him and finally settled on sticking out my tongue. *Take that, Your Highness!*

His dimples deepened as he laughed, unfazed by my reaction.

"As I told you, my father was killed in the civil war several years ago. The remainder of my family has been living in exile. The powers that be seem content to leave us alone as long as we make no attempt to regain the throne. The king decided that if a Nidolan were to become the heir, the attentions of those currently clamoring to have *him* removed would be refocused on me, thereby giving him more time to - hopefully - produce an heir of his loins."

"True. Your royal blood would have made you a target soon enough, but something still doesn't add up." My brow furrowed as I thought.

"What do you mean?"

"I was tasked to kill the heir to the throne – *whoever* he might be." I slid closer to Nef and took his hand in mine, idly stroking his fingers with my thumb as I pondered. "It seems to me that the purpose of the hit was to keep the king from having a viable heir, thereby making it easier for him to be removed from power."

"That is exactly what is wrong with this country!" Nef's eyes flashed in anger. "The most powerful of the noble families vie constantly behind the scenes for control of Manah. Each family works against the others, stooping to intimidation, blackmail, and when necessary, murder to elevate their own to the upper echelons. It's this mindset that has allowed the Va'Shile to arise to such a position of influence. They don't care who is in control; they will kill for whoever provides them with sufficient coin for the hit. If the Nidolan family had remained in control of the throne, the Va'Shile would be nothing more than a inconsequential group of murderers with no major sway in political circles."

I sat in silence for a few moments, considering the information that Nef had provided. I didn't like the conclusions that I was reaching. "If the Nidolan family regained the throne, what would become of the Va'Shile?"

Nef became very serious. "The kindest way to put it would be to say that their ranks would be thinned. Such an organization could not be allowed to continue to exist. Without the Va'Shile to hide behind, few of the noble families would be willing to do their own dirty work. They would have to fall in line behind the new regime or be recognized for the traitors that they are."

"Don't underestimate the Va'Shile, Nef." My heart began to pound as the pieces fell into place. "Vido, the Guild Master, raised me; he is a smart man, and cruel. He knows that if the Nidolans regain the throne his life and his livelihood are in danger. He will not allow that to happen. Even if none of the nobles came forward to have you killed, Vido would have it done himself." As I spoke, I became more and more certain that this was what had happened. Perhaps Nef's plan to hide in plain sight as a servant had not worked as well as I initially thought.

"How well do you know Vido?" Nef broke into my reverie quietly.

I shrugged. "I would like to say 'as well as anyone,' but that wouldn't be true." I struggled to explain. "The Va'Shile recruit many children, through many avenues. As Guild Master, Vido takes an interest in all of the recruits. We are taught to think of him as our 'father.' However, thinking back on it, I now realize that Vido took an uncommon interest in me. He made sure that I was kept well fed and healthy, even though he wasn't obvious about it. Doing anything to call attention to me would have made me the victim of the other recruits.

"He also made sure that I trained with the best. Of course, Vido considers all of his trainers to be good at what they do or they would not be in his employ. However, some are better than others. I was always trained by the best of the best. Vido seemed to have some sort of vested interest in making sure that I became a top assassin. I have no idea why. Why would it matter to him that I succeed any more than any other recruit?"

"Could it have something to do with your parents? Do you know anything about them - other than what he told you?"

Nef sat up and urged me closer, until I was sitting beside him, our hips touching.

Warmth flooded my body from the contact. I struggled to keep my awareness of him from interfering with my thoughts. It didn't work very well. I fought down my libido and returned to the discussion at hand.

"I don't know. I don't remember them." I hung my head. "Vido said that they sold me because I was 'bad' and they chose to exchange me for food and coin." My head jerked up as I remembered.

"What?"

"Just before I left the kitchens, Mama L told me that there was more to my birth than I knew. She urged me to find the truth. Her exact words were that I should 'become what I was born to be.' What in the name of the Maker's Mother does that mean?" I tilted my head to look Nef in the eyes.

"I have no idea." He stroked his thumb lightly across my lips, his pupils widening in desire. "But, I think that we have talked enough for now."

He wrapped his arms around me and pulled me close for a kiss that left me breathless and wanting more. Apparently he did too - his hands wandered to the fastenings on my clothes and began yanking at them eagerly.

"Don't you think that you need to reserve your strength?" I placed my hands on his arms, offering a token resistance. "After all, you *have* been very ill."

"I feel much better," he insisted as he pulled open my top. "Besides," he added, giving me a playful glare, "I shouldn't be the only one in a whorehouse that isn't getting laid."

Nef acquitted himself nobly during our lovemaking before collapsing into an exhausted sleep. I dressed quietly and left him to his dreams as I went in search of Brava. I needed someone to talk to.

"Ah, child. It is good to see you." Brava looked up at my knock and beckoned me in. "I could use a break." She motioned me to the nearby couch then stood and stretched in a very feline fashion before joining me. A smile played over her face when she looked at me. "So, tell me, is your young man a good lover?"

"How did you know?" I found myself blushing and wondered why Brava had that effect on me. I was never overly modest and she knew it.

"Little one, I have been in this business for many years. I know the look of a woman that has been well bedded." She sniffed delicately. "Also, you smell of sex."

The blush spread down my neck and onto my chest.

"What can I do for you, child?" Brava asked gently, ignoring my plight.

"I have so many questions that I don't even know where to begin looking for answers." I threw my hands up in exasperation, or possibly despair, I wasn't sure which. "I need someone to talk to, someone to help me order my scattered thoughts. So, here goes. First, I have no money except the little that I have hidden away in other areas. I need to gather money and supplies, without attracting the attention of the Va'Shile." I met Brava's eyes as I continued, "Next, I need to know who wanted Nef killed. Was the hit ordered by one of the nobles, or did Vido arrange it himself?"

Brava's expression had not changed as I spoke, until now. Her elegant brows arched in surprise. "Why would Vido arrange a hit himself? Unless..." Her eyes narrowed in thought; it didn't take her long to reach a conclusion. "Perhaps, your lover is somehow a threat to him?"

"Nothing gets past you, does it?" I laughed.

"Very little," she stated matter-of-factly. "People think that I am in the business of selling flesh, which of course I am. What they *don't* realize is that I am also in the information business. Men talk to the women that they bed - even if those women are whores. I don't pick my girls just for their looks; they have to have brains as well as breasts. They are trained to listen and to retain what they hear. They meet with me daily to pass on any interesting tidbits. I record the information - as well as who it came from - until I can find a way to use it." She gave a throaty chuckle. "You'd be surprised how well people will pay to keep some things quiet."

"Pay? How can your clients pay you anything? Most of them are from The Narrows; the fee for an hour with one of your girls would break most of them. How would they have anything left to give?"

"My *clients* may not have much, but many of the ones that they earn coin from *do*. It is these people that pay me well not to reveal what I have learned." Brava leaned forward and patted my knee. "As I am sure that you learned during your time in the palace, the well-to-do frequently forget that their servants are people, with perfectly good ears and minds. They say things in front of them that they would never say in front of each other. It is these servants that are my clients; they are the ones that reveal their master's secrets. All I have to do is put the pieces together to determine who I should blackmail." She leaned back, her expression satisfied. "My targets are always astounded by the information that I have, yet they are never able to figure out how I know. They are so self-righteous, yet so clueless. I find it amusing. As a reward to those who provide me with important information, I give them a free night with the girl of their choice. It keeps them coming back." She gave a hearty belly laugh at her choice of words. "Getting the goods on someone and seeing the expression on their face when they realize that they are trapped is almost as good as sex. But only almost." Unselfconsciously, Brava began stroking her nipple, sighing in pleasure at her own touch. "What else would you like to talk about, child?"

"There is more, but that is a conversation for another time. For now, I think I know where I need to start. I am going to need clothes. May I borrow some from the outfits set aside for the girls?"

"Of course, of course. Help yourself to what you want. If anything needs to be altered, just speak to Mistress Rowns; she is my live-in seamstress, laundress, and sometimes midwife. Let her know that I sent you and she won't give you any problems. At least, no more than she gives me."

"Thank you, Brava." I gave her a hug of appreciation.

As I turned to leave, she stopped me.

"Let me know if you need any help pleasuring that man of yours. It has been quite a while since I bedded one so young."

"I'll let you know, but don't hold your breath. I am quite capable of satisfying even his wildest desires. After all, I learned from the best." I gave her a saucy curtsy and swept from the room to introduce myself to Mistress Rowns, making sure to tell her that Brava sent me.

"Humph," the seamstress said. "I don't know what that woman was thinkin' when she recruited you." She put her hands on my shoulders and turned me from side to side, eyeing me critically. "Men come here lookin' for girls with breasts as big as melons and quim big enough to take in a draft horse's cock." She wheezed amiably at her own humor. "Cuz they all think that's what they've got, even the ones that can't find theirs with both hands."

"I'm not a new employee; I'm a friend of Brava's. She said that I could borrow some clothes and that you are just the person to assist me." I figured it wouldn't hurt to flatter the woman a little. "She is quite proud to have you on her staff."

Her weather-beaten face practically glowed at the praise.

"Well, that's a relief. She would've lost money on you. Come in, lass, and let's see what you need."

Mistress Rown's quarters resembled a large closet. Rods hung with female garments of all sizes and stacks of materials lined the walls. It was like walking into a somewhat suffocating rainbow. Sometime later I left with a bag stuffed with a variety of garments that might be of use. I wasn't worried about the fit; these clothes were to serve as a disguise more than as a fashion statement.

I stopped by the kitchen for food before returning to my room. My attempt to enter quietly without dropping any of my items resulted in a sound only slightly less noisy than that made by an invading army. Needless to say, Nef was no longer sleeping by the time I shut the door behind me.

"Maker's Teeth, Lillie! How in all the hells does someone so small make so much noise?"

"It's easy when I'm trying to carry this much stuff! I can barely see where I'm going." I managed to set down the food with only minor tea spillage before dumping the bag of clothes on the floor. "All right, you. Out of bed and into the chair. No more eating in bed for you." I smiled to take the sting from my words.

Nef made the transition easily and was pleased to see that I had brought a more substantial meal for him. Stew, complete with vegetables and meat. I wouldn't make any wagers on the type of meat, but I wasn't in the mood to be picky. I was starving. We ate in a companionable silence.

"I'm going out for a while to pick up some supplies," I explained once we finished. "I should be back in a couple of hours."

"Is it safe?"

"As safe as it can be." I shrugged. "I know The Narrows and I can disguise myself with the clothes that I borrowed. I'll be extra careful." I dug through the bag of clothes and pulled out what I needed, leaving the rest in a pile on the floor. I didn't care if they got wrinkled and dirty; it would make my future disguises more realistic.

Once I made my selections, I stripped down to bare skin in order to prepare my costume. All right, I admit that it wasn't really necessary to undress completely, but it did make it easier for me to seduce Nef. Although that really wasn't very hard; like me, he seemed to stay in a constant state of slight arousal. All I had to do was fan the flames a little to turn the ember of excitement into a roaring conflagration of desire. Once the fire was burning, it would have been rude to walk away and leave Nef to suffer. Or for that matter, me.

Sated - for the moment at least - I dressed and left Nef sleeping once again. This was becoming a habit. Garbed in layer upon layer of non-descript clothing, I bound my hair in a turban like a washer woman and slung the borrowed bag over one shoulder; the garments peeking out of the mouth completed the image. Grabbing a piece of fruit off of the lunch tray and giving Nef a quick kiss, I headed out.

I made a quick stop by the stable to check on Elah. She was happy to see me and even happier with the apple that I brought.

"See, I haven't forgotten about you." I rubbed her neck as she munched. "I owe you my thanks for getting us to safety. Nef is feeling much better; he will come to see you soon."

She whickered and rubbed her soft muzzle against my arm in understanding.

A washer woman would be sweaty and grimy after working at the river all day, so I swiped my hand across the floor and rubbed dirt on my face. A quick check out the back door of the stable revealed no tell-tale shifting of shadows that shouldn't be moving, nor any sounds out of place. I stepped out, a woman worn out before her time, hunched over with the weight of the laundry on her back and limping slightly, perhaps from an old injury. Even though my head hung as if in exhaustion, my eyes were alert, searching every shadowy doorway and corner; my ears listened for sudden footfalls.

I wound my way slowly through the maze of alleys. Many women had taken advantage of the warm weather to hang their laundry out to dry. As I worked my way along, I stole various articles of clothing that I thought Nef and I might be able to use. I felt bad about stealing from those with so much less than I, but our survival was more important to me at the moment. Someday, hopefully, I could find some way to make reparations.

I made my way to the safe house that I visited earlier; the place where my poisons were kept. I selected a few poisons - and the antidotes, of course - and added them to my pack. I also chose a variety of weapons from the small cache there; a short sword for Nef and a couple of my favorite daggers. I wrapped the weapons in purloined clothing before adding them to my bag. The purpose was twofold; the padding would camouflage the shape of the weapons and prevent them from making any noise if they clanked together. Finally, I opened the secret panel at the back of one of the drawers and withdrew the coins hidden there and dispersed them throughout the various pockets in my voluminous skirts.

As I approached the doorway I got the sense of a presence outside. The alley was well-lit by the afternoon sun, but I saw no one through the peep holes. I stepped out only to once again find Master Jaidon waiting on me.

"Lillie." He spoke so quietly, that I almost didn't hear him. "You must get back inside. Now."

My years of obeying the Masters without hesitation kicked in and I did as told, almost against my will. Master Jaidon followed me in.

"Master." I put down my bag and bowed respectfully. "Once again, I know that I was not followed, yet once again you found me here. How did you know? What gave me away?"

"This safe house has been compromised, little one. I am living in the hovel next door and have rigged the door so that I will know when it is opened. I also have a few peep holes of my own so that I may see who enters." He leaned against the counter and crossed his arms over his broad chest as he studied me. "So, it has finally happened. You have taken a lover. I believe congratulations are in order." A small smile creased his cheeks; for a moment, his scarred face was a thing of beauty.

"Am I so obvious?" I was more than a little cranky. "I may as well wear a sign around my neck that says 'I like to get laid.'"

Master Jaidon actually laughed. I didn't think I had ever heard him laugh before.

"You wouldn't be your father's daughter if you didn't."

My throat closed. I could barely force the words out. "You knew my father?"

"Very well. We were friends. I promised him that I would look after you if anything ever happened to him." Another fleeting smile. "You don't think I that I continue to work for Vido for his winning personality, do you?"

"I've never really thought about why you work for Vido." My temper began to rise. "I would assume it was for the same reasons as anyone else. You like to kill, or you know no other way of life." I glared at him. "And what the hells has my sex life got to do with being like my father?"

"Your father was a bit of a ladies' man. He was quite popular at the local brothel – at least until he met your mother. The first time he laid eyes on her, he was

hooked. He was never with another woman after that."
Master Jaidon shifted slightly, glancing over his
shoulder as he did.

My gaze dropped to the slight hump on the Master's
back. In a flash of insight, I saw him as he must have
looked in his younger days; slightly hunchback, pock
marked face. No buck teeth, but those were easy
enough to fake. A smile of my own crossed my face.

"I believe you are acquainted with a woman named
Brava?"

He froze, his eyes locking onto mine.

"You know Brava?'

"Yes, I do. She told me of an evening that she spent
with someone fitting your description - except for the
teeth."

"What did she say?" He choked the words out.

"She said that if he were ever to return, she would
bed him again gladly, for free."

His dark skin flushed a shade darker.

"Master, who has compromised my safe house?
What purpose could it serve?"

Jaidon shook himself as if to bring himself back to
the present. "I don't know. During the time that I have
been watching, no one other than you has entered. Not
knowing who limits my ability to guess why, but I
suspect that you are being set up to take the fall for
something big. Something that will result in your death
at the hands of the authorities."

"I don't understand." I struggled to push down my fears. "Why would I be singled out? Why me, out of all of the Va'Shile? There are many who have done things far more heinous than I."

"Lillie, there are things about your past, your parents that you don't know." Master Jaidon stepped closer and rested one hand on my shoulder. "My guess is that someone in the Va'Shile, someone higher up than I, knows the truth and has found a way to use it to his, or her, advantage."

"You are the second one in the past few days to tell me that there is more to my birth than I know." I propped my hands on my hips and worked up my sternest glare. "I'll start my search with you. You said that you knew my father and promised him that you would look after me. This implies that you knew my mother as well. What can you tell me about her?"

With a sigh, Master Jaidon stepped back and once again leaned against the counter.

"I shouldn't tell you anything, little one; to do so endangers us both." He raised his hand to stop my protest before it was even fully formed. "However, I will tell you a little. Your mother was Southron and very beautiful. Men practically threw themselves at her feet, vying for her attention. No one believed that she would even deign to notice one such as your father, but she did." Once again, a smile softened his features. "Your father changed when he met your mother; she softened his rough edges, helped him to see that a different life was possible. The courtship was short, their marriage both quick and secret. There were those on both sides of the relationship that would not approve. Nevertheless, they were thrilled to learn that your mother was with child. They loved you, Lille. Never doubt it."

"Thank you, Master." Tears ran unheeded down my face. "It has always hurt to believe that my parents sold me. You can't possibly know how much it means to know that I was both loved and wanted." Other thoughts crowded through the surge of joy filling me. "But if my parents wanted me, how did I wind up at the assassin's guild and what happened to them? Why did Vido tell me they sold me? Why didn't he just tell me the truth - whatever it was?"

"I can tell you no more. You are beginning to walk on very dangerous ground; be careful where you tread. As for Vido, he only does what is best for him. Be assured, that whatever he told you was for a reason. You can also be assured that whatever the reason, it was for *his* best interests, not yours. Now, you must leave quickly. Be careful returning to wherever you are hiding. If you are followed, your follower will not be as kind as I. Take care of yourself, Lillie and do not return here - ever."

17

It took me twice as long to get back to the brothel as it had to get to the safe house. I worked my way slowly through the narrow alleys, frequently doubling back on my trail to throw off any followers. Master Jaidon's words had shaken me, but I pushed them away resolutely. Now was not the time to lose my focus. Every shadow loomed ominously; every distant footfall became the harbinger of my doom.

Pausing at the entry to the market I glanced quickly over my shoulder, catching the briefest glimpse of a pale face disappearing behind a stack of crates. Va'Shile – I recognized him from the guild house. He was good, but I was better. I joined the crowd of day workers surging into the square as they returned from MidTown and worked my way into their midst. As I pushed through the press of bodies, I overheard snippets of conversation.

"Did you hear? The new prince is dead – they found 'im smashed on the razorrock…"

"…'e's missin'. I bet 'e's hidin' and waitin' fer everything to blow over."

"The king is dead." The speaker nodded sagely as he pontificated. "That there's his twin on the throne; 'e killed his brother and took 'is place."

"His Majesty is royally pissed."

Listeners chortled in appreciation at the pun.

"Mark my words, heads is gonna roll – startin' with those namby-pamby good-fer-nothin' nobles."

In spite of the fact that I was a marked woman, I *had* to find a way to get back into the castle. I needed to talk to Mama L and find out what she knew about my past. Someone wanted me dead and I needed every bit of information that I could find to help me determine who and why and what, if anything, it had to do with Nef's situation.

I reached the far edge of the crowd and ducked down the alley that led to the brothel. One of my precious coins went to ensuring that the watchman would deny seeing me if questioned; a mild but sincere threat backed it up.

I was more than ready to get back to Nef but had to see Mistress Rowns first. With a little shameless flattery and wide-eyed wheedling I was able to obtain the extra items that I needed for the plan that was slowly forming in my mind.

Entering our room I found Nef awake and pacing; I had been gone much longer than I had anticipated. Relief flooded his face when he saw me, only to be quickly replaced by anger.

"Where have you been?" He grabbed my shoulders and shook me. "I've been worried sick! I had no idea where you were or where to go looking. I don't know anyone here or who to turn to for help..." Just as quickly, his anger faded and he hugged me hard enough to make my ribs creak and then kissed me - hard. He buried his fingers in my hair and pulled back my head, his blue eyes burning into mine. "Don't ever scare me like that again! You're the only part of my world that makes any sense right now. I don't want to lose you."

"I'm sorry; I didn't mean to be gone so long." I hugged him back as hard as I could, pressing my cheek firmly against his chest; the steady thrumming of his heart soothed my jangled nerves. I began to shake with the after-effects of the adrenaline that had fueled my return trip.

"Lillie?" Nef's voice softened as he placed a finger under my chin and forced me to look at him. "Are you all right?"

"Yes. No." I shrugged helplessly and dropped onto the bed. "I don't know." *Pull yourself together girl!* My emotional equilibrium returned slowly. "I have known that my life is forfeit since I made the decision not to kill you." I tried to grin to ease the sting of my words, but wasn't very successful; it felt more like a grimace. "However, having it confirmed for me by a member of the Va'shile was rather unnerving."

Nef slid onto the mattress beside me and wrapped his arms around me, pulling me with him as he lay back against the pillows. I snuggled against him, basking in his warmth. My shivers slowly subsided as I filled him in on the events of the afternoon.

"So where do we go from here?"

"I'm not sure. Master Jaidon is the second person to reference my parents and my past." I shook my head. "I'm missing something somewhere." I forced my next sentence out in a rush. "Which is why I have to go back to the castle."

Nef leapt to his feet and the expression on his face said quite eloquently that he thought I had lost my mind. In a way, he was probably right. Escaping the castle with my life had been relatively easy; walking back in was potential suicide.

"I'll be disguised; no one will recognize me." I waved my hands to fend off his words as he opened his mouth to interrupt. "I've got to talk to Mama L and ask her a few questions. I can't shake the feeling that she has information that I need."

"It will have to be a damn good disguise. You're well known to most of the servants; they will recognize you on sight, even if you change your clothes or your hair."

"Actually, they *won't* recognize me, because they won't be looking for me. By now, it's widely known that a small, red-haired servant girl vanished at the same time as the prince. Everyone will assume that I had something to do with his disappearance. Which, of course, I did." I shot him a grin. "Besides, you would be amazed at how often people don't see things that are right in front of them simply because they don't want to see them or aren't expecting to. No one would expect me to show back up at the castle, so they won't be looking for me. Even if they were, they would be looking for a girl. When I go back, it will be as a boy."

"A boy?" Nef's eyebrows disappeared into his hairline in surprise. "And exactly how are you planning to pull *that* off, pray tell?" He eyed me critically. "You definitely look like a woman to me." His perusal turned into a playful leer. "And I should know; after all, I have inspected you thoroughly."

It was safe to say that Nef was now fully recovered from the poison; his sense of humor had come back.

"Ah, but you are forgetting one thing, my dear young man." I waggled a finger in his face before beginning to unwind the turban from my hair. "I am well-trained in the art of disguise." After flinging the length of cloth to one side, I dumped the contents of my bag onto the bed.

"I, ah, 'borrowed' a few articles of clothing while I was out today; they will help with the authenticity of any disguises that I may require." Rummaging through the pile, I pulled out several items and set them aside as I talked. "A simple band will be enough to hide my breasts, especially when covered by a loose shirt and vest that will also cover the curve of my hips. A pair of trousers and worn shoes will cover my legs and feet. I know how to walk with the more loose-legged stride that men use. It will be all right"

"What about this?" Nef ran his fingers through my hair which, freed from its restraints, tumbled loosely over my shoulders. "No boy on Manah has hair like this."

"That is where *these* come in." Reaching into the bag, I pulled out the scissors that I had gotten from Mistress Rowns.

"You're..." The words seemed to catch in his throat and he swallowed manfully before trying again. "You're going to cut off your hair?" His voice was tinged with sadness. "But, you're so proud of it." He trailed his fingers lightly down the side of my neck before running them through the silky fall of my hair to my breast.

Goose-flesh pebbled my skin in the wake of his touch and heat blossomed in my belly. I shivered as desire woke from its slumber and spread languorously through my limbs.

"And what will I run my hands through when we make love?" His voice grew husky, his gaze distant.

Nef's fingers tangled in my hair, his body – glistening with sweat - arched above me as he cried out in completion. Shaking my head, I forced the memories away. Were his thoughts similarly occupied?

"You'll, ah, you'll just have to find something else to occupy your hands." I straightened slightly, pushing my breasts forward in not-so-subtle suggestion. "Besides-" I forced myself back to the discussion at hand - "it's just hair; it will grow back." The tears running down my cheek gave lie to my casual words and I dashed them away angrily. "I'm sorry. I know that you like my hair as well. I hope..."

"Stop right there," Nef admonished as he wiped away the tears. "Yes, I *like* your hair but I *love* you - Lillie, the person. It doesn't have anything to do with how long or short your hair is. But..." His expression grew sheepish. "You aren't going to cut it *all* off, are you?"

"No, *I'm* actually not cutting my hair at all." I offered him the scissors, handle first, as if offering him a sword. "You are. I don't think that I can bring myself to do it."

His eyes widened and he licked his lips nervously as I ran a brush through my hair then wove it into a thick braid that I tied off at both ends. I instructed Nef to cut the braid off just above the upper tie. He hacked at the thick tail, gritting his teeth as he worked. I swallowed hard when the braid fell away. I didn't remember ever having short hair.

I surveyed the damage critically in the small mirror above the dresser. The ends of my hair fell just to my shoulders in a ragged cut. I ran the brush through the mass again to remove any loose pieces, then retrieved the last item from my bag of tricks - a bottle of the dye that some of the "girls" at the brothel used to darken their hair when streaks of grey appeared. I rubbed the dye through my hair and applied it to my eyebrows. Nef helped me rinse it out once it had had time to set. The resulting color was sort of a chestnut brown with just a hint of a reddish hue. Now that my hair was shorter, the natural curl had gone wild, the curls clinging tightly to my head. I could, however, still brush them out enough to pull my hair back in an acceptable queue. Standing, I quickly stripped out of my washer-woman attire and donned the breast band – wincing at the unexpected tenderness in my breasts - and the rest of the purloined clothes comprising my "young boy" disguise.

Nef whistled in appreciation as he turned me side to side. "I'm impressed. You look more like a boy than I thought possible." His eyes narrowed slightly as he studied my profile. "However, your face still has a definitely feminine shape."

"I'll rub a little dirt on it to soften the outline. It won't be perfect, but it should allow me to pass fairly easily as a pre-pubescent boy - one young enough to not have a developed Adam's apple. I definitely can't fake that. Oh! Speaking of faking...." I once again rummaged through the clothing scattered across the bed until I found what I was looking for. A few quick snips of the scissors and I relieved a garment of its pocket which I then stuffed with small pieces of rag before folding it over to form a tube of sorts. I held it up for Nef's inspection.

"What, exactly, are you going to do with that?"

I gave him a grin as I stood shoved the tube into my pants. "Well, I can't exactly be a boy without a cock, now can I?"

Nef's eyes almost bulged out of his head. "They actually teach you this stuff?"

"Of course." I lifted a newly brown brow at him. "Along with many other things. You never did ask me how I know Brava."

"You're right. And now I'm almost afraid to ask." He closed his eyes and inhaled deeply. "How do you know Brava?"

"She was one of our trainers; she was in charge of teaching us the art of seduction as well as how to pleasure both men and women."

"I take it that you didn't exactly have scrolls on the subject." Nef paled slightly.

"No, no scrolls," I laughed as I shook my head. "Only classroom training. We were a room full of young vo-yeurs. We watched Brava and her girls as they illustrated various methods of seduction and pleasuring one's partner during sex. Sometimes Brava was a participant; sometimes she was the instructor and stood by to narrate what was going on and provide details of the actions that perhaps couldn't be seen well from a distance."

Nef's shock was obvious. "You mean her clients let you *watch* them have sex?"

"They not only let us watch, they paid for the privilege. You'd be surprised how many people like performing for an audience; they find it arousing. We saw women with men, women with women, men with men, and various combinations in two and threesomes."

"Did you find it exciting?"

"I'd be lying if I said 'no' - it's hard to *not* be aroused by such. Some were more roused by the visual stimulation; others, such as me, were more aroused by the sounds. I'm a very aural person."

"That would explain why you are so noisy during sex." Apparently Nef was somewhat aural as well; he began to remove my clothes slowly, his fingers lightly teasing.

"By this point in our training, we were a bunch of hormonal teenagers – sex was never far from anyone's mind." Nor was it far from mine then as I shifted to give him easier access to my body. "The added stimulus of watching - and hearing - others have sex every day was almost unbearable. That was why nights in our room were spent in such frenzied sexual activity." My brow furrowed in realization. "Looking back on it, I think that was why it was done that way. What we saw was not sex based on affection; the masters didn't want us to associate sex with love or any sort of emotion. They presented us with this training at a time in our lives where it would be most difficult to control our reactions, and our living arrangements virtually ensured ferocious coupling with nothing more than raw need behind it, reinforcing the notion that sex has nothing to do with affection."

"And yet, you remained a virgin?" Nef sounded somewhat skeptical.

"Do you think I lied to you?"

His doubt, while understandable, still stung. I knew that my hurt was reflected on my face.

"I believe you, Lillie, but..." Nef shook his head, still seeming unsure.

"But what?"

"You said that you were a virgin, and I had no reason to doubt you. However, I had always been told that a woman's first time was painful, due to the tearing of her uh, her... maidenhead." He looked away, focusing his attention on the removal of my trousers.

"You're right. I suppose that is the normal way of things, but you must remember that little about my life has been 'normal' – I was Va'Shile. The masters leave no yaren unskinned, so to speak. Recruits are supposed to become masters of seduction and sex but there are those of us that do not become sexually active. What if I had to seduce a man, leading him to believe that I was wise in the ways of the world and well acquainted with the pleasures awaiting me from the member between his legs? If he were then to take me to bed and rupture my maidenhead, causing me pain and bleeding, he would become suspicious, and rightly so, about everything I had told him. To avoid such situations, the Va'Shile simply rupture the hymen of all female recruits before we begin our sexual training. Problem solved." However, now *my* curiosity was peaked. "Do you mean to tell me that you never bedded a virgin before?"

"Well, to be honest, I uh..." He cleared his throat. "I never bedded anyone before."

I almost fell over. "What! You were a virgin as well?"

"Well, yes, but it wasn't from lack of *trying*," he spluttered indignantly. "Aneri, my first sweetheart, said that she loved me — and that she was willing. We picked the day and snuck off behind the chicken coop..."

"The chicken coop!" I snorted with laughter. "You're such a romantic."

"We thought that we had less of a chance of being interrupted there. I had her skirts hiked up and just as I move to enter... she changed her mind. She ran off, tugging her clothing into place leaving me standing there with a massive hard-on. That sort of thing is rough on a man's confidence."

"Well, I'll be damned. You could have fooled me. Actually, you did. You certainly didn't show any hesitation and definitely seemed to know your way around." I shrugged out of my vest and raised my arms. "A handsome guy like you? Girls probably throw themselves at you all the time; you could have had your way with any one of them - or all of them. Why didn't you?"

"My mother." He stripped my shirt off over my head. "It has been pounded into my head for as long as I can remember that my family is of royal blood, and there are many that would love to carry a royal bastard. It is up to each of us to prevent that occurrence. I was implored from a young age to consider the course of my actions and to not spread my seed indiscriminately. I was told that I shouldn't have sex with anyone that I didn't care about - or anyone that I would not wish to wed to should a child be born of our lovemaking. I took those lessons to heart."

"And you chose me? I'm honored, but... why?"

"Because I *love* you, silly." He pressed himself against me, his arousal evident. "I was attracted to you from the beginning. This small girl..."

I glared at him.

"Correction." He laughed. "This young woman with something about her that caused even the most recalcitrant animals at the palace to fawn at her feet." He reached behind me and released the binding on my hair before turning his attention to my breast band. "This woman that somehow seemed so innocent and yet so worldly all at the same time. You were interesting; I was attracted to you. As I got to know you, the attraction grew and became love. And then, on the island, you offered me the most amazing gift. How could I not accept?" One work-roughened hand caressed my cheek.

I turned my head and pressed a kiss into his palm then teased it lightly with the tip of my tongue.

"Besides, with the show that you put on I had two choices: I could take you and we could pleasure each other or I could leave you there to pleasure yourself while I did the same in the bushes. Of the two, only one was acceptable." As he spoke, he dropped his hands from my face and rapidly removed his own clothes.

I cried out in ecstasy as Nef entered me. I hoped that someday I could last more than a few thrusts before exploding into orgasm, but he didn't seem to mind my hair-trigger. We came, we rested, then we did it again until we were sated or simply too exhausted to continue. If we survived this mess that we were in the middle of, I hoped that things would always be this way. I never wanted to be one of those who grew tired of their lover or complained about his "needs."

18

The next morning as I dressed in my disguise and prepared to go to the castle, Nef was in an exceptionally foul mood.

"What is the matter with you?" I finally asked.

"What am I supposed to do while you're gone? I feel fine. I don't want to keep staying in this room, but I don't know what else to do."

"Well, for a start, you can go visit Elah. She is looking forward to seeing you again. She was worried about you while you were sick. However, don't venture out into the streets; we can't take any chances on someone recognizing you." I ticked off points on my fingers as I continued. "Brava might have some things for you to help with around here, but there's a good chance that they would involve you bedding her." I narrowed my eyes in warning. "I wouldn't take that very well."

"Oh ho," he exclaimed, the corners of his eyes crinkling in amusement, "are you the jealous type then?"

"Very much so. *And* I'm not the type to just get mad and stomp my feet or throw things. I have the training to do *far* worse than that."

Nef laughed. "Don't worry; I'm not interested in bedding anyone else. I suspect that I have my hands full with you." He gave me a hug. "And that's all right with me." All signs of amusement disappeared as he added, "Be careful; come back safely."

"I will." I hugged him back then quickly turned and left the room, still wondering what excuse I would give as my reason for requesting an audience with Mama L.

Maybe Brava would have a recommendation. I found her in Mistress Rowns' quarters going through the clothing that lined the walls. They were busily preparing the cold weather apparel for storage until the next winter, as well as pulling out the items requiring repair.

"Good morning, ladies," I called as I entered the room.

Both women stared and Mistress Rowns obviously did not like what she saw; she plowed her way through the sea of fabric like a barge. It was obvious that she planned to bodily remove me.

"Young man, I don't know how you got in here or why you are here, but I must ask you to leave at once." She flapped her apron at me in a shooing motion as she approached.

I stepped back but didn't leave and continued to look at Brava steadily. She returned my gaze calmly. Mistress Rowns reached for my arm.

"Stop there, Rowns," Brava said. "He may stay." She stepped closer and studied my disguise critically. After turning me in order to get the full effect from all sides, she nodded in satisfaction. "Well done, child. Please wait for me in my quarters. I will join you shortly."

I gave a small bow and retreated as directed. I had not missed the fact that she did not reveal my identity to Mistress Rowns, who apparently still did not recognize me.

Brava did not rush to meet me, nor did I expect her to. She would complete her current task first. I was too restless to sit quietly and took advantage of the opportunity to explore her parlor. I had not been there in several years and had been in no condition to look at the details when Nef and I made our hasty, unannounced arrival.

The room was elegantly decorated, probably not what most would expect from a madam. The furniture was of high quality, the wood burnished to a warm gleam. The upholstery on the chairs and sofa was plush, the padding comfortable. Candlelight flickered from sconces on the walls. Woven rugs covered the floor and wallpaper in alternating stripes of pink and burgundy covered the walls. It was not my taste, but everything worked well together. However, when examined closely, small details pointed to Brava's sense of humor. For example, the candlesticks placed on the low tables throughout the room were actually dildos. The artwork lining the walls was really quite lovely, but there were a few pictures that made me giggle upon closer inspection. My particular favorite depicted what appeared to be a couple picnicking beside a stream, the gentleman's head resting in his companion's lap as they relaxed after their meal. Only a closer look revealed the truth; the front of the woman's skirt was shoved up around her hips and her head was thrown back in ecstasy as the man's mouth pressed firmly between her legs. Brava was a woman with both class and high standards, but she was not ashamed of her chosen profession, as displayed in those subtle reminders.

Eventually, Brava swept into the room closing the door behind her. She leaned against it, crossing her arms on her chest and surveying me critically. "I hope you have a good reason for cutting off your beautiful hair?"

I nodded. "Vido is trying to kill me. I suspect that is has something to do with my parents and my birth, but I don't know what. Mama L, the head housekeeper at the palace, knows something; I've got to talk to her, find out what it is. The only way I stand a chance to get back into the palace is as a messenger boy, or something similar. I couldn't successfully disguise myself as a male without cutting my hair." I couldn't help but sigh as I repeated what was becoming my silent mantra. "It will grow back."

"True enough. I suppose that Mistress Rowns' reaction was enough to let you know that your disguise is a success. However, I suspect that that is not the reason that you came looking for me. Is there something that I can help you with?"

"I hope so. I have altered my appearance enough that I should be able to infiltrate the palace successfully." I began pacing as I talked. "However, I haven't come up with a good excuse to request an audience with Mama L. If I don't have a decent reason, I won't get past the gates, much less into the palace itself."

"I'm sure that I can come up with something." Brava crossed the room, moved the tabby tom that was sleeping on her chair and sat at her writing desk, pulling out parchment, ink, and a quill. She tapped the feather thoughtfully against her cheek as she considered. She brightened as inspiration struck. "Yes, yes, that will do nicely." The quill scratched faintly against the paper as she scribbled busily. Once the ink dried she sealed the letter and gave it to me. "Tell the guards that I hired you to deliver this message to

Mama L and that you have been instructed to give it to no one but her."

"Thank you." I shoved the letter into a pocket and strode to the door. My steps faltered as I reached the threshold and I rested one hand on the doorframe as I turned back to face Brava. "Nef is becoming restless. If you have any chores that you can give him to keep him occupied, I would appreciate it. Keeping in mind," I continued with a scowl, "that his 'services' belong to me - and I don't like to share."

"Don't worry, child." Brava laughed girlishly as she tucked a strand of hair behind her ear. "I won't poach on your territory. I'm sure that I could teach him a thing or two, but I have no doubt that you can teach him as well as I."

Giving her a wave, I turned to leave once again.

"Do you remember your lessons on how to prevent pregnancy?"

Uh oh. I could almost feel her gaze on my back.

"Yes, of course." I looked at my mentor but couldn't quite meet her eyes. I spoke directly to her left earlobe. "Why do you ask?"

"I just want to make sure that you are taking the proper precautions." Her unspoken question demanded an answer.

"We are careful." Wincing, I braced myself for a well-deserved tongue-lashing when I added, "Sometimes." When no outburst was forthcoming, I forced myself to meet her dark brown regard.

I couldn't help but be suspicious when she waved me away, almost casually.

"Ah, well, be careful, little one. Your life is not the only one in danger."

"I know. That is why I am leaving Nef with you. He will be safe here."

Brava gazed at me steadily as she shook her head. "Yes, your Nef is in danger, but that is not the one of whom I speak." She glanced pointedly at my abdomen. "I speak of the child that you carry."

The blood drained from my face as my legs forgot how to support me. I slid down the doorframe until my ass hit the floor and then rested my forehead on my knees. I probably should have seen this coming but I didn't. Or maybe I did; I had brutally silenced any little voices that tried to tell me what I didn't want to hear. My reaction startled Brava into action; she rushed to kneel by my side and patted my hand gently.

"How long have you been lovers?"

"Several weeks. I knew this could happen. I just didn't want to admit it, especially with the recent turn of events." I looked at her, my confusion evident. "How did *you* know?"

"I saw you naked the other day – remember? In this business, I've seen enough women with child to recognize the physical changes. Your breasts are tender, are they not? And you feel the need to piss all the time?"

I nodded in response to both questions.

"You must take care of yourself, little one, for everyone's sake. After all, you are carrying an heir to the throne."

The blood that had started to return to my face retreated. I should have known; Brava probably knew Nef's true identity all along.

"I'm not even going to ask how you knew who Nef is." I closed my eyes, struggling to ward off the lightheadedness that threatened to overwhelm me.

The swish of skirts was followed by the sound of liquid being poured.

"Drink this." Brava returned to my side, pressing a cup into my hand.

I accepted without question and gulped eagerly at the contents — fruit juice.

"The sugar will give you energy. Stop by the kitchen and get a snack before you leave. You're eating for two now." She patted my knee in an almost motherly fashion, before rising to her feet and returning to her desk. "Please let me know when you return. I will rest easier when I know that you are safe."

Once the shock passed and I felt capable of walking, I proceeded to the kitchen as instructed and grabbed fruit to munch during my journey to the palace.

19

"Eww – lookit the guts!"

"And the bugs!"

"Them ain't bugs – they's maggots."

A group of boys in ragged clothing knelt in the dirt at the side of the road. I decided to delay my trip to the palace long enough to put my disguise to the ultimate test and joined them. As I walked up, one industrious soul – apparently the leader of the group – poked at the stiffening remains of a cat with a stick, his bravado eliciting more sounds of fascinated disgust from his followers.

"What happened?" I asked, dropping to my knees and leaning over to peer at the corpse, my stomach roiling at the smell.

"I bet it got stepped on by a horse," a tow-headed boy offered.

"Or run over by a cart." This statement came from a lad with hair the color of flame and a face dotted with freckles; he looked ready to argue his point.

"Nuh-uh," I disagreed dropping my voice slightly. "Look 'ere," I pointed to wounds on the side of the cat's neck. "See them holes? It got bit by somethin' big – probably a dog."

"Oooh!" The circle grew smaller as the boys' heads moved closer together while they examined the body.

I pushed to my feet. "I gotta go before I git in trouble." I backed out of the group, struggling with the urge to brush the dirt from the knees of my pants; doing so might make them suspicious. What boy would be worried about a little dirt on his clothes?

I trotted the rest of the way to the palace bridge, flush with satisfaction.

"Stop right there," a uniformed man growled. "Where do you think yer goin'?"

I stopped my forward momentum as ordered, but fidgeted from one foot to the other. Palace security had been obviously been tightened; normally one didn't encounter sentries until the palace gate proper.

I dug in my pocket and pulled out the rather crumpled parchment. "I got to give this -" I waved it absently - "to some lady named Mistress Lalane."

"Give me that!" He snatched the letter from my hand and scowled, his dark brows almost meeting as he flipped the paper over, studying the wax seal. "Hmph. Looks real enough." He handed it back, flicking his free hand toward the palace. "Go on."

Just to irritate him, I dawdled as I crossed the bridge, gazing in fascination at the muddy water flowing beneath my feet. I even leaned out far enough at one point to spit over the side and watch the fish rush to the surface in search of food.

The sentinel at the entry to the palace courtyard grinned as he watched my approach; he was a much more amiable sort. "Well, well. What have we here? What brings you here, young man?"

"Madam Brava hired me to bring a note to Mistress Lalane." I patted my pockets frantically as if searching for the missive and heaved an exaggerated sigh of relief as I pulled it out and presented it for his inspection.

"Madam Brava? *The* Madam Brava?"

"I guess." I shrugged. "Is she important or somethin'?"

"*Important* is one word that could be used I guess." The guard chuckled, scratching thoughtfully at his crotch. "I won't damage your tender ears with the others. I don't know what the madam could have to say to Mama L, but that's between them I guess. Proceed, young man." He opened the gate and motioned me into the courtyard with a playful bow.

I passed many familiar faces, but their expressions were grim. The atmosphere of the palace had changed

- even the dogs seemed serious. One of the lurchers recognized me and got to his feet, the tip of his tail twitching in greeting. I sent warm, but warning thoughts his way. *It's good to see you but it's important that no one recognize me; you must stay away. I'm sorry.* I included a mental pat on the head. He seemed to understand and sat back down, but still panted happily in my direction.

I couldn't walk directly to the kitchens; a young messenger on his first trip to the palace wouldn't know his way around. I stopped the nearest person and asked where I could find Mistress Lalane; he pointed vaguely across the courtyard. At the kitchen door, I asked again. I was in luck; she was on the far side of the room.

Entering the cavernous room felt like coming home and my heart ached with a sudden sadness. Tamping down my emotions, I scampered between the servants busily preparing for the midday meal and stopped before Mama L, waiting for her to acknowledge me.

"May I help you?" Her violet gaze was as inscrutable as ever.

Still, it was as if she saw straight through me.

"This is fer you." I handed her the crumpled letter. "It's from Madam Brava."

Only the raising of one elegant brow hinted at Mama L's feelings at receiving the note.

"She -" I waved vaguely in the direction of The Narrows - "told me to stay here until you write her back." I crossed my arms over my chest and widened my stance as if to make myself immovable.

"Wait there, please" she directed, pointing to a table in the corner. Raising her voice, she called out, "Cook, please give our young friend here a snack while I address this message." Mama L stepped into the small room that served as her office and closed the door.

Cook brought me a cup of fresh milk and a slice of freshly baked chocolate cake. There were definitely advantages to the messenger business. I munched happily, swinging my feet as I ate. I was just finishing my snack when Mama L opened her door slightly.

"Young man," she called, one slim hand beckoning me to join her.

Stepping into the small room, I closed the door behind me and, at her gesture, took the empty seat on the far side of the small table that she used as a desk. She stared at the table top for a long moment, seemingly gathering her thoughts. Taking a deep breath, she looked up.

"I know who you are."

Who I was, not *what*. At least we had taken a step in the right direction.

"Ma'am?" I tried to sound, and look, confused – it wasn't difficult.

"You can drop the pretense, Lillie." She looked me over carefully, a small smile playing at the corner of her mouth. "Although, I have to give you credit. Your disguise is excellent; I probably wouldn't have recognized you without this." She held the letter out to me. "See for yourself."

I took the paper and read.

Cissy,

I am sending you this note in order to aid a mutual friend. The messenger delivering this epistle is actually Lillie, a young woman that until recently worked as a servant under your authority. Lillie's life is in danger. She needs the information that you have concerning her family. For the sake of our friendship, I ask that you tell her what you know. Please do nothing to reveal her identity to others.

Remembering you fondly,
Brava

"*You* know Madam Brava?" Doubt tinged my voice; the two of them couldn't be any more different.

"Brava and I were close many years ago; she helped me during a very difficult time." She looked away, into the past. "Would it surprise you to learn that I was raised in The Narrows?"

Surprise? *Shock* was more like it. Her air of calm reserve was not one that I associated with life in The Narrows. I nodded vigorously once I realized that it wasn't a rhetorical question.

"I was an exceptionally foolish young woman, thrilled to catch the eye of a handsome man." She smiled sardonically. "Of course, I was only one of many to share Vido's bed."

"Vido! As in the head of the Va'Shile?"

"Yes." She shrugged. "I found the air of danger surrounding him... exciting." She smiled. "Few things in my life to that point could be considered so. And the fact that a simple girl such as I had caught the eye of someone like him, well... I considered it an honor." She began toying with the inkwell on her desk as she talked.

"My enthusiasm wore off quickly; it didn't take me long to learn that Vido was a cruel man. He was abusive and enjoyed - for lack of a better word - 'torturing' others." She looked back at me, her frown aging her. "I remember once when an informant came to Vido at the tavern where we were dining. The poor man looked like a whipped dog. He had given Vido false information; he had decided, poorly as it were, to attempt to be a double agent and had tipped the victim off to the fact that Vido was planning to kill him. The victim paid the man to lie to Vido." She shook her head. "A very big mistake. The man practically crawled to Vido, apologizing profusely, and begging for forgiveness." She looked at me intently, her violet eyes narrowed. "Vido does not forgive - *ever*. Never believe otherwise."

She stood and attempted to pace, unsuccessfully, before taking her seat again. "Vido did everything except pat the man on the head as he assured him that all was forgiven. He even invited him to dine with us. It was sad to watch the poor man as he fawned over Vido, sure that he had escaped with his life. He had not. When the man stood to leave, Vido stood with him, placing his arm around the man's shoulder in a friendly fashion. A knife appeared in his free hand and he slit the man's throat. As the man lay on the floor, his blood staining the floorboards, Vido knelt over him. 'No one double-crosses me and lives,' he said.

"The only sounds in the room were the crackling of the fire and the gasps of the dying man. Vido looked at the others patrons and added, 'Let this be a lesson.' No one said a word; everyone returned to their meals in silence. However, I knew that before morning, everyone in The Narrows would know what had happened and that people would be lining up at the door of the guild house to tell Vido the location of his intended victim.

"It was then that I truly realized just what sort of man I had become involved with." Mama L's slim fingers trembled slightly as she plucked absently at her skirt. "However, I dared not break off the relationship. Vido was not one to have his wishes thwarted; it was best to let *him* tire of me and cast me aside so that he could move on to new conquests. It happened soon enough.

"Early one evening we were walking through the streets of The Narrows, on our way to whatever hovel he had chosen for the night's liaison." She looked up at me through dark lashes as she continued, "Vido never slept in the same bed two nights in a row, and there was no pattern to his choices. He knew that there were those that would gladly kill him and he did nothing to make it easy for them. Those of us that he took as lovers slept in the nude; we were not allowed to keep our clothing with us during the night so that we wouldn't be able to smuggle in a weapon and kill him as he slept.

"But, there was something different that night. I could feel the tension in Vido; he radiated an excitement that had nothing to do with impending sex. As we walked, I got the sense that he was looking for someone. I was correct. One of the small squares contained merchants selling various goods; a few people lingered near the stalls, surveying the wares. Among these people was a family; a man with golden hair and green eyes accompanied by a striking Southron woman. They were holding the hands of a small child with glorious red hair that fell in ringlets to her shoulders."

I gasped.

"Yes, Lillie." Mama L nodded. "It was you. You were all laughing together as your parents shopped. You were happy." Both her head and her voice dropped. "Vido walked up behind the man and spoke quietly. The man wheeled around; a look of fear flickered briefly across his face, only to be replaced by a small smile as he said 'Hello Vido.'

"Vido nodded agreeably enough, but I saw his hand twitch at his side. 'Yes, Marco. You knew this day would come. No one walks away from the Va'shile - especially not to marry a Southron whore.' Marco turned to the woman and the child, pushing them away, urging them to run. Vido grabbed Marco by the shoulder, turning him around. As Marco turned, Vido plunged his knife into his chest, then pulled it out and slit his throat as he crumpled to the ground. The woman was stunned and had only taken a few steps." Mama L closed her eyes as if to shut out the memories. "Vido was on her before she could move farther and murdered her as well. However, it was not enough for him to simply kill her; he also mutilated her body in ways that he apparently felt appropriate for a 'Southron whore.'"

When she opened her eyes again, they were filled with pain.

"Fortunately, you saw little of his actions. I pulled you to me, pressing your face into my skirts. You clutched at me, crying in fear. Vido calmly surveyed his handiwork, wiping the blood from his hands and knife onto your parents' clothing. He then came and watched you for a moment. You looked at him with tear-stained eyes, still calling for your parents. Vido slapped you, told you to shut up. I pulled you closer, but he snatched you out of my arms.

"When the smell of the blood reached me, I vomited in revulsion. Vido watched with disgust. He tossed a couple of gold coins at my feet and announced that my 'services' were no longer required - it was obvious that I was too weak to be with him. Then he turned and walked away, taking you with him.

"I was free – and not a moment too soon." Mama L rested one hand lightly on her abdomen. "I was with child and had longed to get away from him before it became obvious. I returned to my family, but they put me out on the streets when they learned of my condition - and who had fathered the babe." She fell silent, watching me.

My thoughts – and stomach - whirled as I struggled to process what I had been told; the chocolate cake was in grave danger of reappearing. Mama L recognized the warning signs and discretely slid the chamber pot that had been hidden in the corner into easy reach should I need it.

I finally found my voice and plucked a statement from the swarm that buzzed around me vying for attention. "My parents didn't sell me, that bastard killed them!" An anger stronger than anything that I had ever felt before surged through me.

Mama L laid a soothing hand on my arm. "Yes. Your father turned his back on the guild – on Vido. A man like that would consider raising you to become an assassin the ultimate revenge. But, there is more that you should know."

"I really don't think I can handle any more right now." I wanted to curl into a ball and sob helplessly –

right after I finished throwing things. Breakable things. Lots of them.

"You must." Mama L's voice grew stern. "I do not know if we will have the chance to speak again. I must take this opportunity to tell you what I know. As I said, your mother was Southron but she was also royalty and..."

And? Oh, joy.

"I don't know how much you know about the ruling family of the Southron continent, but they are said to have special powers; some would call it 'magic.'"

"My mother really was a Southron witch?" My voice held a note verging on hysteria.

Mama L nodded.

I threw up. Then, I fainted.

20

When I regained consciousness the ever efficient Mama L knelt by me, applying a cold cloth to my forehead.

"Welcome back." She smiled as she looked me over carefully. "Do you think you can sit up?"

I nodded and she helped me into a sitting position, my back against the wall for support before returning to her chair.

"How often does the sickness strike you? How far along are you?"

Color rushed to my face. "Is my condition so obvious to everyone? You're the second person today to confront me - Brava was the first. You have both seen easily what I was not willing to admit to myself.

And yet, everyone else seems to accept me as the young boy that I appear to be."

Apparently deciding that I was no longer in danger of fainting again, Mama L helped me get up and back into my chair. "Brava and I both know that you are, in fact, not a boy *and* we are both very familiar with young women that are with child. You will be able to carry off your current disguise for now, but not much longer. It won't be long before you will begin to show and, as your milk comes in, your breasts will be too sore to be bound so tightly. Is Nef the father?"

I nodded. Again. I was getting good at it.

"Then your child is doubly royal which means that you are in even greater danger than you know. Vido will want your life for your failure to kill Nef. But, if he were to learn that you are with child - and by whom - he would not hesitate to take you prisoner until the child is born and then kill you. With such a child, he could blackmail the ruling families of both continents and perhaps even find a way to be made ruler himself as regent."

The mere thought made my stomach churn again. It was amazing how I wasn't affected by sickness at all until I knew that I was pregnant.

"That *will not* happen." I forced the nausea away and pushed to my feet, speaking through gritted teeth. "Vido will not do to my child what he did to me. I must go." I stumbled toward the door.

"Wait. Let me prepare a reply to Brava. After all, she is expecting a response." She pulled out a fresh piece of parchment and wrote quickly as I read over her shoulder.

B -
I thank you for your concern, but the services of your girls are not required. There are women enough in the palace willing to spread their legs; outside assistance in providing 'stress relief' during this difficult time is not required.
Regards,
C

I snorted.

Silence fell as we waited for the ink to dry.

Never having been one to tolerate quiet for long, I resumed my seat and asked "How did you meet Brava?"

"After my family kicked me out I took odd jobs where I could, but my baby was born early. I had no one to care for her while I worked and she was too small and weak to take with me. I resorted to sleeping in stables and scrounging scraps from the trash." She grimaced as she remembered. "I was starving – and so was my daughter. Brava found me behind the brothel, picking up moldy bread thrown out by the cook. She took us in, gave us a room and nursed us back to health. We owe her our lives."

"And the Va'Kyrian?"

"I thought they were just a… a… fairy tale told to the children of The Narrows to give them hope. The hope of a better life, the hope that someone cared enough to make a difference for those of use that weren't born to nobility. Once I regained my strength, I ran errands for Brava in exchange for allowing us to stay at the brothel, but we couldn't stay there forever. One day when I was in the market I was approached by a woman; she acted like she knew me." Mama L stared at the candle on her desk, the flame flickering as she spoke.

"She said that she had been watching me and asked if I wanted to make a better life for myself and child or if I wanted to stay at the brothel and eventually become a whore." Her expression grew grim. "That was the *last* thing that I wanted – never again would I be dependent on a man for my well-being.

"She took me to meet the leaders of the Va'Kyrian; it wasn't pleasant." Her nose wrinkled as she remembered. "They grilled me about my family, my time with Vido, and my daughter. Once they were satisfied that I had no ties to the Va'Shile, I learned that they protect the throne, guarding it for its rightful owners. They also protect those who can't protect themselves. I joined them and learned to fight – and how to protect what is mine. They gave me a home, security, and a purpose - I would give my life for the Va'Kyrian, if necessary."

"And your daughter? Where is she?"

"She is with the Va'Kyrian – for now." A pained look flashed briefly across Mama L's face. "My daughter is beautiful and intelligent. She is also restless and wild. I fear that she is very much her father's daughter. We have agreed – after much arguing – that she will complete her training with the Va'Kyrian. After that she is free to leave and make a life for herself however she sees fit."

Bringing our discussion to an end, she folded the now dry letter and sealed it with a bit of wax. As she moved, her sleeve fell back revealing the gold and ruby bonding bracelet purchased by Jehrold in MidTown. I reached for her wrist and held it so that the light glittered off the stones.

"You said *yes*? What about never depending on a man again?"

"I do not *need* Jehrold to defend me or pay my way in the world – I am more than capable of both." Her face softened as she pulled her sleeve back down and smiled up at me. "However, I *love* him and want him to be a part of my life - and to be a part of his." The smile became decidedly wicked as she added, "Besides, he makes a rather pleasant bed warmer."

"Good. I like Jehrold – I hope that you will be very happy together."

Mama L placed the sealed note in my hand, folded my fingers around it and squeezed gently. "Please tell Brava that it was good to hear from her and that I remember her friendship with great fondness. Now, you should go so that you can get back to her before it grows dark." She gave me a brief hug. "Take care of yourself – and your family."

My family. By the Makers! I finally had the one thing that I had wanted for as long as I could remember. Now all I had to do was figure out a way to keep us alive.

I rambled slowly on my return to MidTown as would any young boy, stopping to throw stones in the river and wandering through the market gazing in feigned awe at the wares displayed there. One industrious entrepreneur had taken advantage of the warm weather to set up a stall selling freshly cooked meat pasties. The savory smell had drawn a crowd; I allowed myself to be drawn into the edge of the throng.

A noblewoman crowded against me, which struck me as odd; there was plenty of room, she didn't need to be so close. I understood her intentions when she placed herself between me and the vendor, casually maneuvering me away from the crowd. I stumbled over a cobblestone and caught myself, my back against a wall. This position played into her desires nicely. She pressed closer and stroked my cheek, almost purring.

"Such a smooth young face, just the way I like them." Her hand began to drop lower, caressing my neck and wandering to the buttons of my shirt. I attempted to move away, but she was stronger than she looked. "You look hungry. I'll buy you as many pies as you like if you will come back to my house with me."

Without warning, her hand dropped to my crotch; I jumped in surprise. Fortunately, her hand brushed the codpiece as I turned away.

"Very nice, young one." She practically purred. "You will be quite a marvel once your growth spurt hits, I'm sure. In the meantime, I can instruct you on how to use this equipment with which you have been blessed."

I managed to get my hand in front of hers before she could discover that my "equipment" wasn't real. "I... I'm sorry my lady, but my... my mistress is saving me for a special occasion; I think she intends to provide my instruction herself."

The noblewoman laughed, drawing away reluctantly. "I'm sure she is! Such a shame." She waved me away. "You should return to your mistress quickly, little one, before I change my mind."

"Yes, my lady." I managed an appropriately awkward bow and worked my way quickly through the crowd, the woman's laugh following. Her willingness to do everything except molest a young boy in broad daylight had my fingers itching. My dagger was in its usual location on my thigh – I was willing to remove one more pedophile from the world. I could do so easily – but not in front of so many witnesses. I gritted my teeth and continued my journey.

Once back at the brothel I went to Brava's office to deliver Mama L's response but she wasn't in. I left the note on the desk, under the watchful eye of her faithful tabby, for her to peruse at her leisure.

When I got back to our room, Nef wasn't there. I stomped my foot. Not necessarily the best way to rid myself of my childish persona.

"Where *is* everyone?" I spoke to the empty room.

The stairs creaked slightly; I whirled just as the top of the elderly cleaning woman's head came into view. She was stooped almost in half from age and arthritis and moved slowly and deliberately.

"Can I help you, child?" she wheezed.

"Yes, please. I am looking for the young man that I was told is staying in this room."

"Oh, that one. I believe that the madam has put him to work in the stables. Perhaps you can find him there."

"Thank you, old one." I gave her a respectful bow before darting around her and scampering down the steps.

A familiar tune drifted from the stable door as I approached; Nef's happy whistle. I darted in, eager to see him, and skidded to a halt on the straw strewn cobblestones at the sight of the blond head just visible over the top of the nearest stall.

"Excuse me," I called, not wanting to startle the stranger. "Have you seen a dark-haired young man? In his early twenties?"

The blond turned to face me, his eyes creasing at the corners. I heard the smile in his voice.

"Lillie, it's me."

The voice was Nef's, but the face was not. Or was it? As I moved closer, I realized that it was indeed Nef's amazing blue eyes looking back at me and his dimples when he smiled, but his hair...

Nef's wavy black locks had been replaced by straight, golden brown hair; small braids ran from his temples around the back of his head, where they were held in place with a plain wooden clasp. Even his eyebrows had been lightened to the same golden shade. It was such a basic change, but the effect was astonishing.

"Impressive." I circled him slowly, studying the changes.

Master Jaidon taught us that the best disguises were usually the simplest. The more elaborate, the more opportunities for something to go drastically long. With just a few changes, Nef had become almost unrecognizable.

I stepped closer, reaching up to touch his face, still needing to reassure myself that it was really him. Nef slid his arms around me, backed me against the wall of the stall and kissed me enthusiastically. I stood on my toes, sliding my arms around his neck and deepened the kiss.

Nef chuckled, the vibration rumbling through his chest.

"What?" I mumbled against his lips.

He pulled away, his eyes twinkling. "Anyone walking by will think that I have a marked preference for young boys." He stroked my hair, playing with the shortened curls.

"That would only give extra credence to your disguise. People would wonder if Brava had a pederast as a stable boy, or if she was expanding her business to include those with a more... varied taste."

"Perhaps we should go inside then." Nef glanced around uneasily. "Either would draw unwanted attention to both Brava and myself."

I kissed him again for good measure. "That's fine; the three of us should talk. There is a lot that we need to discuss."

Hand in hand, we went in search of Brava.

21

We sprawled sleepily across the couches in Brava's parlor, the remains of a sumptuous meal scattered on the table in front of us. Brava handfed the cats choice tidbits from her plate.

Stretching noisily, I broke the silence. "Vido is behind the attack on Nef and he wants me dead. I'm not certain, but I think that he's making a power play. He believes the king to be weak - which he is - and feels that his position has been further damaged by the lack of a viable heir. Obviously, that's the reason that he wanted Nef out of the picture. We need to know what his plans are so that we can develop one of our own."

"Vido is dangerous, yes, and we must get rid of him, for both of your sakes - and the lives of untold others;

he will not hesitate to kill anyone that he feels stands in the way of what he wants." Brava was quick on the uptake as always. "However, the Va'Shile is made up of more than one man. When Vido dies, there will be someone more than willing to step into his place; someone that may turn out to be even more brutal than he is."

When Vido dies, not *if*. I liked the way Brava thought.

"We need someone on the inside," Nef chimed in.

Both he and Brava looked at me expectantly.

I shook my head. "No. It's too risky for me to try to infiltrate the Va'Shile. Vido knows me well and there are too many others that might recognize me."

"Neither of us wants you to put yourself in danger," Brava assured me.

Nef nodded vigorously in agreement.

"However, you know the Va'Shile. Is there someone on the inside that you can trust? Someone who you can approach for assistance?"

I sat in silence for a few moments, considering. A few days ago, my immediate response would have been "No." We all knew that most, if not all, of our fellow assassins would stab us in the back – possibly literally - just as easily, if not more so, than they would help us. However, my recent conversation with Master Jaidon caused me to hesitate. His revelation that he had been keeping an eye on me as a promise to my father had come as a surprise, but I believed him. If there was anyone who I was willing to trust, it would be him.

"Master Jaidon. I know where he is staying, but I can't go there myself. My safe house has been compromised; he warned me not to go back - to do so would be to put myself back into Vido's hands."

"I have an idea."

Nef and I listened carefully as Brava outlined her plan to bring Master Jaidon to us. We offered our thoughts and tweaked the idea until it was acceptable to everyone.

"Very well, I will implement it tomorrow." Standing, she rang the bell for the serving girl. "Now, you should return to your room and rest. I suspect that we are going to be busy for a while."

Nef and I were quiet as we returned to our room. It was late and we began preparing for bed as soon as we arrived. I undressed slowly, examining my body. The slight physical changes of pregnancy that Brava had pointed out to me earlier were now very evident. I must have been in serious denial not to have been aware of them earlier. My breasts, while still small, had developed a certain fullness that they had not had before; my nipples and the surrounding skin had also taken on a slightly darker hue. I slid my hand casually over my belly as I removed my trousers, noticing the slight fullness there as well. I looked up to find Nef watching me curiously.

Ablutions complete, we crawled into bed and spooned together, still quiet. Nef began stroking my hair idly, speaking softly, almost as though he were afraid of breaking the silence.

"Lillie? Is everything all right? You've seemed a little... distracted this evening."

"Yes, everything is fine. At least, I think it is." I pulled away slightly and rolled on my side to face him before continuing. "I'm not sure the best way to say this, so I'm just going to come out with it. I'm pregnant." I held my breath as I waited for his response.

"Really?" An amazing array of emotions crossed his face, finally settling into one of incredulity; his tone was one of wonder.

"Really." I began breathing normally again.

He rolled me gently onto my back and propped himself up on one elbow so that he could look at my body; a fairly easy task since we had fallen into the habit of sleeping in the nude. He studied my breasts, carefully cupping them in his hand as if feeling the extra weight for the first time. He then gently traced the darkened skin around my nipples before finally sliding his hand lower to spread it almost reverently across my belly. He turned his face away as he caressed his unborn child. When he turned back to look at me, his eyes shimmered with tears.

"My child? Our child?"

I nodded again, relieved by his reaction.

"Lillie, I don't know what to say. That is... amazing. Thank you." He leaned over and kissed me passionately.

I returned the kiss happily.

"Why didn't you tell me sooner?"

"I didn't know. Or, I guess maybe I did, but I hadn't admitted it to myself. However, after having it pointed out to me today by two different people, I couldn't deny it any more. So, I told you as soon as I could."

"Who told you?" Nef laid back down next to me, his head on my shoulder, his hand still splayed protectively across my stomach.

"Brava and Mama L. They've both been around enough pregnant women to recognize even the earliest signs. However, Mama L told me something else that you should know."

"What?" He moved his hand from its position on my abdomen; its current location displayed an intent more amorous than protective.

"Do you remember when you teased me about being a Southron witch?"

His head nodded against my shoulder, his explorations making it increasingly difficult to concentrate.

"It's true, my mother - *ah!* – my mother was a member of the Southron royal family - she really *was* a Southron witch."

Nef's head jerked up, his fingers stilling.

Damn. Just when things were getting interesting.

"Your mother was of royal blood? Our child is heir to two thrones?" He sounded more than a little shocked.

"Apparently so - yet another reason that Vido must be dealt with. He knows my parentage. As Mama L pointed out, if he were to learn that I am with child by you, he would kill you and hold me hostage until the birth of the child and then kill me." I rolled my hips, pressing myself against his hand, encouraging him to return to his earlier actions. "With our child, he would have power in both countries and could conceivably even rule in its place as regent someday."

"Maker's teeth, Lillie! You were only gone a few hours and you come back and tell me all of this? I'm not letting you go anywhere else; I'm not sure I could handle the debriefing."

"Well, if you are going to keep me here, you are going to have to find a way to keep me occupied..." I grinned as I let my hands begin some explorations of their own.

"I can do that," he began as he rolled on top of me then froze. Just as suddenly, he rolled away.

"What's wrong?"

"The baby. I don't want to hurt it."

I couldn't help but giggle. "Brava assures me that unless there are difficulties with the pregnancy, it's all right for a woman to remain sexually active." I slid my hand between us and wrapped it around the length of his erection, squeezing gently.

It responded enthusiastically.

"Besides, I'm fairly sure that conception occurred during one of the first times that we were together and we have made love several times since then, so don't worry. He will be fine."

"He?" Nef looked at me curiously.

My words surprised me as much as they did him. Spreading my hand over my belly I became aware that I could actually sense the new life growing in me - a boy. Once again, I couldn't describe *how* I knew, but I definitely *knew*.

Filled with wonder, I looked back at him and nodded. "Apparently Southron witches can do more than just communicate with animals; our child is unquestionably a boy. And he will be fine if you make love to his mother."

Nef obliged me graciously, touching me as if I were something delicate, precious. It was a feeling that I could get used to. The presence of our child and the knowledge that we would be parents in a few months, coupled with the untold dangers still ahead took our love making to a completely different level.

22

The next morning, Nef and I joined Brava in her quarters for breakfast. In the middle of our meal, there was a knock at the door and a young boy entered without waiting to be acknowledged. Brava merely raised an eyebrow at his impudence.

"My cocky young friend here has proved himself useful on many occasions. I have full confidence in both his ability and his discretion."

His small chest swelled with pride as she spoke.

I told the boy where I suspected that Master Jaidon would be found and quizzed him until I was certain that he knew the correct location. I also gave him a sealed message to deliver, instructing him to wait for a response. I gave him a general description of Jaidon, but assured the boy that he would deny being the man that he sought. I told him to give him the message only if he were relatively certain that the man to whom he spoke was the one that we required. Hence, the physical description - Jaidon might be disguised, but there were some characteristics that he could not easily change.

Brava gave the boy a small basket filled with bits of ribbon and lace. He would go from house to house selling the tidbits as his cover while searching for the master. With the note securely in his pocket and basket firmly in hand, he scampered out the door as only a child could, letting it slam behind him. His footsteps quickly faded into the distance.

Now that the messenger was gone, the waiting began. Have I mentioned that I was never very good at waiting? Apparently, neither were the others. We were all somewhat used to being in charge of our own destinies; putting our fates into the hands of a small boy, no matter how capable, put us all on edge. It wasn't long before we were all sniping at each other. Brava finally kicked us out, insisting that we find some way to amuse ourselves. She promised to send for us as soon as her errand boy returned.

I didn't think it was a good idea for us to return to our room; the close quarters and our nerves would not be a good combination. Instead, we went to the stables to visit Elah. We arrived to find her curled up in the hay, a couple of Brava's cats snuggled against her. The cats appeared to be supremely happy with themselves for finding such a warm, sheltered location; Elah looked extremely pleased to have the company.

Nef and I split up; he fed Elah some fruit he had stashed in his pocket, then got her to her feet and gave her a thorough brushing all the while talking to her like the good friend that she was. Elah whickered contentedly, happy thoughts rolling off of her like water. I took advantage of her preoccupation to replace the used straw bedding with fresh.

The physical activity did us both good and gave us a chance to work through some of our nervous energy. Chores completed and nerves settled, we leaned against the stall wall as Elah and her new friends settled down for a nap. I slid my arms around Nef's waist, laying my head on his chest; he kissed me gently on the head. We stood quietly, neither of us speaking. The silence was shattered by one of Brava's girls entering the stable.

"Excuse me, um... sirs. Brava asks that you attend to her at your earliest convenience." She bobbed a quick curtsey and walked away, glancing at us a couple of times over her shoulder.

I buried my face in Nef's chest in an attempt to muffle my laughter. "Apparently, our disguises are still working. It will be all over the brothel by nightfall that Brava is entertaining a couple of pederasts." Stretching, I kissed him firmly on the lips, wondering if our messenger was watching from around the corner. "Come on then, we don't want to keep our hostess waiting." I took him firmly by the hand and led him back inside.

Brava was waiting for us patiently. She had changed out of her dressing gown into a simple, but elegant muslin gown. As we entered, she held up a note.

"Is that...?" I began.

She nodded, smiling. "I haven't opened it yet. I will leave that honor up to you." She handed it to me with a flourish.

My hands shaking in anticipation, I ripped it open and read quickly, a sigh of relief escaping from my lips.

"Good news?" Nef asked.

I nodded. "Master Jaidon says that he will meet us here after nightfall."

"Lillie, are you sure that you trust this man?" This time, Brava spoke.

"Yes. He was one of our many masters during my training with Va'Shile. Master Jaidon is the master of disguise. He is the one that told me that one of my safe houses had been compromised. He also revealed that he knew my father and that he has been keeping an eye on me all these years in order to honor a promise that he made to him." I considered before adding, "I'm beginning to think that he may actually have a genuine fondness for me."

It was only a couple of hours before dark. We whiled away the time by playing cards. No one bothered to keep score; we were just going through the motions. But, at least we weren't biting off each other's heads as we had been earlier in the day.

As darkness fell, we stopped long enough to light the candles. It was not a task for the faint of heart - I counted no less than fifty. Brava believed in filling a room with light, even when doing so was almost enough to set it on fire. We froze as slow footsteps sounded in the hall.

The door opened to reveal the youngest of Brava's girls, bearing a huge tray; she sweated with the effort of carrying it, her arms trembled slightly. The tray bore the makings for tea, a variety of finger sandwiches and assorted sweets. The slightly threadbare red carpet was definitely being rolled out in preparation for the appearance of Master Jaidon.

We were just beginning to relax, feeling somewhat foolish about our nerves, when the door opened with no warning and Master Jaidon stood amongst us. I should have known that we would have no advance notice of his actual arrival. After all, he was the master of stealth. Only someone that knew Brava as well as I did would have seen the flash of surprise that crossed her face; she recovered her composure quickly. Getting smoothly to her feet, she folded her hands at her waist, the very picture of calm.

"Master Jaidon, I presume?" She glanced at me for confirmation.

I gave her a small nod.

Master Jaidon swept the hood from his head, took one of Brava's hands in his and kissed it gallantly. "Madam, it is good to see you again."

Brava's mask of serenity not only slipped, it shattered completely. For a brief moment, it seemed as if all of the air had been sucked out of the room - even the candles flickered. It then returned with a rush, bringing a rosy glow to Brava's cheeks. I had never seen her blush before.

"You!" Brava choked then began again, struggling to gather the shredded cloak of her dignity around her again. "*You* are Master Jaidon?"

"The one and only." He swept into a low, formal bow, the swirl of his cloak only adding to the effect. He straightened, a small smile on his face as he took Brava's hand in his once again. "Come, my lady. Let us be seated. We have much to discuss." He led her to the unoccupied couch and made sure that she was seated comfortably before settling himself close to her, just a hair over the invisible line that intimated a more personal relationship between them.

Struggling to hide my grin, I poured tea for everyone - making sure to obey all of the many rules that applied to the providing of refreshments in a formal situation. However, I suspected that the formality of this particular situation was draining away rapidly. I gave Brava her cup first as was proper; she was the lady of the house. The tea was also strong and I suspected she needed its soothing effect.

"Master." I spoke to Jaidon for the first time as I gave him his cup.

He gave no indication of surprise at my voice and surveyed me critically.

"I give you credit, little one. You have given yourself completely to this disguise, and it is effective. However, I do regret the loss of your lovely hair." He scowled at me slightly as he continued to study me. "However, you will only be able to carry this off for a few weeks at best; after that your condition will become obvious."

"Oh, by all the hells! Not you too!" I glared at everyone in the room for good measure. "Does everyone in Ramalda know that I am with child?"

"Not yet." Jaidon chuckled. "But as I said, it will be obvious to all before too much time goes by." He nodded in Nef's direction. "Is this the father?"

"He is." I nodded as I resumed my seat next to Nef. "Master, this is Nef Nidolan. Nef, this is Master Jaidon."

Nef responded with a very proper "Pleased to meet you, sir."

"I know who he is," Jaidon replied as he surveyed Nef critically. "I was at the palace the night of the Naming." He gave me a respectful nod. "You did well, young Lillie. You smuggled Nef out of the palace with no one the wiser. I couldn't have done it better myself."

I flushed with pleasure. Master Jaidon did not give compliments lightly.

"However," he continued gravely, "you two have definitely complicated matters by bringing a child into this situation. And not just any child, a child that is heir to two thrones." He held up a hand for silence as we all started to speak. "Of course, I know. I know the lineage of both parents, so it is only logical that I know the lineage of the child. And now that there is a child, we cannot allow anything to happen to it."

"Master, we are in a difficult situation and there are few that we can trust. I believe that I can trust you. Will you help us? We need to find Vido's weak spot." I made my point bluntly. "We need to know how to kill him."

If my instincts about Master Jaidon were wrong, I had just slayed us all.

"Your trust is not misplaced, child. As I told you, I promised your father that I would watch over you if anything happened to him. I have done so for most of your life. That is why I watched over your safe house, so that I could let you know that it had been compromised. I will help you. Vido is a dangerous man. He needs to be removed from power, and quickly."

"Can you tell us what Vido is up to?" Brava asked, "Why he wants both Nef and Lillie dead?"

Although they did not touch, the air between Brava and Master Jaidon practically crackled with the electricity of their attraction.

"Lillie's life was forfeit the moment that she failed to kill the new heir. There is no room in the Va'Shile for an assassin who fails to kill his or her target; especially such an important one. As Vido's protégé, she is doubly doomed. He does not look kindly on failure and especially not the failure of one in whom he invested so much personally." The Master stood and removed his cloak, tossing it over the back of a nearby chair before resuming his seat.

Brava's nostrils flared ever so slightly as she inhaled his scent. She pulled a fan from her pocket, flicked it open and fluttered it gently in front of her face. I snorted with laughter that I tried to disguise as a cough. She may have been cooling herself, but she was also waving her own scent toward Jaidon. The impact was rather like twisting the nose ring on an ox. Master Jaidon's words stumbled to a halt and his eyes glazed over. At that moment Brava could have led him anywhere, done anything and he wouldn't have protested. After a moment he shook himself and continued where he left off.

"As for Nef, he must die so that the king once again has no heir. Vido is a man with a great desire for power. He made the Va'Shile what it is almost single-handedly, but he wants more. He desired to make the king look like such an incompetent buffoon that he couldn't even keep his heir from being killed on the night of his acknowledgment.

"Vido plans to remove the king from power by whatever means necessary. He has been blackmailing the nobles for years so that when he makes his move, they will not resist. Once the king is gone, someone will need to take control of the country and Vido intends to be that man. May the Makers help Manah if Vido is on the throne. Murder will become both legal and a convenient way to remove anyone who gets in your way."

"What about the Va'Shile?" My mind raced. "Who will take over the guild if Vido becomes king?"

"Good question. There are many that would vie for the role, none of them good. The primary contenders would be older, most vicious members of the guild. The bloodshed would begin immediately. They would kill most of the younger members and replace them with others like themselves - those who kill for pleasure of it. It wouldn't matter that they have not had the training to make them true assassins; they would simply be killers - in the purest sense of the word. Finesse would no longer be a requirement." He sat back, rolling his head from side to side as if to relieve the tension in his neck. "I'm sure that I would be among the first to be terminated; stealth would no longer be a requirement. The new regime would simply murder their targets boldly in broad daylight. Who would stop them? Certainly not King Vido. And not the nobles. They would fear too greatly for their own lives to attempt to stand up to the Va'Shile."

"What do we do?" I whispered.

"Actually, the timing of all of this couldn't be better. Vido is marshaling his troops, preparing to make his move. Soon there will be a gathering of all of the Va'Shile that can possibly attend. He will announce his plan to ascend to the throne and his chosen henchmen will begin the slaughter of the less fortunate then and there."

The room fell silent, each of us lost in our own thoughts.

Brava rose to her feet abruptly, brushing non-existent wrinkles from her skirt. "Thank you, Master Jaidon. You have given us much to think about. I recommend that we all retire to our quarters and meet again in the morning, when we have had time to process what we have learned thus far." Turning to Jaidon, she added "However, I have been remiss in my duties as hostess. I hope that you will join me for an evening snack before leaving. I would not want to send you away on an empty stomach.

Master Jaidon stood as well. "An excellent idea, my lady. I appreciate your concern."

Nef and I bade everyone good night and stepped into the hall. He glanced worriedly over his shoulder as Brava closed the door behind us. "Do you think it's safe to leave her alone with him? What if he plans to kill her?"

I laughed. "I assure you, Brava is in no danger. Master Jaidon came here, not only to help us, but to bed her. I wouldn't be surprised if they haven't already begun to, well, let's just say 'get reacquainted.'"

"Are you serious? We just walked out the door." He gestured to the wooden portal. "Surely it would take a little while. They've only been in the same room for a few minutes and neither displayed a particular interest in the other."

"Are you kidding?" I grabbed his arm and began tugging him down the hall. "It was like sitting atop a primed powder keg in there. The smallest spark would have set it off."

As if in confirmation of my statement, something shattered behind us, as if a tea cup had suddenly hit the floor. A brief moment of silence was followed by a muffled thump, as of a body impacting a solid surface. The thump was almost immediately followed by muffled groans, both male and female. The groans developed a steady, pulsing rhythm which slowly became louder.

Nef looked at me with wide eyes. "Was that...? Are they...?"

The groans escalated into cries that crescendoed simultaneously.

"Yes, it was and, yes, they are."

Footsteps in the room behind us were followed by the sound of what I thought was Brava's bedroom door flying open. My suspicions were confirmed when the slam was soon followed by the rhythmic squeaking of Brava's bed.

Nef's eyes grew even wider.

I grabbed his hand and pulled him toward our quarters explaining as we went. "You were probably too sick to remember, but Brava told me about a man that bedded her many years ago; a man that left, um, shall we say, quite an impression on her. Such an impression that she said that she would gladly bed him for free should she ever see him again. Master Jaidon was that man. Apparently, she left an equally good impression on him."

I shut the door to our room, and quickly stripped out of my clothes. "How about we do a little bed squeaking of our own?"

"Gladly." Apparently Nef was a bit of an aural voyeur as well. He was eager enough that he didn't even fully undress; he simply loosened his breeches and took me.

We achieved maximum climax with minimal bed squeaking, but that was only the first round. I undressed Nef and we put the bed through its paces several times that night.

23

When Nef and I returned to Brava's quarters the next morning, she and Master Jaidon sat side-by-side, thighs touching; they both wore smug expressions and seemed well-pleased with themselves. The plunging neckline of Brava's dressing gown revealed several faint hickies; I felt sure that they would bloom into a lovely rich color over the course of the day. If Master Jaidon bore similar marks they were hidden by his clothing.

As Nef and I took our seats, I couldn't resist any longer.

"Good morning. Did you sleep well?"

Brava gave a peal of girlish laughter. "Child, we did not sleep at all. You have a quick mind. I'm sure you have realized that your Master Jaidon is the man that I told you about - the one that bedded me so well so many years ago."

I grinned. "I did." Glancing between them, I continued, "Apparently his ability to satisfy has not faded with time."

Brava slid her hand down her lover's thigh. Fortunately, his clothing hid any physical reaction to her touch.

"Faded? Not at all. As a matter of fact, he has made a few very pleasant additions to his repertoire."

Beside her, Master Jaidon exuded a thoroughly masculine self-satisfaction, although I was sure that his contentment was not entirely due to his own abilities.

I arched my eyebrow at them in what I hoped was an appropriately stern manner. "Are you two going to be able to focus on the tasks at hand, or do I need to separate you?"

Master Jaidon snorted. "We are quite capable of focusing on many tasks at once. We discussed the current situation last night during our other nocturnal activities and neither the discussion nor the screwing lacked for attention to detail. However, should we decide that we can no longer restrain ourselves, we will retire to the bedroom for a few moments until we can regain our composure. Does that meet with your satisfaction?"

I rolled my eyes. "I guess it will have to do. However, before we get down to serious discussion, I really must eat; I'm starving. Apparently, now that I have acknowledged his presence, our son is going to insist on being fed on a regular basis." I immediately began filling my plate with the provisions that the cook had so generously prepared, pleased to note the addition of fruit juice to the usual tea and coffee. Brava was not one to overlook even the smallest of details. I gave her a smile of thanks, my mouth stuffed with a marvelous egg and cheese mixture.

"Your son?" Brava and Master Jaidon reacted at the same time.

I nodded, my mouth still full, glancing at Nef for assistance.

"Yes, a son," he explained, "Lillie seems to have inherited the ability to communicate with animals from her mother. Apparently the ability extends beyond just animals; Lillie can feel the consciousness of our child and knows that it is a boy."

"Yes." Brava nodded thoughtfully as she spoke. "Yes, that would hold true. However - " her gaze fell on me - "if you have inherited the full range of your mother's capabilities, you will find that there is much more to it than what you currently know. You are just reaching the age where a Southroner comes into his or her full powers. It would be wise to find someone with the necessary skills to teach you what you need to know about the gifts that you possess."

Her comments surprised me, although I didn't know why they should. Brava *was* Southron. She would know much more about their abilities than I.

"True enough," Master Jaidon interrupted, "but that sort of training will have to wait until the current crisis has been dealt with. There is no need to discuss training for her abilities until we make sure that Lillie will survive long enough to require such."

I finished the last of my meal and pushed aside my plate, then allowed myself a luxurious stretch. I rested my hand lightly on my abdomen as I slid back to sit closer to Nef, who had also finished his morning repast. He smiled at me and I suspected that his thoughts mirrored my own. He kissed me on the head and put his arm around me, pulling me against his side. I snuggled in happily. Our lives might be in danger, but that didn't mean that we weren't going to make the most of the time that we had - the here and now.

I turned back to face the others. They were sitting in a similar position. Master Jaidon had pulled Brava close and rested his arm lightly but possessively across her shoulders. We all share somewhat foolish grins.

Pushing aside the sudden sleepiness that threatened to overwhelm me, I said, "All right, let's get this meeting started." Why I was the one suddenly taking charge? "Did your nocturnal discussions turn up anything useful? In regards to the current situation?" I clarified quickly.

The older couple nodded in unison.

"The guild house is going to be a hive of activity over the next week or so as Vido prepares for the gathering," Master Jaidon explained, "I must return to the house soon, as I will be expected to play a part in the upcoming events." Slightly crooked white teeth flashed against his dark skin. "Vido doesn't know that I am aware of his plans to kill me and he will want to keep me close so that it will be as easy as possible."

Brava smiled affectionately at her lover, but then her gaze turned serious. "Jaidon and I discussed many options and there is no way around it – the two of you must infiltrate the guild house."

Jaidon twined his fingers in Brava's as he resumed speaking. "I know that you are probably thinking that to do so will be suicide, but I think that it will not. Vido knows that you have gone into hiding; he is too arrogant to believe that you would attempt to do so not only in plain sight, but in his home. Your current disguises are a good start." He looked us over critically before continuing. "We may have to make a few adjustments, but overall, you have done well."

He focused his attention on Nef. "Your role will not be as critical as Lillie's; your submersion will not have to be as complete. Fortunately, very few from the guild actually attended the Naming ceremony, so few know what you look like. The simple change to your hair color and style has made you almost unrecognizable." He squeezed Brava's hand in acknowledgement of her part in the changes.

Nef smiled, which caused Jaidon to frown.

"Until you smile, that is. Dimples are not that common and yours may trigger someone's memory. Yet another reason for you to play a smaller role."

Then it was my turn to fall under Jaidon's implacable gaze.

"The guild will have to temporarily increase the number of servants in its employ in order to complete all of the necessary preparations on time," he went on. "I will secure you a position on the kitchen staff for this event. Your appearance as a young boy will mean your involvement in a variety of tasks and give you access to most of the guild house. It is good that you already know your way around. It will also give you the opportunity that we need for you to put your poisoning skills to good use at the big meal."

I shifted uncomfortably. "Master, you should know that I don't *want* to be an assassin. I'm not comfortable killing innocent people – which is why I couldn't kill the prince. I went to his quarters to remove the poisoned wine and found Nef there drinking it; I gave him the antidote and brought him here to recover. I know that we have to do something, but I don't know think I am comfortable killing so many that may have nothing against us. There will be those in attendance that I grew up with, trained with; we may not be the best of friends, but I don't know that I can kill them in cold blood."

Master Jaidon's gaze hardened. "*You* may not want to kill in cold blood, but Vido will not hesitate to do so. Rest assured that many of your fellow assassins will not live to see the assembly. Vido will make sure that the gathering is populated primarily with those who will support his plans. Any that he is not sure about will inexplicably not be in attendance, nor will they ever be seen again. I will be there with enough antidote on hand to assist those that I think would work with us against Vido. The rest, dear Lillie, are not deserving of your mercy. If left alive, they will kill you, your lover, and your child, not to mention being the harbingers of a reign of terror from which Manah may never recover."

Of course, he was right. None of us would come out of this without blood on our hands – both literally and figuratively; I would do everything in my power to minimize the amount. My hand still lay on my belly and I could feel the reassuring presence of my son as he slept. Very briefly, I thought I felt a flicker of something else, but it faded. I focused on that presence, that life within me. If I had to kill in order for him to survive, I would do so with no regret.

I met Master Jaidon's steady gaze and nodded, signaling my understanding.

"I will need to choose a poison that is tasteless and fast-acting, yet not so fast that you don't have time to give the antidote to those who require it. My stocks have been compromised and possibly tainted. I have time to brew a new batch, but I require supplies; I can't risk being seen by going shopping for the necessary ingredients."

"I may be able to assist," Brava interjected. "Are there any poisons meeting the criteria that you specified that involve ingredients such as those that would be used to induce a spontaneous abortion, say perhaps in a whore that does not wish to bear the child that she carries?"

My training included not only instruction on how to prevent sexually transmitted diseases and how to avoid conception, but how to end an unwanted pregnancy should it occur. Such practices were common, even among non-whores that did not wish to bear a child, and I never felt strongly about it one way or the other. Now, knowing that I carried a life inside of me, my perceptions had changed somewhat. My stomach rolled, the sumptuous breakfast it contained threatened to reappear. I tamped down the nausea firmly.

Putting my personal feelings aside, I nodded.

"I keep a small store of such supplies on hand," Brava continued. "I will need you to look at what I have and determine if it suits your needs. You will also need to give me a list of any other ingredients that you require; I should be able to procure them without any significant difficulties."

"Good." Master Jaidon spoke. "I need to return to the guild house soon to put our plans in motion. I recommend that you have your list of supplies to Brava later today. After I leave, our communications will be limited. However, it will not seem suspicious if I feel the need to come to the brothel periodically. After all, organizing such an unprecedented gathering of assassins is a massive undertaking and a man occasionally needs to blow off steam. Many guild members are already frequent customers here; I will just become one of the throng." He grinned wickedly at Brava, his eyes twinkling dangerously. "Would you prefer that I turn my attentions to one - or more - of your girls as I relieve my needs? Some might find it strange that I rate the attentions of the Madam herself."

Brava fluttered her lashes at him coyly. "Bed one of my girls and I will relieve you of the equipment of which you are so fond."

Jaidon threw back his head and roared with laughter, pulling Brava against him in a hug.

She elbowed him playfully as she continued, "No one need know that you are here to bed me. I will simply let it be known that I am striving to establish a working relationship with the Va'Shile in which my girls will be the only ones used during the assembly. As the guild liaison, I will be required to work closely with you to determine which girls will temporarily be assigned to the guild house." She rose to her feet and stretched languorously, angling her body so that Jaidon was sure to get the full effect. "Now, you should make your way to the store room to begin your survey, Lillie. Cook can tell you where I keep my private stores. Nef, you should help."

Knowing a dismissal when I heard it, I went quickly to Jaidon and bowed respectfully. "Be careful, Master - and, thank you."

He surprised me by getting to his feet and enveloping me in his arms.

"You should be careful as well, little one. You and the rest of your family." He nodded his head at Nef.

I glanced over my shoulder as Nef and I reached the door; Brava and Jaidon were already standing close together.

"One word of advice before I leave."

They looked at me curiously.

"If you don't want anyone to know that the two of you are sharing a bed, you need to be a little quieter. Nef and I could hear you very well last night and we were well down the hall."

"We will take your recommendation under advisement, child. Now, be on your way." Brava sniffed somewhat haughtily.

I gave her a grin and ushered Nef out. As I pulled the door closed behind us, Master Jaidon already had Brava's dressing gown open, his face buried in her ample bosom. Her eyes were closed in ecstasy. I shook my head as the latch clicked and moved to Nef's side.

"They're at it again. I hope that Brava is beyond child-bearing years or that they are using one of the methods that she taught us for avoiding conception. Otherwise, those two could find themselves becoming parents unusually late in life."

Nef laughed. "When did you become such a mother hen? Brava has been in this business a long time. Does she have any children that you are aware of?"

"No. You're right, of course. I'm glad that they found each other again and that they have this time together. Who knows how long it may last?"

Nef gave me a hug. "Don't get all glum on me; we need to stay positive. Now, let's go check on Brava's stores. I'll be the recorder if we can find writing supplies." He nuzzled my neck. "Once that is done, I recommend that we go to our room for a little one-on-one recreation ourselves."

"Again?" I rolled my eyes. "Don't you ever get tired of making love?"

"Are you kidding? I've got twenty-two years of virginity to make up for. We're just getting started!"

"I like the way you think." I slid my hand into his, twining our fingers together as I stretched up to give him a lingering kiss. "Now, let's go take a look at these supplies. As we work, maybe I'll tell you what sort of things I have in mind for later."

"Be still my heart." His dimples flared and deepened as he led the way to the kitchen.

Cook's eyebrows rose as we entered, still hand in hand. I asked her where Brava kept her private stores, indicating that the Madam had instructed us to do an inventory.

"The supplies is over there." She motioned with her head to the corner. "Behind that door. The key is here." She reached into her ample bosom and pulled out a small key on a sturdy chain. Looking us over again, she huffed, "At least she don't have to worry about the two of you making off with anything. Yer too young to get with child, even if you was female."

Her last remark was aimed at me, of course. I grinned as I turned away. *Wrong on both counts!*

Brava was as good as her word. The supplies that I needed were quickly procured and I spent the next two days concocting my poison and antidote, while Master Jaidon returned to the guild to take on his role as faithful - and hopefully indispensable - advisor to Vido.

Nef assumed his mantle as the new stable boy for the brothel. Brava felt that that would be a suitable role as her business would increase as more and more assassins flooded into town for the upcoming assembly. She felt it important that her customer's horses be accommodated at least as well as their owners - minus the sex, of course. Putting Nef in that position would allow others to get used to seeing him, and it wouldn't seem unusual should she need to send him on an occasional errand to the guild house.

Master Jaidon put in an appearance a couple of nights later and we all made our way, individually of course, to Brava's sitting room. Jaidon looked tired, but his face lit up when Brava entered. People sighed and got all doe-eyed over "young love," but I had to admit, there was something to be said for middle-aged love as well. The way that the two of them looked at each other warmed me all the way to my toes. I hoped that Nef would still look at me that way when we were that age - provided of course, that we survived that long.

Jaidon sat Brava next to him and pulled her close, inhaling her scent deeply. He seemed much like a man savoring every moment with the one he loved, storing away memories to recall during the cold and lonely nights should he lose it.

I suddenly had the urge to grab Nef's hand and run - as far and as fast as we possibly could. But I didn't. To do so would mean living our lives in constant fear and hiding, which would be no life for us or our child. It would also mean leaving Master Jaidon to face his death alone and leaving the people of Ramalda and Manah to deal with the reign of a tyrant. I suppressed my fears; running was not my style. If I was to fail and to fall, it wouldn't be without a fight. I might be bloody and beaten, but when the final blow came, I would be on my feet. I would stand.

I slid my hand into Nef's and squeezed hard; he returned my grip. He understood both my fear and my reality. If it was in his power to do so, when the end came, he would be by my side.

Wow. Where did all of that come from? Apparently my hormones were raging. I shook myself, both literally and figuratively, and focused on the discussion at hand.

"As expected," Master Jaidon began, "Vido keeps me close. I have been assisting with the assessment of those that will be in the temporary employee of the Va'Shile as servants. Tomorrow, Lillie will join the staff." Nodding at me, he continued, "I will escort you to the guild house in the morning and introduce you to the cook; you will be assisting him. What name will you go by?"

So much for the completeness of my disguise; I had not considered a name. I chewed the corner of my lip thoughtfully.

"What about 'Laisle?' It is similar enough to my real name to keep me from slipping up and not responding should someone call me."

"Good enough, Laisle. I will see you in the morning. We -" he motioned to our group – "will meet again in a few days to discuss the plans for the final stage."

We all said our good nights and returned to our own quarters for our more intimate farewells.

24

The morning sun was barely making its presence known on the eastern horizon when Master Jaidon escorted me to the guild house. I only half-feigned stumbling with fatigue as he led me into the kitchen and presented me to the chief cook.

"Cook, this is Laisle. He will be joining the kitchen staff until the assembly is complete. I will be bringing you a few more recruits over the next few hours. Put them to good use."

Fortunately, the cook was not one that I remembered from my time at the guild house, so there was no danger of him recognizing me as he looked me over.

"Laisle, is it? Tell me boy, what can you do?"

I pulled myself up to my full height and mumbled "I can do whatever you tell me to do, sir - I'm a quick learner." I gave him what I hoped was an earnest look. "Please sir, I'll do good; I promise. I need this job. My dad's been drinkin' again and I need to help my mum."

He gave me a noncommittal grunt, but there was a slight twinkle in his eyes. "Well, lad we'll see about that. For starters, you can fill the pot over there." He gestured toward the fireplace and the large iron kettle hanging there. "We'll be needing plenty of hot water for tea and coffee."

"Yes sir." I walked across the kitchen, thinking quickly. There was no way that I could carry the heavy metal pot when it was empty, much less when it was filled with water. Fortunately, I spied a pitcher sitting on a nearby shelf, and after checking to make sure it was clean, I made several trips to the pump, where I filled the pitcher and then returned to dump the contents into the pot. Once finished, I pushed on the swing arm to move it into position over the fire.

Cook was watching. He seemed pleased with the way that I solved the problem and promptly began giving me other tasks. He ran his staff with the ease of a general commanding his troops - the kitchen was well-organized chaos. Everyone had a job to do and Cook knew what they were and who should be doing them. There were those who thought that they would be able to get away with shirking their duties by simply hiding in plain sight; they felt sure that the sheer number of people and the amount of activity would conceal that they weren't carrying their weight. They were wrong. Many the young boy or girl suddenly found themselves almost lifted off their feet by Cook's firm grip on their ear. They also received a hearty chewing out, heard by everyone in the large room. Miscreants were given a second chance, but not a third. After the first few people were literally thrown into the street with very loud orders to never darken the doorway again, the rest of the staff buckled down to the tasks at hand and soon we were working together smoothly.

I quickly learned that being the "youngest" member of the kitchen staff meant answering to everyone else, from the cook all the way down to the scullery maid. My days began before the sun rose and ended long after it set. I was glad that I was in good physical condition before this began, or I would have worried about the toll that my new lifestyle was taking on my unborn son.

However, my position allowed me to observe the inner workings of the guild - which servants were allowed where, which were the most trusted, and so forth. I also became privy to the plan for the feast that would be presented to the assembly. Cook was pulling out all the stops with a multi-course meal featuring something for every taste. In any large crowd, the tastes of the attendees would vary; not everyone would partake of every course. However, everyone would be expected to participate in the toast to Vido and few assassins were unwilling to partake of alcohol. To ensure that the poison was ingested by as many as possible, it would be best to fall back on my standard methodology and poison the wine.

Breakfast was served buffet style in the main dining room, but a few of the senior masters preferred to dine in their rooms. I made sure to be busy with other tasks when it was time for those meals to be delivered; they were the individuals that stood the best chance of recognizing me, so it was important that I avoid them at all costs.

The guild house wasn't large enough to accommodate both the assassins arriving for the assembly and the temporarily increased staff. Therefore, those of us who lived in The Narrows were allowed to go home in the evenings and return for our shifts the next day. I staggered back to the brothel well after dark every night.

As soon as I could scrounge a few minutes of free time, I began snooping through the wine cellar, trying to determine the best way to get the poison into a large quantity of wine. I had not been in the room long when an older boy came down the steps, apparently sent to retrieve the wine for the evening meal. He started when he saw me.

"Hey - what're *you* doin' down here? Cook sent me to get the wine!"

I shrugged. "Ah, don't get your breeches in a bunch. I ain't poachin'. I took a wrong turn and wound up here. Go ahead and get the wine and I'll follow you out."

He looked around for a moment, seeming confused. He peered near-sightedly at different flasks as if he couldn't read. He finally shrugged and said, "Cook sent me for red wine, but they all look the same to me. I'll just take these."

"Those aren't the right ones." I tugged at his arm, pointing to a rack farther down the aisle. "The ones that you want are over there."

"What do you know? Yer no better'n me." He grabbed the original flasks and rushed back up the stairs, with me hot on his heels.

"I'm trying to help you, idiot. That's not the right wine. Cook is going to be angry."

We puffed up to Cook and the boy handed him the flasks.

Cook's face turned red. "Boy, this ain't what I sent you for. Now, go back and get the right stuff." He gave the boy a shove.

"See, I tried to tell you," I hissed as he went past.

"Wait, boy." Cook turned to me. "What was that?"

"I tried to tell him that he had the wrong wine, but he wouldn't listen."

"What were you doing in the wine cellar? And how do you know so much about wine?"

"I got lost. My dad drinks - a lot; whatever he can beg, borrow, or steal. I may not know exactly which wine goes with which foods, but I know that what he got is a dessert wine, not the stuff that goes with the main course. I kin also read a bit and I kin tell one kind from another."

Cook arched a brow in surprise. He took the flasks from the object of his disapproval and gave them to me. "Prove it. Put these back and bring me the Fletcher's Red."

I took the flasks, hurried back to the wine cellar, returned them to their proper location and went in search of the requested vintage.

That sneak. I smiled. *He's testing me. There is no Fletcher's Red.* I did a quick scan of the available wines, made my selection and returned upstairs.

Cook was waiting, arms crossed across his broad chest. "Well, boy, let's see what you have."

"I'm sorry, sir." I handed him the flasks, panting as though I had run. I couldn't find no Fletcher's Red. The closest I could find was Arrowmaker's Red."

Cook looked at me in astonishment and then laughed; a rich, full sound that started at his toes. His face turned red with the effort and tears streamed from his eyes.

"Well done, lad. Well done." He slapped me on the shoulder, almost hard enough to knock me down.

I beamed with pride.

From then on, I was in charge of bringing the wine selections to Cook before every meal which fixed one of the biggest holes in our plan to kill Vido. Now, it would be easy to poison the wine - I would simply slip it into the flasks before bringing them upstairs.

25

The end was in sight – finally; the assembly of assassins was the next day. Our small band of saboteurs met one final time in Brava's parlor. The atmosphere was glum. There was a very good chance that three of the four of us might not survive. Well, four of the five, counting the child that I carried.

Our final plans were in place. The menu was set and the kitchen staff at the guild house had been cooking for days. The wine had been selected, but I wouldn't put the poison in until the last minute, just in case it was changed. Jaidon would be seated on the dais with Vido as his second. Once the toast had been made and the poisoned wine drank, Jaidon would be able to get the antidote to those that he had selected as survivors. Nef would be lurking outside, prepared to intervene if needed. I was to remain in the kitchen with the rest of the staff as all hell broke loose in the main hall.

However, even the best of plans could go awry and ours did so in spectacular fashion.

As the assassins gathered in the main hall to feast, I slipped the poison into the wine without incident. Servants moved through the large room filling glasses in preparation for the toast. Vido waited on the platform. He would spring his announcement of anarchy on the assembled after its completion.

As many servants as were able crowded in the hallway vying for a glimpse into the main hall. I edged my way through them, struggling to get close enough to see the action. I peered around the arm of the ridiculously tall man ahead of me. The crowd was on their feet, glasses raised in toast. Tribute completed, they drank; Vido, as the recipient of the toast did not. He rose slowly to his feet, drawing all eyes to himself. In the far corner of the room first one, then another person doubled over in pain and collapsed. Soon others did the same. The crowd's gaze was drawn from Vido to the growing chaos around them.

Jaidon stepped forward, knocking Vido's glass from his hand. "Master, the wine has been poisoned!" He started from the platform as his gaze darted around the room. "I must go and help the others - maybe it's not too late."

Just as he shifted his weight to step down, Vido grabbed him by the collar of his cloak and dragged him back, pressing a knife against his neck.

"I think not, Jaidon. Or perhaps I should say *traitor* - I know that you played a role in this, and you will be made an example to the others."

Jaidon twisted free, his own knife flashing toward Vido; they locked into combat.

Movement caught my eye. Several senior masters moved through the crowd with brutal efficiency, killing those that were in the throes of the poison. They seemed unaffected; apparently they had not participated in the toast after all.

"No!" A familiar voice rang out nearby.

Nef.

He had worked his way through the crowd, to the foot of the platform and now struggled to reach Master Jaidon. Light gleamed as his short sword flashed from the scabbard at his side. The other masters abandoned the ailing to their fate and advanced toward Nef.

I shoved and elbowed my way through the doorway, screaming, "Nef, look out!"

"Where d'you think *yer* going?"

The other servants reached out to stop me. I swung my arms, pulling free of their grasping hands. I ripped my dagger free of its sheath, slashing blindly, uncaring if I inflicted damage on them - even if they were innocent bystanders. Struggling free, I ran toward Nef, sparing a brief glance for Master Jaidon as I ran past. Blood ran down his arm from a gash in his sleeve. Vido was also bleeding, but not as badly.

Nef battled with two men, both bigger than him. This was the first I had seen of his skill with a sword and I was impressed. Apparently his family didn't take their status as royals lightly; he was obviously well-trained. He ducked, lunged, and succeeded in running his blade through the thigh of one of his assailants effectively ending his attack. Before he could turn, the second attacker slammed the flat of his blade against Nef's head, dazing him; he staggered, throwing his arm up to block the next blow.

I missed what happened next. I was so focused on Nef that I made a rookie – and potentially fatal – mistake; I failed to keep an eye on my surroundings. A blow from behind knocked me to the ground. I rolled to the side, narrowly avoiding the blade that slammed into my previous position. As I rolled, I slashed at the feet of my attacker. A grunt from above indicated that I had struck home. Struggling to my feet, I assumed a fighting stance facing my assailant.

The man was large, and I didn't recognize him. He was probably one of the killers that Vido had recruited for his new regime. He sneered at me, showing rotten teeth. We circled, each of us looking for weak spots in the other's defense. His size gave him the advantage in reach, and he wore leather armor - a definite improvement over the servant's garb that I wore. I lunged, slashing at his thigh, and whirled away. The sounds of fighting filled the air nearby as both Jaidon and Nef continued their own battles. Nef yelled. I clenched my teeth but I couldn't risk looking toward him.

My attacker returned the lunge, but it was a feint. When I dodged, he anticipated the movement and grabbed my knife hand, twisting it brutally. I screamed as my dagger slipped from nerveless fingers. Tears blinded me, I wiped at them frantically with my free hand.

"Just the way I like 'em – young." He pressed against me, his erection straining at his trousers. Leaning over, he swiped his tongue across my cheek, laughing at my attempts to escape. "That's right, fight. I like it when you struggle." A callused hand fell to my neck and began to squeeze. "Dead or alive – it don't matter to me. You'll be a good fuck either way."

I brought my knee up into his groin. *Hard.* He dropped like a rock, his hands grasping at his crotch as he hissed in pain. I snatched up my knife with my off hand and planted my knee on his chest.

"I don't think so," I growled, slitting his throat with one sure motion. As his blood poured over us and the light faded from his eyes, I wiped my blade on his clothes and staggered to my feet, moving in search of my friends.

Vido and Jaidon circled each other in a brutal dance. Nef was once again outnumbered. My head was pounding from the blow I received and I flexed my fingers madly, trying to get the feeling back to something resembling normal.

I would like to say that I ran down the stairs and threw myself on Nef's attackers in a whirlwind of death but, sadly, that was not the case. It had been some time since I had participated in hand-to-hand combat and I was already feeling the effects; apparently, my pregnancy was having an effect on my stamina as well. I felt as though I were running through mud.

"The girl lives," Vido called from behind me. "She is mine."

Damn. I had hoped that it would take a little longer for him to see through my disguise – preferably only when I revealed myself to him as I watched him die.

Nef's eyes widened slightly when he saw me. I gave him a grin and swung into action, hamstringing the nearest opponent who fell to the ground screaming. Reversing my knife I brought down the handle with as much strength as I could muster on the head of the next man, staggering him. I was now close enough to see that Nef was bleeding from several wounds, but I couldn't determine the extent of his injuries.

I said that when the final blow came, I would be on my feet and I was. It came from behind with only the slightest of sounds. I whirled to see a gloved fist coming at my face but there was no time to react. The impact knocked me off my feet, slamming me into the wall. Much to my surprise, there was no pain. The last thing I saw as my vision faded was Nef taking a vicious sword slash to the face.

26

Something warm, wet, and slightly sticky swiped across my face again and again. I tried to turn away from the sensation, but the pain that shot through my head caused me to reconsider such a rash course of action. My eyes refused to open so I reached up to push away the wetness and encountered...

Fur? I traced the firmness of what could only be a dog's muzzle. With a supreme effort I finally forced my eyes open and fought to focus. Slowly, the face of my oldest friend came into view - Grau, Vido's guard dog and my long-time companion.

Grau whined at me encouragingly, nudging me with his muzzle; I could feel his concern. I pushed myself up onto one elbow and waited for the room to stop spinning. Once the motion had eased, I used the big dog's collar to help pull myself into a sitting position.

"Grau! I'm so glad to see you." Burying my face in his fur, I hugged him for all I was worth - which at the moment wasn't a whole lot. I hadn't seen him since I went to the palace.

Grau's tail thumped the floor behind him; he was glad to see me too.

"Such a touching reunion. It almost brings a tear to my eye," Vido mocked.

We were in his personal quarters; he sat on an throne-like chair on a small dais.

"I never have understood the effect that you have on animals Lillie. Grau, as you like to call him, has always been my most loyal protector. A look from him will stop even the bravest of men in their tracks. But you - you have always been different. He has always treated you gently."

"Perhaps because I have always been gentle with him. He knows that he can trust me."

Grau pushed his muzzle into my hand, asking to be petted.

"Isn't that right, boy?"

He woofed in agreement.

"He is growing old and can no longer serve as a guard dog; I will put him down soon. I have no need for a pet."

"No! You can't kill Grau. I won't let you." I reached for the knife on my thigh only to find that it wasn't there. Big surprise.

"Ha!" Vido gave what I could only assume was a laugh. "You can't stop me, girl. But, since I'm going to kill you as well, maybe you will see each other again on the other side of death." Vido leaned back, draping one leg casually over the arm of his chair before pulling out his dagger and cleaning out his fingernails with the point. "But don't worry. His bloodline will live on. He has sired many pups during his lifetime - the newest litter is in the next room. A fine bunch, newly weaned and ready to step into their sire's place."

"Why?"

"Because you deserve to die." He didn't pretend to not know what I was talking about. "You failed your mission." He looked at me again, his eyes cold. "You are too much your father's daughter. He failed me, turned his back on me and you have done the same." Shoving himself to his feet, he paced angrily. "Your father and I were friends. We trained together, came up through the ranks of the Va'Shile together. He was my right hand man. Until he met *her*." He made the word an epithet.

"Her? I'm assuming that you mean my mother?"

"Yes, your mother. The whore. The Southron bitch. Once he met her, he changed. He no longer wanted to kill - he spent his days and nights with her. Only, I knew the truth. I knew what kind of a man your father really was. I couldn't allow him to turn his back on the life he was born for, the life that we shared. He had to die, and *I* had to be the one to kill him." A cold smile spread across his face. "And your mother. I treated her like the whore that she was. But that left you. Training you to be the assassin that your father refused to be would be the ultimate irony - the ultimate retribution for his betrayal." He began slowly twirling his knife through his fingers as he moved toward me.

I forced myself to my feet, trying not to waver. My right eye was almost swollen closed and I had no weapon but the fists clenched by my sides. Grau stepped between us, facing Vido, his front legs spread, his head down, a warning growl rumbling from his chest.

"Apparently your father's weakness breeds true. Look at you, doing the same thing. Turning your back on the Va'Shile, on all that I gave you. For what? For *love*?" He spat the word at my feet. "But, before you die, I want you to see what your actions have caused."

Pressing his fingers to his lips, Vido whistled shrilly. The door opened and two men entered, bowed under heavy burdens. They dropped their loads at Vido's feet; as he toed the bundles one of them groaned. My stomach churned, those bundles were people, *my* people - Nef and Jaidon. I couldn't tell who had groaned. If they were alive, it was only just. Even though we had all known that it could come to this,

Vido was right. It *was* my fault. However, I refused to let him see my pain.

"No, Vido. Not my actions. Yours. *You* were the one who ordered a hit on an innocent man - all because of your lust for power. Am I a killer? Yes. But I will not kill an innocent man - not for you; not for anyone. I will not let you complete your goals. You. Will. Not. Become the power behind the throne of this country – or on it."

"And just how do you plan to stop me? You are unarmed. You can't touch me." Vido lunged.

Grau leaped, teeth bared, a snarl tearing from his throat. He hit Vido in the chest staggering him, then screamed in pain. The huge dog collapsed to the ground and lay there, whining. I rushed forward to find Vido's knife buried to the hilt in Grau's chest.

"No!" I fell to the ground, pulling Grau's head into my lap. Tears fell on his greying muzzle. "Grau, I'm so sorry. I never meant for this to happen."

Grau whimpered, his tongue flicking over my hand. I felt his thoughts as his life drained away. He had no regrets. He was old and had willingly given his life for me. For love.

"I love you too," I whispered as he took his last breath then buried my face in his fur, sobbing.

"Everyone – every*thing* – that you have ever loved is gone." Vido's low growl shattered my mourning. "And now you must die as well."

Gritting my teeth, I pulled the knife from Grau's body; it snagged briefly on bone before sliding free.

Once armed, I pushed myself to my feet and turned to face my former master. He was wrong – there was still one living being that I loved – my son. I wasn't about to let him take him away from me as well.

Vido looked at me with pure hatred, another dagger in his hand. This would be dangerous. Yes, I was fast, but he had reach and years of experience. We began to circle slowly, each looking for an opening, a weakness to exploit. He had the advantage. We were in his quarters; he knew every inch of his surroundings – I did not.

He feinted once, twice. I moved away easily, watching him carefully. The real attack, when it came, would be quick – he would not telegraph his true intentions so blatantly. I lunged and he parried easily, nearly knocking my blade from my hand. He had earned his position as guild master simply by being the best of the best. He was not a man to be trifled with.

Vido pressed his attack, pushing me back steadily. I attempted to feel for obstacles with my feet, but he moved too quickly and I stumbled over Grau's body and fell, the impact knocking the wind out of me. Before I could recover, Vido was on top of me. I swiped my dagger at him, aiming for his face. The swing was wild and he blocked it easily, disarming me in the process.

I fought with everything I had – arms, legs, even teeth. I struck at his face attempting to gouge him in the eye, but it was no use – my arms simply weren't long enough. Vido was bigger, stronger, and heavier. I was completely at his mercy.

"You will die, young Lillie, but it will not be fast." He straddled me, pinning my legs and simply ignoring my arms and the blows that I rained upon him. He placed one large hand on my throat; the pressure prevented me from breathing easily but did not restrict my airflow completely. "No, I will kill you slowly as your father did me."

"What...?" I croaked.

He immediately pressed harder and I stopped struggling as I desperately sought for some way out of this mess.

"Marco and I were recruited at the same time. We became fast friends and swore that we would always be so even when our masters sought to end all such relationships."

A sharp yip sounded nearby and I remembered the pups that Vido mentioned earlier. I reached for them with my mind – called to them as I had called to their father when I was trapped in the root cellar. *Help me!* I could sense their confusion; young and untrained as they were, they didn't understand. *Come!* It was all I could manage.

Vido pressed harder; I could now get only the smallest amounts of air. The world began to go grey, but I could still hear.

"It was *my* body that he sought solace in after a bad day – or simply when he needed release."

I stiffened at his words.

"Yes, Lillie, that's right – your father and I were lovers." He squeezed slightly harder. "I thought we would always be together. And then we went to that damn brothel. Once Marco bedded his first whore, he no longer wanted to fuck me." Tears strained his voice.

Suddenly, we were surrounded by barking, bumbling lurcher pups. They had responded to my call! They whined when they discovered their father's body but they were too young to be concerned for long. They were delighted to find people on the floor – at their level. This must mean it was time to play. They swarmed over us, barking and yipping. Vido released his grip on my neck as he flailed mercilessly at the pups, beating them away.

I fought madly to get away, but only succeeded in moving a few inches; Vido still had my legs pinned firmly beneath him. I struggled to drag in air with only slightly better success. Even though I was free from his grip, my throat was beginning to swell.

"You bitch!" Vido backhanded me. "You called them! A Southron witch - just like your mother." He hit me again.

My lip split under his first blow, my brow on the second; both wounds poured blood. In spite of my efforts, a whimper escaped me. *I'm sorry*, I apologized to my son. *I tried.*

Vido placed his hands back on my neck and began squeezing with a purpose. This was the end.

"I begged Marco to come back to me, but he refused. He said that our time together had never been anything more than youthful experimentation." He pulled me up by the neck then slammed my head down onto the stone floor.

I was developing tunnel vision.

"I was left to watch while he bedded every female in the dorms. Once we began earning coin regularly, he returned to the brothel. And then he met your mother – and I knew that he was gone for good." *Slam. Slam.*

I teetered on the edge of consciousness. The whining of the pups began to fade, only to be replaced by a high-pitched ringing in my ears.

"I kept you to turn you into the assassin that your father refused to be. But seeing you every day – a living, breathing reminder of *him* – was almost more than I could bear." *Slam.* "I *loved* Marco – and he left me. For your mother. For you." He was sobbing openly now. "You have no idea how much I *hate* you."

I was hearing things. The ringing in my ears had taken on the sound of metal singing, the sound of a sword being drawn. I braced for the killing blow, but Vido froze, his grip on my neck loosening slightly. Gasping, I fought back the blackness enough to see the blade of a sword pressed against Vido's neck, but couldn't see who wielded it.

"You killed my husband. You will *not* kill my child."

The blade flashed briefly in the firelight. A warm wetness covered me and the smell of rust filled my nostrils as blackness claimed me.

27

Warm. Soft. Dark.

Vido assured his recruits frequently that there was a special level of the seven Hells reserved just for us; somehow, I didn't think *warmth* and *softness* would describe it. Dark, maybe. I also didn't think that being dead would hurt quite so much.

Where was I? I struggled to remember through the pounding in my head.

You will not *kill my child!*

Vido, dead. His throat slashed, blood flowing over me.

I opened my eyes, and then slammed them shut immediately. Sunlight filled the room, its gentle beams like daggers in my eyes. The pain in my head worsened and tears poured down my face.

"You're awake." A tender hand placed a slightly dampened cloth over my eyes. "Relax, Lillie."

Brava.

"You took some pretty nasty blows to the head; you've been out of it for a while. Open your eyes under the cloth and let them adjust to the filtered light."

I grabbed her hand and held on for dear life then did as she instructed. My chest ached with sobs struggling for release but I fought them back. If I lost control, I wasn't sure that I would ever regain it.

In a few moments, my eyes adjusted to the reduced lighting, and I squeezed Brava's hand to let her know. My voice didn't seem to be working.

"Close your eyes while I remove the cloth and then open them again slowly."

Once again, I did as I was told. This time, the light didn't cause pain.

"Welcome back. You had me worried. How do you feel?"

"Like hell," I croaked, my voice rough from disuse.

Much to my surprise, Brava laughed. I was a bit taken aback until I noticed the tears running freely down her cheeks. I suspected that her reaction was one of relief. Still shaking with laughter she leaned over and pressed her forehead gently against mine.

"Oh, child. I was afraid that I had lost you. I didn't think that I could bear it."

You will not kill my child. That voice…

"It was you! *You* killed Vido."

Brava sat up but would not look at me.

"You called me your child."

She still refused to meet my gaze.

"But that's impossible. Vido killed my parents – Mama L saw it happen."

"No." Brava finally looked at me, her face drained of all color. "The woman with your father was my sister." She closed her eyes, her pain evident on her face. "I was ill, so I didn't go to the market with them that day."

Mother. All my life I had wanted a mother. Now that I had one, I was furious.

"You abandoned me!" The force of my cry left me coughing.

Brava poured a cup of water and helped me take a sip. It was the most marvelous thing that I had ever tasted. I wanted to drain the cup, but if I did it would come right back up. I made myself drink slowly. Once my throat was moisturized, I tried again.

"You left me to be raised by that... monster. To *become* a monster." I flung the cup at her.

Brava sat without flinching, even as it bounced off of her shoulder.

"If I had revealed that I was your mother – that I lived - Vido would have killed me as well." She wiped away the water trickling down her cheek before looking at me again, her heart in her eyes. "Then you would have been truly alone in the world. If I kept my identity secret, I could watch you from a distance, be sure that you were well."

We stared at each other across an awkward silence. I looked away first. Brava was my friend. Our relationship had just shifted drastically and I was clueless as to how to proceed. I closed my eyes and laid back. Memories returned in a rush.

"Nef! Jaidon!" I sat up abruptly, the sudden movement making my head pound.

"Easy, child!" Brava grabbed me by the shoulders, stilling me. "You have been through a lot. You need to relax."

I hated the weakness that suffused my body. I lost the battle with my sobs; they burst from my chest, tearing at my already tender throat. "They're dead! And it's all my fault. They died because they were helping me."

Brava pressed my head to her shoulder, rocking me as she would a small child.

"Shhh. Shush, little one. Nef and Jaidon are not dead; they both live. Like you, they sustained serious injuries, but also like you, they are getting better. Jaidon will be relieved to know that you are conscious again." Brava held me until the soul-shaking sobs subsided.

Only then did I remember. I dropped my hand to my abdomen and relief flooded through me as I felt the life that was my son. Once again I felt the brief flicker that I had noticed before, only this time I recognized it for what it was. A smile spread across my face.

"Is everything all right?" Brava asked.

"With my pregnancy? Yes. With us? No." My smile faded. "Everything has changed too fast - I'm going to need some time to adjust." Changing the subject, I asked "When can I see the others?"

"Soon. But for now you are still too weak to get out of bed. Rest. When you are stronger, I will take you to see them."

Brava's manner was brisk as she tucked the covers tightly around me. Once satisfied that I was comfortable she swept from the room without speaking, leaving me alone with my thoughts.

Rest should have been impossible. After all, I had done nothing recently *but* rest. I was wrong. I was asleep again almost immediately. When I awoke, the wonderful smell of food assailed my nostrils and my stomach growled in response.

Brava – *Mother?* - was just placing a tray on a low table near the bed. She helped me sit up and placed several pillows behind me to keep me in an upright position, then carefully fed me the broth that she had brought. It was delicious; even so, after only half a bowl, my stomach began protesting, threatening to bring back up its contents. I stopped eating but even the small amount of nutrition that I had taken in seemed to have cleared my head. My thought processes were working smoother. I suddenly realized what Brava had said earlier.

"You said that *Jaidon* would be relieved to know that I am conscious. What about Nef?"

Brava dropped her gaze for a moment. When her eyes met mine again, her sadness was obvious. "Nef lives. His wounds are healing, but he has not regained consciousness."

I swung my feet over the edge of the bed and, once again, the room spun around me, the world going grey. I set my teeth and fought the weakness with all of my will.

"Take me to him," I ground through clenched teeth.

"No. You are too weak. I will not risk you damaging yourself or your child."

"My child and I will not be fine if Nef dies. Take me to him - *now!*"

Have I ever mentioned that I was somewhat strong-willed? Brava would probably call it hard-headedness. Actually, she called me several things - none of which bear repeating here - but she did take me to Nef. And she was right - I was too weak. Even though he was only in the next room, by the time we got there I was shaking and dripping with sweat. All I could do was climb into the bed next to Nef and take his hand in mine. He was pale and a bandage covered half of his head. I looked at Brava with concern.

"Nef took a sword to the face," she answered my unspoken question. "It just missed his eye. I think that his vision will be unimpaired, but he will never again be as pretty as he was before. Like you, he also took some nasty blows to the head, which probably explain his continued unconsciousness, but I am worried that he is not showing any signs of awakening yet. However, all wounds heal at their own rate; all hope is not lost. He may just require more time to mend."

"Nef, I'm here. I live and I am here." I reached out and stroked his unbandaged cheek then pulled his hand to my mouth and kissed it.

He sighed; I didn't know if he heard me or if it was coincidence. Try as I might, I could do no more and drifted to sleep again, still holding his hand.

I awoke once again to the smell of food and was able to consume an entire bowl of broth. It might not seem like much, but I was extremely proud of myself nonetheless.

Brava changed the dressings on my wounds and the bandage on Nef's head although she insisted that I turn my back while she did the latter. There was still an awkwardness between us, but Brava seemed determined to make the best of the situation; she was smiling when she finally allowed me to turn around. "Perhaps I should have brought you to Nef sooner; his color has improved and he seems to be resting better. Keep doing whatever you are doing - let him know that you are near."

I talked to Nef, read to him, touched him, told him that I was with him and that I loved him. And all the while, I gradually grew stronger. Brava finally let me out of bed after two extremely long days and I was allowed to walk all the way across the room to sit in a chair in front of the window. It was too bad that there were no witnesses; I'm sure the applause would have been thunderous.

The sunlight streaming through the window felt marvelous. I leaned back, resting my head against the upholstered chair back and closed my eyes, soaking in the warmth, simply enjoying being alive, when I felt it. For the first time, I felt the movement of the new life that I carried within me. My hands covered my abdomen of their own accord, both in benediction and protection.

"Hello there," I whispered.

"Hello," a raspy voice responded.

After a moment of stunned silence, I realized that the voice came from the bed. I whirled around quickly enough to make myself dizzy. One gorgeous blue eye stared at me over the rumpled covers.

"Nef!" Count on me to state the obvious. I made my way back across the room a bit quicker than I should have, considering my own still somewhat less than complete recovery. Climbing onto the bed, I showered the uncovered part of Nef's face with kisses until he weakly attempted to push me away.

"Lillie? You're alive? I thought you were dead - that guard hit you so hard." He struggled to sit up.

I placed my hand in the center of his chest and was able to hold him down without even exerting any pressure.

"No. Stay there - Brava would be very upset with me if you were to get up. Not that you could." I lay down next to him and carefully pulled his head onto my chest.

Nef draped one arm over me, while I wrapped both of mine around him. By the Makers, it felt wonderful to hold him again! We lay there in silence, basking in the fact that we were alive and together. I slowly became aware of a moist warmth spreading across my chest as Nef cried quietly, his shoulders beginning to shake under my arms.

"Nef? What's wrong?" I stroked his arms and back soothingly.

He moved his hand slowly until his fingers splayed across my belly. "Our child..." His voice broke and he couldn't continue.

"Shhh." I placed my hand over his. "Hush, my love. Our son is fine." I let him hear the smile in my voice as I added, "And so is our daughter."

Nef stiffened in surprise. He tilted his head to look at me as best he could between his position in my arms and his bandage.

"Our daughter? Are you sure?"

"Absolutely. She has been a little shy about making her presence known, but she is there. Keep your hand there - I felt them move for the first time a little while ago. Maybe they will let you feel them too."

In spite of our waiting patiently for several minutes, the children were uncooperative - I could tell that Nef was disappointed.

"Don't worry," I said to cheer him up. "They are getting bigger by the day, I'm sure you will be able to feel them soon." I hugged him ferociously.

He gave a small gasp of pain.

"I'm sorry!" I apologized. "I'm just glad that their father will be here to help me raise them." Tears of relief flowed down my cheeks.

Before Nef could respond, there was a knock at the door and Brava breezed into the room with Master Jaidon trailing her. Jaidon moved slowly and had one arm bound tightly to his chest. He made his way to the chair that I had vacated and settled into it with a slight grimace. He sat stiffly, but relaxed slightly as the warmth from the sun soaked into his muscles. Pain had deepened the lines in his face.

Brava went to Nef and laid her hand on his cheek to check for fever and smiled as she found none. "Welcome back. I'm glad you could finally join us."

28

Brava removed a couch and table from her parlor and replaced it with a bed, thereby turning it into a temporary bedroom for Nef and me so that we could all be in close proximity as our healing continued. Jaidon, of course, shared Brava's bed. Our days were spent in discussion of how to proceed now that our actions had precipitated so many changes.

"The Va'Shile is in total disarray." Master Jaidon tugged irritatedly at his sling as he spoke. "Not only is Vido dead, but the majority of assassins in attendance at the gathering died since I was unable to deliver the antidote as planned."

"Jaidon plans to assume leadership of the Va'Shile." Brava moved to his side and repositioned his sling as she spoke, her look daring him to move it again.

"Under his leadership the organization will change – no longer will it be something to fear."

"Exactly what it will become remains to be seen – perhaps we can join with the Va'Kyrian and aid in bringing peace and safety to our country." He stood and stretched carefully; his wounds were not fully healed. "I must move quickly, before someone else attempts to assume the mantle of leadership. Word of Vido's demise will travel quickly and others will come – many looking to take his place. I must act now if I am to keep that from happening."

"What about the king? And the nobility?" I asked. "Surely they will not be content to sit around and see what unfolds. There are more than a few among the nobles that will be glad to take advantage of the chaos in The Narrows to strengthen their own bid for power while everyone's attention is directed elsewhere."

"We already thought of that." Brava glanced at Jaidon as she spoke.

He grinned and motioned for her to continue.

"While the rest of you were focused on bringing about the fall of the Va'Shile, *I* worked with Cissy." Her voice rang with pride. "Members of the Va'Kyrian are stationed at the palace and at the homes of each of the noble families. They will remain there until such time as the loyalties of each can be determined." She turned her gaze to Nef and me. "We did not include you in these plans so that Vido could not torture the information out of you if you were captured."

"Speaking of captured," Nef chimed in, his dark hair sticking up rakishly over his bandage. "Just how did you come to be at the guild house to rescue us?" He had taken the news that Brava was my mother much better than I had.

"The link that a Southron 'witch' has to her child never fades." Brava waved an elegant hand. "I knew that something was wrong – that Lillie was in danger. When I reached the guild house, all hell was breaking loose. It was simple enough for me to walk in; no one even tried to stop me. However, I didn't know my way around." Her dark eyes glistened with tears as she looked at me. "Had you not called out to the pups as you did, I might not have found you in time."

Silence fell as we each pondered what might have been. Had Vido succeeded in killing me, he would have then made short work of Nef and Jaidon as well. Brava's actions had saved us all. My heart softened when I looked at her. I might not agree with all of the choices that she had made, but she had done what she thought was best for me.

"Now, young man." Brava dashed away her tears, cleared her throat and focused on Nef. "What are your intentions toward my daughter? After all, you have both deflowered and impregnated her."

"What! She... I mean, we... Well, I..." Nef stammered, his cheeks flaming.

I snorted with laughter and laid a calming hand on him. "Relax. She's kidding. Sort of."

Nef gave me a crooked grin and pulled back my sleeve to display the bonding bracelet on my wrist, then raised his arm to show its mate. "Surely you have seen our bracelets. Lillie and I exchanged them the night of the Naming – before she learned my identity and before I knew that she was with child. My love for her is as unbreakable as these strands. I intend to marry your daughter – the sooner the better." He slid to the edge of the bed, got gingerly to his feet and approached Brava. Steadying himself with one hand on the arm of the couch, he bowed gallantly. "Madam, it would give me the greatest of pleasure if you would agree to give me your daughter's hand in marriage."

"Well it's about time." Brava grabbed Nef's face before he could stand and kissed him soundly on each cheek. "Of course I will. You have my blessing – both of you." She shooed him back to his seat next to me. "We can begin preparations for the nuptials immediately." She glanced back and forth between us. "That is, if you don't mind a small, intimate wedding?"

"I don't mind small..." Nef's voice was tinged with sadness and his face fell.

"But..." I encouraged him, my heart in my throat. What could possibly be wrong?

"I just wish my mother could be here."

"Well, why can't she? All we have to do is send her a letter, right? I mean, it's not like we have to get married tomorrow."

There was a knock at the door.

"Come in," Brava called, an oddly expectant look on her face.

A hooded figure entered. Both Jaidon and I leaped to our feet, knives at the ready.

"Put those away," Brava chided. "Is that any way to treat our guest?"

A slim hand appeared from the folds of the cloak and pushed back the hood, revealing a woman that could only be Nef's mother. Though their coloring was different, the resemblance was undeniable. Although it was impossible to do so, I suddenly wanted to hide. What if she didn't like me?

The woman stepped in front of us. There was a pause while we studied each other. She was tall and slim, although with the more rounded curves that came with age and child-bearing. Long blonde hair hung unbound to her waist and her brown eyes sparkled with what I hoped was good humor; a light scattering of freckles dusted the bridge of her nose. Her face suddenly split into a wide smile and I knew where Nef's dimples had come from; the lines at the corners of her mouth and eyes indicated that smiles were a common occurrence.

"Mother?" Nef's voice was a whisper.

"Nef!" she cried, cupping his bandaged face gently in her hands. "My poor baby." She pulled her son close for a long hug.

Pulling slightly away from his mother, Nef reached for my hand and drew me into their group. Sliding his arm around my shoulder, he looked at me with eyes full of love. "Mother, I would like for you to meet Lillie, my soon-to-be wife. Lillie, this is my mother, Lady Marona."

Lady Marona released Nef and took my hands in both of hers and studied me carefully from head to toe. I struggled not to blush under the scrutiny. Her eyes widened slightly as her gaze passed over my midsection. She lifted her eyes to mine at which point I lost the battle and my cheeks assumed a rosy hue. Her eyes twinkled as she shifted them to Nef and then back to me.

"Apparently congratulations are in order?"

"Yes! Oh, Mother, isn't it wonderful?" Nef laughed. "Lillie is carrying my children!"

His mother seemed stunned. "Children? More than one?"

"Yes, my lady," I assured her emphatically. "Twins. A boy and a girl."

My future mother-in-law's mouth was almost hanging open. "Twins? How can you be sure?"

"It is a gift of her Southron heritage," Brava's husky voice intervened.

"You are Brava, I presume?" Lady Marona turned to face my mother.

"I am."

"Thank you for taking care of my son." Lady Marona took Brava's hands in hers, pulled her to her feet and hugged her.

"You are most welcome." Brava picked up the orange tabby lounging in the only available chair and indicated that Lady Marona should be seated. "*And you are just in time. We were about to discuss wedding plans.*"

The next months were busy ones. Nef and I - as well as Brava and Jaidon - were married in a small double wedding. Lady Marona, Mama L, and Jehrold doubled as both our guests and the required three witnesses.

After the wedding, Nef and I moved into the palace for the remainder of our recuperation. I insisted that we take Grau's pups with us. Their father gave his life for me; the least I could do was give them the best lives possible in honor of that sacrifice.

Nef very nearly lost an eye courtesy of the sword slash to his face; the blade gashed a line from his temple across the outer corner of his eye and then continued down his cheek, where it nicked the corner of his mouth before exiting across his chin. The scarring caused the skin at the corner of his eye and mouth to crinkle, giving him the appearance of being slightly amused about everything. While the scar would fade over time, it was currently a vivid red weal that shone brightly against his fair skin. However, Nef had gotten his revenge against his attacker, even if it had been more a stroke of luck than skill. Blinded by the blood pouring from his wound and in excruciating pain, he lashed out blindly with his own sword, catching his attacker in the crotch and very nearly gelding him.

My own convalescence proceeded smoothly – to a point. Four months into my pregnancy the midwife insisted that I remain in bed for the safety of both the children and myself.

I thought that I was going to go out of my mind.

Konal, the farrier's apprentice, came to my rescue with a wheeled chair that he designed. Maerie – now my lady's maid – rolled me outside for fresh air occasionally, weather permitting. Nef joined us whenever possible. Between my outings and the antics of the pups, my confinement was bearable. Mostly.

The twins were born on the coldest day of the winter. We named our son Marco Garrard after our fathers, but agreed to call him Marco since "Garrard" and "Jehrold" were a tad too similar; no need to make life any more confusing than necessary. Our daughter, Aliyana, was the spitting image of her Southron grandmother and was named after the aunt that died at Vido's hands.

I thought that my heart would burst with pride the day that Nef assumed the throne of Ramalda, returning the crown to its rightful family. I stood by his side as best friend, wife, lover, mother of his children and the first Assassin Queen of Ramalda.

ABOUT THE AUTHOR

Isabella Norse scored major "cool mom" points by playing the same video games as her sons and their friends. In these virtual worlds she slayed demons and destroyed machines bent on galactic extermination while simultaneously wooing cocky assassins and sexy aliens. She fell in love with the make-believe worlds and rich characters that inhabited them and now writes her own sci-fi, fantasy and paranormal tales of love, romance and adventure.

Still a gamer – and still cool – Isabella lives in Georgia with her husband and a herd of rescue cats.

Find out more about the author at isabellanorse.com.

ALSO BY ISABELLA NORSE
(All books available on Amazon.com)

Virtually Yours

Phoebe Link, nerd extraordinaire, has several lovers - all virtual. The men in her favorite video games are cocky, witty, and self-assured. They are also safe - they will never cheat on her or break her heart. Of course, they will also never hold her close or warm her bed.

Kyle Shepard has been smitten with Phoebe for years, yet she remains oblivious to his hints that he would like to be more than friends. With subtlety getting him nowhere, he must channel his inner ladies' man - surely all of those reruns of Space Trek have taught him something - and ask her out.

Can Kyle convince Phoebe to take a chance on love? Can Phoebe bring herself to risk her heart in a relationship with a living, breathing man? Or, will they both get more than they bargained for when they discover that the lines between fantasy and reality can blur when romancing a nerd?

The Purrfect Partner
(Book 1 in the *Paws and Effect* Series)

Lorelei Stevens, newly certified veterinary technician, faces the future with a mix of excitement and dread. Freedom from the meddling of her well-intentioned friends is finally within reach. All she has to do is spend Valentine's weekend dodging the unwanted attentions of strangers during the annual singles gathering at The Lodge. In return, her friends promise to never, ever set her up on another blind date.

Dalton Freeman, laid-back rancher, receives a getaway to The Lodge as a gift from his brothers. The catch? The gift is only good during Valentine's weekend. So what if all of his attempts at online dating have failed miserably? There's no reason for his brothers to play Cupid. Really.

When these two strangers pretend to be a couple for a weekend, will it be a disaster or will fate - and a half-frozen kitten - lead them to the purrfect partner?